Fashionably Fanged

The Hot Damned, Book 8

By

Robyn Peterman

D1739298

Edition Notice

This book is a work of fiction. Names, characters, places, and incidents either are the product of the author's imagination or are used fictitiously. Any resemblance to actual persons, living or dead, businesses, companies, events, or locales is coincidental.

This book contains content that may not be suitable for young readers 17 and under.

No part of this book may be reproduced, or stored in a retrieval system, or transmitted in any form or by any means, electronic, mechanical, photocopying, recording, or otherwise, without express written permission of the author/publisher.

Cover art by *Rebecca Poole* of *dreams2media*
Edited by *Meg Weglarz*

Copyright © 2017 Robyn Peterman
All rights reserved.

Praise for *Fashionably Dead*

*Uproariously witty, deliciously provocative, and just plain fun!
No one delivers side-splitting humor and mouth-watering
sensuality like Robyn Peterman.
This is entertainment at its absolute finest!*

~ Darynda Jones, NY Times Bestselling Author of the
Charley Davidson Series

Acknowledgements

This book was a blast to write. It took me on a wild ride. I knew Venus would get her story from the moment I created her in Book 1 of the Hot Damned Series. However, writing the story is only part of the journey to getting a book published. There are many people to thank and I'm a lucky girl to have such a talented and wonderful support system.

Rebecca Poole—your covers are brilliant as are you. Thank you.

Meg Weglarz—your editing always makes me look better than I am. We are both WONTON women. LOL Thank you.

Donna McDonald and JM Madden—a gal couldn't ask for tougher, brilliant and more awesome critique partners. Thank you.

Kris and Donna—your insight into my technical needs for this book ROCKED! I'm a slight disaster on the computer… You saved me big time! LOL Thank you.

Wanda and Melissa—you are the best-est beta readers in the world. The journey this time was extremely helpful and a ton of fun. Thank you.

Wanda—you rock hard. Thank you.

My family—none of this would be worth it without you. Thank you for being mine. I adore you.

Dedication

For Melissa. I'm so very lucky to have you in my life.

Chapter 1

"Listen to me," Astrid said frantically, pacing my suite like a Vampyre on fire. "I'm seriously worried I might behead them accidentally on purpose. That would be so, soooo wrong even though they technically deserve it. I need your help."

"You want *me* to behead them?" I choked out, running my hands through my wild curly black hair while trying to figure out where my best friend was going with her line of thought. With Astrid, one could never be certain.

"No! I mean, yes... but *no*. Absofuckinglutely *not*. We can't behead them. Samuel loves the sequined old nut jobs and they saved his life," she went on, still making very little sense.

"Your son loves everyone. He's a child," I reminded her. "Would Sammy really miss Martha and Jane?"

"Fine point. Well made," Astrid agreed thoughtfully. "But I'm the jackwad that gave the okay to have them turned. It would be like committing patricide if I had them offed. Right?" she asked, clearly looking for someone to give her permission to eliminate the banes of her existence.

"Actually, you've already done that," I told her, trying not to laugh.

Astrid halted her pacing and looked wildly confused. "I've done what?"

"Committed patricide," I replied.

"Wait. What the hell does *patricide* mean?" Astrid asked, flopping down on the over stuffed Shabby Chic chair in the cozy den of my suite.

"It means kill your father."

Her groan echoed in my suite. "Oh, well... shit. I guess I have done that. He was a total dick."

And that was the understatement of the century. Her father had been one of the most vicious and deadly Demons known to our world. Even his brother, Satan, appreciated Astrid for ridding the Underworld of such a blight on humanity.

"Then what does matricide mean?" she asked with a wrinkled brow.

"Kill your mother."

"Well, hell, I've done that too," she shot back, letting her head fall to her hands. "You know when you say it out loud like that, I sound like a bad fucking person."

"Yes... but your mother was literally ingesting your father-in-law, our King. Not to mention she'd tried to kill you numerous times," I told her as I slipped into my running shoes and tied them.

"This is true," she said with a shudder. "I'm not that bad then."

"No, my friend, you're not. You're Compassion. And you're my hero—not to mention my Princess. I'd go to the ends of the earth for you. However, even though Martha and Jane make me want to grind my fangs down to nubs—committing wrinkly old lady *batricide* would be, um..."

"Satisfying?" Astrid asked with a wide grin.

I laughed at her toothy smile. "Yep and wrong."

"Okay then, is it *wrong* for it to be my secret fantasy? I won't actually do it, but can I dream about it?" she inquired, looking frazzled.

"If it's wrong, I don't want to be right," I told her, unsuccessfully trying to bite back a grin. "I daydream about it frequently."

"Crap. You might be the wrong person to train them," she mumbled through splayed fingers.

"Wait. Whoa. Train them?" Wincing, I shot Astrid an alarmed glance. "They already know how to fight. They've killed plenty of Demons, and Dark Fairies, and God only knows what else—and shockingly, lived to tell about it—in great and gory detail."

"I know," Astrid lamented in her outdoor voice. "But they're sloppy and short in the brain cell department. I don't want the old fuckers to get killed. I mean, don't get me wrong, I totally want to kill them, but I don't want anyone else to do it. And since there's no way in hell I would do the deed, it can't happen. Does that make sense?"

"Alarmingly, it does." I shook my head, amazed that I could follow her discombobulated train of thought. That possibly made me as crazy as she was, but then again we were all a little crazy. Immortality did that to a person.

"Apropos of nothing, are you still bumping uglies with Edward the German exchange weenie?" Astrid asked with a raised brow, clearly searching for a less life-threatening subject.

"Umm… no." I cringed and covered my eyes with my hair. "As usual, you were correct. He's a gaping butthole and annoying as hell."

"In your defense, he *is* pretty and the German accent is a novelty around here in Kentucky," she offered up a pathetic excuse to make me feel better.

ROBYN PETERMAN

"Yep." I nodded and groaned. "But pretty doesn't make up for vapid, conceited and loser-y."

"True," Astrid agreed with a shrug, and began picking through my laundry basket of clean clothes. "What about Gareth?"

"What *about* Gareth?" I shot back with my eyes narrowed to slits.

"Hmm..." Her smile grew wider and I wanted to slap it off her face. "Your reaction is very, umm... passionate."

"He's a disgusting, manwhore, pig from hell. You're mistaking passion for intense dislike."

"Interesting. Maybe you should try online dating."

"Maybe you should shut your cakehole. I might have horrible taste in men, but I'm not desperate. I have no problem getting them. I just don't want to keep the ones I get," I informed her, as I removed three pairs of brand new Lululemon leggings from her sticky fingers.

"Roger that," Astrid replied, giggling. "If you change your mind let me know. I would love to set you up with a hot, smexy Vampyre."

"I'll keep that in mind. Not." My eye roll made her laugh harder, but I wasn't joking at all.

"Fine, little missy. Back to business. I'll make training the fashion-challenged dorkholes worth your while," Astrid promised, dangling a metaphorical carrot in front of my nose. Metaphorical because the undead couldn't eat food.

"*How* worth my while?" I asked and then smacked my own head for even considering doing something that could end in actual death—either mine or theirs.

"Three full shopping days in Milan. My treat."

"Oh my hell, you're a mean, heinous, undead woman," I hissed, knowing I was going to cave. Prada was Prada after all.

"I know. Right?" She punctuated her glee with a little dance around the room.

"Materialistic hooker," I snapped, mentally cataloging all of the shops I wanted to visit.

"Takes one to know one," she shot back with a laugh.

"True," I admitted.

Now I was the one pacing. Could I actually train Martha and Jane without tearing their heads off? I enjoyed a good challenge—*and* Prada—but...

Thankfully my suite in the Cressida House—the massive Vampyre compound we all lived in—calmed me. It was one of the very few places in the world that was totally mine and reflected me. I favored Shabby Chic—big overstuffed furniture in soft cottons and fuzzy chenille mixed with rich crushed velvets. The patterns were faded cabbage roses in peach and pale pink, mixed up with equally faded tulips and daisies in lavender and periwinkle. The walls were a pale celery green dotted with pieces of crazy cool folk art and Aboriginal Dream art I'd collected over the years. None of it went together individually, but together it was perfect—eclectic and weird—just like me.

However, at the moment even my sanctuary didn't help. Decisions sucked. Decisions involving Prada and training trash-talking, politically-incorrect, dumbasses really sucked.

"Can I damage them?" I inquired, running my hands over the velvet pillows on my couch.

"Of course," Astrid replied. "Dismembering is completely acceptable too. Arms and legs grow back. No biggie."

"Not sure that a shopping spree is a big enough incentive," I muttered.

11

"You know what? You're right," Astrid said, making me realize I'd spoken my thought aloud. "How about I throw in pole dancing classes with Mother Nature?"

"Um... how about no freakin' way in hell?"

Astrid's grandmother was every kind of insane rolled into one frighteningly beautiful package. Even her sons, Satan and God, feared her. Mother Nature *aka* Gigi was under the very mistaken belief that she could pole dance. She couldn't. However, that didn't stop her.

"Not for you," Astrid insisted quickly with an evil little smirk hovering on her lips. "For Gareth."

Now *that* stopped me in my tracks. An enormous belly laugh escaped me as I pictured Gareth—the Vampyre Prince of the Asian Dominion—pole dancing. The ridiculously gorgeous brother of our Prince Ethan was a thorn in my ass and a wildly regrettable notch in my bedpost.

"No way you can make that douchebag pole dance," I told her.

"Dude, dude, dude." Astrid shook her head in mock-insulted horror. "I'm a True Immortal—one of only nine in the Universe. You underestimate me. With the title comes a lot of bullshit and apparently an assload of clout. Normally, I use it wisely and for the good of our people, but Gareth deserves a little payback—he's been a royal pain in the ass—pun intended. Besides, I've got dirt on everyone—or at least the baby Demons do. You teach the foul-mouthed sorry excuses for Vampyres to fight better and Gareth pole dances."

"The shopping spree still included?" I asked, mentally weighing the pros and cons.

"Absolutely," she swore.

"You drive a hard bargain," I said, laughing at the crazy woman who led our people. "I'm in."

"Excellent. You won't regret this," Astrid promised as she stood up and hauled ass out of my suite before I could change my mind.

Smart girl.

Plopping down on my smooshy couch, I let my head fall back and grinned at the impending stupidity of what I'd just agreed to do. I would so live to regret this. But life was long for a Vamp—very, very long. Challenges helped pass the time and pushed the loneliness of living forever to the back of my mind.

As long as removing a few limbs wasn't off the table I could do this—I hoped.

The thought of Gareth's utter fury at having to pole dance delighted me. That bastard had been starring in my dreams for months—not to mention we couldn't be in the same room together without wanting to kill each other. Wait. That wasn't exactly accurate. I wanted to kill him. He wanted to shag me—his words—definitely not mine.

Hell would freeze over before that would happen again. I'd made that mistake once in a moment of weakness and stupidity. He was a manwhore-jackass. Sadly—for me—he was an ungodly beautiful manwhore-jackass who was outstanding in the Big O department. I'd even thought that maybe we were... Whatever. Wishful thinking did not real life make.

Letting reality hit me for a moment, I curled into a ball on my couch and buried my face in the soft pillows. Gareth was aging and dying. He'd been cursed by Vlad—the evil bastard now on the run from every Vampyre in the world. Prince Ethan and Astrid were certain Vlad and the Angel he'd worked with would be found and the curse could be broken. I wasn't as positive.

As much as I despised Gareth, the thought of him dying was unacceptable. Why? I didn't know. The man made me angrier than anyone I'd come across in my over two hundred years on earth.

Tossing the pillows aside, I pushed my panicky thoughts away. I was good at that. Time and experience had taught me to compartmentalize. A brain can only hold so much information without breaking. Sometimes to make it through each day of my eternal life, I had to focus on only the immediate. The future was vast and uncertain. The past was the past.

Screw introspective thought. It would just get me in more trouble when I was in enough trouble as it was.

I had some unpleasant old bags from hell to teach and I was going to train the living shit out of them.

Martha and Jane had no idea what they were in for.

Unfortunately, neither did I.

Chapter 2

The training facility was another favorite comfort zone—second only to my suite. Nordstrom ran a close third. However, it was frowned upon to scissor kick shoppers in the head, which was why it was in third place.

Fight training at the Cressida House was ugly and painful—just the way I liked it. The training facilities were top notch, including a huge gym with every machine known to the undead—triple reinforced due to our strength. There was a boxing ring in the back corner and a one-mile indoor circular running track rimmed the facility.

The training center also encompassed a very large empty area covered in mats for sparring. There was an observation deck on the north wall about forty feet up. It was accessible from an outside set of stairs. The adjoining building contained a shooting range and a cavernous room filled with weapons—swords, daggers, katanas, throwing stars, guns, and then some.

The weapons building also housed a room used for knife throwing. I tended to steer clear of that section since the profane idiots, Martha and Jane, spent hours a day practicing in there. Anyone brave or stupid enough to venture in when the old gals were hurling weapons usually left with something sharp impaled in their head.

"Home sweet home," I muttered as I put down my gym bag and scanned the area for my new students.

Maybe they wouldn't show up. That would be incredibly awesome. I could find a sparring partner, work out some of my pent up aggression, and call it a day.

Or I could run a few miles, and then work on some sword skills, and then...

Shit. No such luck.

"Hey gurrrl, gimme some skin," Jane shouted using what I could only assume was her attempt at what some would call an African-American dialect.

Not killing them was going to be almost virtually impossible.

Ignoring the greeting and crossing my arms over my chest, I gaped at them in open-mouthed shock. "What in the hell is on your head?"

"You like it?" Martha bellowed, preening and posing.

The outfits were appalling enough—gold lame booty shorts paired with feather trimmed pink workout bras, black socks and green high tops. Clearly the dress code that Astrid had imposed on them had tragically ended. However, it was what I was pretty sure were supposed to be afros on their heads, that made me itch to smack them into tomorrow.

"As you *are* Afro-American, we thought it would be in good mother humpin' form to show our acceptance and appreciation for your culture," Martha said while performing a fucked up version of the Black Power salute.

Watching two eighty-nine year old white women try to be black almost rendered me speechless. The freak shows had caused more trouble in the short time they'd been undead than our entire Vampyre race had in centuries. However, they *had* saved Samuel's life and earned Astrid and Ethan's undying thanks and loyalty. Actually mine too, although I'd never admit it.

"It's *African*-American," I snapped, closing my eyes and praying to every deity I could think of to help me not go Rambo on their bony asses. I was proud of myself that I'd come unarmed. God only knew what would have happened if I'd been carrying a sword.

"I told you," Jane grunted, backhanding an unsuspecting Martha in the head. "You and your stupid ideas. This is worse than the time you pulled your hair back too tight so you could fit in with the Asians."

"That was your idea, you fucktard," Martha reminded her, adding a gut punch to make her point.

Maybe if I just let them go at it, they'd kill each other, and I'd get out of my side of the bargain. I watched in horrified amazement as they tackled each other, swearing like sailors and accusing each other of crimes so politically incorrect I had to laugh.

Bizarrely, their age didn't reverse when they'd been turned—but then again, most of us were turned in our youth. They looked every second of their eighty-nine years even though they behaved like un-medicated, rabid squirrels.

"Enough," I growled, extracting them from each other and tossing them onto separate mats. "While I somewhat appreciate the heinous effort, the reality is insulting and wrong. Remove the wigs, stop attacking each other, and I might train you today."

"No can do, sis-tah," Martha said, wiping the blood from her broken nose with the edge of her 'fro.

"I'm *not* your sis-tah," I told Martha through clenched teeth. "And when we train, I'm in charge. You backtalk and I get a free pass at you. Take off the wigs or I'll do it for you and make you eat them."

"Holy shitbombs, ease up gurl-friend," Jane griped, getting to her feet with effort. "What Martha should have said is that the afros kept slipping, so we stapled them to our heads. We could probably take 'em off, but it would be a goddang bloody fucking mess unless you have a stapler remover."

Letting my chin fall to my chest so they didn't see my grin, I slowly shook my head back and forth. Stupid didn't even begin to cover it. They were a menace to society and themselves. I was actually shocked no one had killed them yet. Martha and Jane were walking targets.

"While I usually carry office supplies in my *gym* bag, I'm all out of stapler removers today," I said with sarcasm dripping off every word. "When we're done here, you'll remove the wigs and burn them. You're white. I'm black. This is a fact. Afros will not make you black. What they will do is piss me off and you *really* don't want to do that. We clear?"

"We are," Jane said, covertly flipping Martha the bird while Martha mouthed *"I told you so"*.

"Stretch for five minutes while I figure out how to torture you," I instructed, still trying not to laugh or scream at their appalling attempt to impress me.

And then a bad day took a turn for the worse...

I felt him before I saw him. His power was unmistakable even in his weakened state. It bounced around the vast room and I noticed many bowing down to his royal ass. He could easily take down any Vampyre in the Cressida House, except for his brother Ethan. At full health, I'd have to call it a draw between the two men.

Female Vamps fell over themselves to get close to him. And why not? His damn cheekbones would make a sculptor jealous. His full lips were sinful and his eyes were a mesmerizing crystal blue. Full, jet black hair—just a little too long—begged a woman's fingers to get tangled in it. The six foot four package was gorgeous—savagely gorgeous. Only problem was that it was wrapped up in an outer layer of gaping, macho asswipe.

"That Prince Gareth is a hot piece of man meat," Jane announced as she sat in the splits with her spindly arms over her head. "I'd do him in a hot second."

"Better lookin' than George W," Martha agreed, getting stuck in what I could only call a human pretzel.

"Since he's a big man hooker, I say go for it," I muttered in disgust as I watched every Vamp in the room with boobs fawn over the asshole. Whatever. I'd stupidly been with him one time—two months ago. A mistake that would never be repeated. Gareth was not my problem. And I was quite sure he'd bedded at least half of the female Vamps in the Cressida House since then.

Turning my back on Gareth and entourage, I attempted to untangle Martha so I could get the session over with. However, minding my own business was not in the cards for me this afternoon. Freakin' great.

"Venus," Edward—*my latest mistake*—called out as he strode across the training area with purpose. "Der you are. I've been searching for you for days!"

"Now that one is smokin' too," Jane commented. "But kinda girly."

"Zip it," I hissed as I put on a polite face for the girly man I was trying to avoid.

He walked up, planted himself, and tapped his Prada clad toe impatiently. I wanted to deck him almost as much as I wanted to deck the old gals. Decisions… decisions.

"Edward, I'm busy right now. How about we chat later?" I suggested, dismissing him with a curt nod of my head. It would be all kinds of inappropriate to physically remove him—not difficult, but not my finest moment. I'd try manners first.

"Vat time?" he demanded.

He was clearly unhappy I wasn't making time for him. "Um… eight?" I suggested.

"Vere?"

"How about…" I started.

"Your suite," he finished, looking quite satisfied with himself. "Very goot. I look forvard to being alone vith you. I vill stay here vith you until eight."

Not going to happen—it was only two in the afternoon right now. His smile made me feel bad, but it also made my skin crawl a little bit. Damn it, why couldn't I be a lesbian? Women were so much easier than men.

"No Edward, I need to concentrate and you distract me," I lied prettily.

He wasn't a bad guy. He just wasn't the Vampyre for me and he definitely didn't know how to take a hint. I needed to cut him loose and be very clear.

"You heard, the lady," Gareth cut in, standing so close to me I could feel the power vibrating off of his body. "You need to leave, my *friend*."

"I've got this covered. I don't need your help," I snapped at Gareth.

He simply laughed—stared at my lips, then my breasts, and then back at my mouth.

This was turning out to be a very shitty day. I now felt naked after his perusal—and horny. His damn eyes may as well have been his hands. Gareth was all kinds of trouble and I wanted no part of him.

"As you wish," he said with a smile. He added a bow that made Martha and Jane giggle like schoolgirls and fan themselves vigorously. "Good day, Venus."

"Vhat vas dat about?" Edward pouted and stomped his foot. "You are mine. Not his."

"I belong to no one but myself," I said flatly—again thanking the Lord above I wasn't armed. "Now if you'll excuse me, I have work to do."

Edward sputtered a bit until he realized he was causing a scene. Turning on his heel he marched out of the gym, his perfectly coiffed head held high.

"That Vamp sounds like the smarmy fuck with the pencil mustache and one testicle from that long ass documentary we watched," Jane said, pursing her lips and wrinkling her nose.

"Shitler," Martha confirmed with a disgusted nod of agreement.

"You mean Hitler?" I asked, bemoaning my taste in men for the millionth time.

"No, gurl friend, I meant Shitler. That lowdown turdass was a total piece of shit. If he wasn't already dead, I'd gut his sorry ass and shove his entrails down his throat," Martha vowed, meaning every word.

"And I'd laugh like a loon," Jane added, still stuck in the splits.

Maybe training them wouldn't be as bad as I thought.

Wait, who was I kidding? Just because we had a few beliefs in common didn't mean the old gals weren't batshit crazy.

"You know what?" I said, thinking out loud. I needed to clear my head and I knew just the way to do it. "Today we're gonna run. Stamina is part of the battle. You old farts ready to put some mileage on those skinny, wrinkly legs?"

"You bet your ass we are," Jane shouted, falling over sideways, still stuck in the splits. "Can someone give me a goddamned hand here?"

"Me too," Martha said with her legs still in some kind of bizarre knot. "We love running. One time we saw Barry Manilow at the mall and chased that hot piece of love muscle right to his limo. Damn bastard locked the doors. We must have run ten miles after that dang vehicle before we gave up."

ROBYN PETERMAN

"Son of a bitch will never know what he missed," Jane said sadly. "We wanted to love him up good."

Both repulsed and curious about their obvious stalker problem, my mouth moved before my brain could stop it. "Was this when you were human?"

"Hell no," Martha grunted as she finally untangled her legs. "It was last week."

Astrid was going to owe me big for this.

"Ground rule number one—no more talking. Ever. In my presence, you're only allowed to ask questions about techniques and that's it," I informed them, pulling Jane to her feet.

"But don't you want to hear about the play dough genitalia contest we've entered?" Martha inquired in complete seriousness. "You know, Titties McBoobyland used to be our art teacher back in our human days."

"Titties *who*?"

"Astrid," Jane clarified, popping every bone in her body in preparation for our run. "We have a few nicknames for her. She loves them."

"I'll just bet she does," I muttered. "Never ever use the words play dough and genitalia in the same sentence again—it makes me want to hurl and I don't have that ability. We're doing at least fifty miles today."

"Hot damn," Martha squealed. "That's great!"

And it kind of was, in an annoying, horrifying way.

The air bags didn't shut their mouths for the entire fifty miles, but they actually made me laugh a few times.

I had to slow my pace in order not to lose them, when I ran at full speed I was virtually invisible. They were in pretty damn bad shape, but their willingness to do whatever I told them to do was in their favor.

22

They would never be perfect, but they would be much better fighters by the time I got through with them.

We all just needed to live through it.

Chapter 3

Tired didn't even begin to cover it. Sleepless nights and unsettling dreams starring a jerk named Gareth with a fine ass made me want to crawl out of my own skin. Fifty miles with Martha and Jane made me want a long vacation or a solid set of earplugs. Dealing with a very soon to be ex-lover was not my idea of a good time—at all.

Who did I screw over in a former life to have to put up with this crap? If I had the ability to sigh, the mother of all sighs would have left my lips.

My nice little breakup chat with Edward had turned into something else altogether.

"Vould you like to explain *dis*?" Edward hissed in the German accent that at one point I'd mistakenly found appealing. He held a stack of books and waved a note in my face like a lunatic.

What in the ever-loving hell had I been thinking to sleep with the idiot? Boredom—pure and simple—or possibly insanity.

Or maybe loneliness.

Whatever. What was done was done—stupid or not. Now I just needed to rid myself of him. The sex wasn't good enough to deal with someone who spent more time on his hair than I did. And I was no slouch in the hair department.

"I vill not be disrespected, Venus. You vill treat me as someone of my stature or dis affair is over," he informed me with a well-plucked brow arched so high I was certain it touched his hairline.

"And what exactly is your *stature*, Edward?" I asked in a polite tone that sent smart people running for the hills. Furthermore, the *affair* was already over. Edward just hadn't clued in yet. And what kind of real man plucked his damn eyebrows?

If he knew me well—or at all—he'd know that me being über polite put him on dangerous ground. Clearly he didn't know me.

"I'm a varrior," he informed me in a condescending voice, flipping his artfully messy blond hair off of his face with a flick of his hand.

Warrior, my ass. Astrid had warned me Edward was a weenie, but did I listen? No. I did not listen. He was here in the North American Dominion on a trade from the European Dominion—kind of a Vampyre exchange program. At this point, I was counting the days until he left.

"Dis is unacceptable," he continued, marching around my suite and wielding the books like weapons.

This Vampyre was treading on very thin ice. He was getting attached and on the verge of being possessive, not to mention rude and annoying. I was not the girl for attached *or* possessive. I was a free dead woman and he was a dalliance that had been over for weeks—plus he was far too young for me. At only a hundred, Edward was a baby with a tremendous amount of growing up to do. Granted he was pretty, but then again, most Vamps were.

"Dude, it looks to me as if you're throwing a tantrum over books and a piece of paper," I replied with my eyes narrowing dangerously.

Edward really didn't want to get on my bad side this evening. Several hours with Martha and Jane was my limit for bullshit. My fangs tingled in my gums and I kept them from dropping with effort. I was itching for a smackdown with someone and if he kept going, he would definitely do.

"It's de complete collection of de Twilight series," he snapped. "I vas *not* named for Edward in dis piece of trash teenage fiction."

"I liked the books—very amusing, albeit unrealistic," I replied easily as I tried not to roll my eyes. "And who said you were named for him?"

"Vell from de vay de note is signed, *you* did," he shouted and stomped his foot like a spoiled child. "And de reference to my sparkling tiny man junk is not appreciated."

"Your sparkling tiny *what?*" I took the note from him and scanned it while biting down on my lips to hold back my laughter.

Oh. My. God.

My Dearest Edward,

I bequeath you these books because you remind me of the skinny, pale-faced, sparkling fuckhole in the story that slightly passes as literature. The one rather violent and wildly underwritten fornication scene in the tome is far more tantalizing than bedding you.

I'm done shagging you and your tiny sparkling man junk. I'm in the market for a real man with balls larger than chestnuts. The simple fact that I could kick your ass to hell and back with my eyes closed while bound in silver is an extreme turn off.

I'd suggest you take yourself and your overly gelled hair and walk quietly out of my life. You'd be far better off with someone named Bella—or possibly Jacob. After your performance in the bedroom, I'm not exactly certain which team you bat for.

I wish you the very best—for the most part. Don't let the door hit you in the ass on your way out.

Auf weidersehen

Venus

"Umm... wow," I stuttered, impressed that someone had forged my handwriting so flawlessly. Unfortunately, I had a very good idea who had written it. However, what surprised me most was that the culprit had clearly read the entire Twilight series. "I didn't write this."

"Of course you did," Edward accused. "It matches de script in your journal exactly."

My fangs dropped and my body tensed. "I'm sorry, *what* did you just say?"

He did *not* say he'd read my journal. Unfortunately—for him—the self-satisfied smirk on his face confirmed he had said exactly that. How he had found my journal was suspect. It was locked in my safe along with keepsakes from my human life. If he'd so much as touched my mother's bible or the lock of my sister's hair, he was about to find out what permanent death felt like.

"I found your description of killing dos dat you perceived as doing you wrong quite entertaining," he said with an unapologetic shrug and a chuckle. "And your descriptions of certain members of the Royal Family vere amusing to say de least. Very silly dat you seem to still carry a torch for de one dat turned you. And interesting dat he cared so little for you to never see you again. However, I do find it tragic dat you still harbor so much anger about being a slave. For de love of God, dat was hundreds of years ago. I dink you should get over it."

If I could breathe, I'd be hyperventilating. If my heart could beat, it would have bounced out of my chest. He'd read my diary, smack talked the kind, beautiful man who'd saved my life and turned me, *and* made light of the horrors of my human life. The son of a bitch had just played a very bad hand.

"Perceived?" I hissed.

"You can't possibly expect me to believe you vere treated like an animal—starved, beaten, used," he shot back.

Since gasping or hurling were out, I chose the next best thing. "Would you like a weapon or would you prefer hand to hand? Honestly, it doesn't really matter since you're going down," I informed him in a voice so soft the idiot had to lean in to hear.

"You are not serious," he huffed indignantly with an uncomfortable flash of fear in his eyes.

"Oh, I'm very serious. Pick or I'll choose for you."

"You are a mere voman," he insisted in a pompous tone, but backed away in caution. "I am an esteemed visitor from de European Dominion. You vill not touch me."

"You're correct, *Edvard*," I said flatly. "Touch connotes gentleness and caring—neither of which I feel for you at the moment. I clearly had a temporary mental break to think you were worthy of my time. You are no warrior or man of honor. No self respecting Vampyre with tiny sparkly man junk breaks into a safe and takes what isn't his. You're a weenie, just like Astrid said you were, and I'm in the mood to kick your ass to Hell and back."

"I vas right! You did write de letter!" he shouted, throwing the books at me and picking up my favorite Mackenzie Childs lamp. "And I'm *not* a veenie."

I closed my eyes briefly and groaned. I had the worst damned taste in men. Breaking into my safe, reading my journal, and boring me to violence was unfortunate—for his undead lifespan. However, if he hurled my one of a kind lamp at me, he'd leave in pieces. It had lions and fish on it. I loved lions and fish.

"Put it down. Now," I growled.

"Or vat?" he taunted, clearly realizing he might have a slight upper hand.

"Put it down and I let you leave my suite undead. Break it and you leave for real dead."

"You dink I'm stupid, don't you? You used me and I vas having feelings for you. You can do no better dan Edvard. I know you vant dat dying Vampyre Prince," Edward sneered, carelessly twirling the lamp and grinning widely.

"I have no clue what you're babbling about," I lied without batting an eyelash.

The dying Vampyre Prince was none of his business—or mine for that matter.

"Here's what I do know. Speaking about yourself in third person is all kinds of loser-y. You took what is mine. Reading my journal is lower than scum. You're holding a one of a kind lamp in your slimy hands right now and I happen to really like that lamp. However," I added, centering myself and letting my anger go so I wouldn't be sloppy or break anything in my suite when I busted his ass. "If I find your finger prints on *anything* else that was in my safe, I will tie you into a knot and hang you by your tiny man junk. Literally."

The idiot simply grinned and dropped the lamp to the ground. The sound of the glass shattering echoed through my sanctuary. *Edvard* had just thrown down the gauntlet—or rather the lions and the fish. It was the nicest thing he'd ever done for me. The son of a bitch had just given me permission to release the enormous amount of tension that had been building up inside of me.

Edward had dropped the ball on the goal line and I was going to pick it up and score.

The game was on.

***

"Explain to me again how a visiting Vampyre to our compound lost all of his teeth and several limbs?" Ethan inquired, squinting his eyes and running his hand over his mouth.

I couldn't be sure, but there was a chance he was amused.

"He broke my lamp, my liege," I mumbled, staring at the ceiling in my Prince's massive office.

I knew it sounded lame. It was lame. It was lame with a freakin' cherry on top.

"Oh for shit's sake," Astrid groused, tossing aside her fashion magazine and throwing her hands in the air. "Edward's a loser—a sneaky loser. He's overstayed his welcome. And he didn't just break a damn lamp. He broke into her safe and read her journal."

"He can pick safes?" Ethan asked in a tone that made the hair rise on my neck.

"Apparently," I told him.

"Did he steal anything?" Ethan picked up his phone and scanned his contacts.

"No. Everything is still there—even my journal. I suppose he read it and put it back."

"Did you leave the safe open by chance?" Ethan asked the logical question.

"No. Never."

"Well then, the bastard will be Raquel and Heathcliff's problem. He's part of the European Dominion and my sister is back in charge over there," Ethan said in a clipped tone as he texted his sister.

Ethan was one of the ten ruling Vampyre siblings in the world. He was fair and good, but no one wanted to mess with him. He was as deadly as they came and didn't ever suffer fools. Ethan was a true champion of our kind.

The only thing he loved more than his people was his mate Astrid and his miracle son Samuel.

Edward was in for a world of hurt from Raquel and Heathcliff. Not only was Raquel a badass leader, she was my friend. And forget about her mate, Heathcliff. He was like a brother to me.

"Done," Ethan said, tossing his phone to his desk. "He'll be leaving tonight."

"Not sure he's in any kind of state to travel," I said diplomatically. "I went kind of Rambo on him."

"Well deserved," Ethan replied with a shrug. "I want him off my property and out of the North American Dominion. He'll be flown on a jet and dumped at the airport in London."

"Thank you, sire." I bowed my head in respect and counted my blessings that I was an Elite Guard for such a wonderful man.

"Are we done with this?" Ethan asked, closing his eyes and clearly communicating with someone in the compound.

"We are," I said. "Do you need me for anything else?"

"As a matter of fact, I do. Please stay, Venus."

It was almost midnight and my lids were heavy, but if the Prince wanted someone to stay—the Vamp stayed.

At least now I could postpone my dreams.

Chapter 4

"Come again?" I asked, closing my eyes and wishing today would just end.

"I'd be delighted. All you have to do is ask, love," Gareth replied with a grin that made me want to smack it off of his face.

The Vampyre Ethan had been communicating with was none other than the very one I wanted to avoid. Awesome.

"Enough," Ethan reprimanded, shifting his focus from chastising his brother back to the paperwork on his desk. "If you have nothing to add other than offensive sexual innuendos, you may leave."

"Someone has his panties in a wad this evening," Gareth muttered with a chuckle as he sat back in the leather chair and made the international zip the lip motion.

"And *someone* is his usual douchenozzle self," Astrid added with a raised brow to Gareth as she made herself comfortable on the couch.

"Touché," Gareth said.

Ignoring the Vampyre in the chair who was burning holes in the ass of my pants with his lecherous eyes, I got back to the matter at hand. I was tired and hungry—never a good combination.

"There's a Vampyre television network?" I asked, sure I'd heard Ethan incorrectly. "How do I not know about this?"

"Do you watch TV?" Astrid asked.

"Um… not much."

"Bingo," she said. "I, on the other hand do. And the Vamp Network is one totally fucked up shitshow—except for the fact they show reruns of True Blood. I freakin' love that show. Anyhoo, I'm not a bit surprised Vlad is addicted to the channel. It's violent, weird and creepy. Very much like him."

"They have wonderful porn," Gareth chimed in to no one's great surprise.

"Define fucked up," I said, blocking Gareth out and doing my best not to pull a knife from my boot and plant it in the middle of his forehead.

"Well, as *Gareth* so helpfully pointed out, there's porn," Astrid confirmed with an eye roll. "Also news, weather, undead style shows, and freakin' cooking shows, which I call total bullshit on since we can't eat."

"Vlad is addicted to *cooking* shows?" I asked, getting more confused as to why this had any baring on finding the bastard who needed a silver stake plunged into his undead heart.

"No." Ethan ran his hands through his hair and then pressed the bridge of his nose. "He's addicted to beauty pageants."

"And this helps us find him how?" I asked wanting to cut to the chase and get the hell out.

As much as I adored my prince, Ethan and Astrid, I didn't have time for useless information. Not to mention, being in the same room with Gareth wasn't my idea of fun.

ROBYN PETERMAN

We were oil and water, and he was getting on my very last nerve. All I wanted was my bed and eight hours alone.

And after my performance earlier tonight, I didn't think Ethan would be too pleased if I removed Gareth's fangs.

"He's reportedly been seen in person at several of the televised pageants—in disguise of course. There's a woman that looks like Juliette among the competitors and he's become obsessed with her," Ethan informed me with very little emotion.

"Isn't Juliette still here in solitary confinement?" Gareth questioned with even less feeling than his brother. There was very little love or concern for Juliette from her family at this point.

Ethan nodded curtly and Gareth relaxed.

Astrid shuddered with disgust. "She's locked down so tight, no one can get to her."

Juliette was Ethan and Gareth's sister and in the strangest twist of fate, she was Astrid's sister as well. Ethan and Juliette shared the same father but different mothers. Astrid and Juliette shared the same mother but had different fathers. There had been a massive freak out on Astrid's part until she realized she and Ethan were in no way related by blood. That wrinkle still took me by surprise... and really, very little surprised me anymore.

Juliette was the one who turned Astrid and then tried to kill her, along with just about every other family member she had. She was the only royal sibling without a ruling territory. She was a dangerous rogue. To make matters uglier—if that were possible—she'd teamed up with Vlad. Juliette was his lover, as well as partner in many horrific and deadly crimes against our race. What she wanted above everything else was power. Redemption for Juliette was no longer an option.

I wondered why she was still being kept alive, but that was none of my business. Vampyre punishment held

34

little to no compassion. It was normally swift, vicious, and over quickly. We were a violent race. Brutality was something that we all understood.

Astrid coming into our world as the Chosen One had changed our modus operandi, much to the displeasure of the Old Guard, but she was a force to be reckoned with and had more power in her pinky that the entire Old Guard combined. Astrid's compulsion for compassion made her far more powerful than the evil bastards.

"Is Vlad daft?" I asked, doubtful of the intel. "He's being hunted by every known Vampyre in the world and he's attending *beauty pageants*?"

"Love—or rather *obsession*—can make a man do strange things," Ethan replied with a shrug. "If the data is correct, he's given us an opening and we're going to take it."

"Where did the information come from?" Gareth asked, no longer the snarky, obnoxious man chuckling on the couch.

He was now in full badass Vampyre mode and it was as frightening as it was hot. The muscles in his jaw worked rapidly and fists clenched in anger at his sides. His jet-black hair was laced with grey at the temples—unheard of for a Vampyre since we stopped aging at thirty, but Gareth had been cursed by Vlad and was slowly dying. However, the stupid grey in his hair made him even more appealing. At this point, Vlad was the missing key needed to save him.

Three of the other eleven royal siblings had been cursed as well and were faring about the same as Gareth. Lelia, Alexander and Nathan were on their own missions to bring down Vlad, but so far no one had been successful.

"Roberto," Ethan said in a clipped tone. "The Angel wants Vlad as badly as we do."

"Yet the Angel gave *us* this information?" Gareth demanded with a raised brow.

"He wants the fucker, but doesn't want to get his hands dirty," Astrid said. "It's tidier if we get him."

"I have no problem with that," Gareth snapped. "Well, I do have a slight concern. If I see him, I'll kill him."

"His ashes will do us no good at all," Ethan reminded his brother. "We need him alive to break the curse. As much as I want to beat the hell out of you on a daily basis, your death is unacceptable to me."

"Compliments will get you nowhere," Gareth quipped with a hollow laugh.

"Alive not dead. A dead Vlad cannot break the curse," Ethan repeated.

"*If* he can break it," Gareth said, pacing the large office like a caged tiger.

"Roberto reports he's boiled it down to three Angels who might have betrayed him and worked with Vlad. He'll find the Angel and we'll find Vlad. *Alive*," Ethan said in a tone that brooked very little need for a response.

"May I speak?" I asked.

"Please do," Ethan said, motioning for Astrid to come to him.

Their need and respect for each other humbled me. It made me long for the same, but I knew it wasn't in the cards for me. I was too set in my ways. If I hadn't come across my True Mate in over two hundred years on this earth, there was very little chance I would do so now.

"Bringing Vlad in alive is more than likely impossible. His power alone makes trapping and holding him inconceivable," I said.

"While you might be correct, I have a plan," Ethan said with a grin on his face that made my own grin pull at my lips. My Prince was brilliant, deadly, and never liked to lose.

"God, that's so hot when you get all Vampyre-y," Astrid said as she laid a big wet one on him.

"With all due *respect*," Gareth cut in with an eye roll and groan. "I'd rather not witness any royal foreplay at the moment. I have no real clue how much time I have left. If you have a plan, spit it out."

"Party pooper," Astrid mumbled.

"Under other circumstances, I'd take you out for a comment like that." Ethan glanced sharply at his brother. "But in this case I agree."

"Plan?" Gareth snapped.

"Venus will be punished for defanging a guest in our Domain. She will be put in solitary," Ethan explained, pulling up a document on his computer.

Wait. What?

"You removed his fangs?" Gareth asked with delight.

"Yes. You've read the Twilight series?" I shot back momentarily forgetting what Ethan had just decreed.

"Yes. Very interesting books," Gareth replied unapologetically with a wide grin. "Quite sparkly."

"I loved those books," Astrid chimed in with a clap of her hands. "And Venus didn't just remove his fangs. He's completely toothless and flying home as we speak with one arm, one leg and a nose residing in his hairline."

"Very intriguing," Gareth said, winking at me.

I closed my eyes and shook my head. My instincts were to laugh, but then I'd be giving the imbecile permission to butt into my life again. I could clean up my own messes without any help from a Vamp who wanted to get in my pants—again. I had enough problems already without adding Gareth back to the list.

"And your reasoning for putting me in solitary?" I asked Ethan, willing to go, but needing to know why.

"You'll be caged next to Juliette," he replied evenly. "She doesn't know you. You'll be on death row—so to speak. You'll have nothing to lose—feel free to trash talk all of us. She'll hear this and hopefully you can get information on Vlad. Anything will do at this point. She's stopped talking to the interrogators and my gut says she has useful knowledge."

"No," Gareth hissed.

Ethan's fangs dropped and his eyes blazed green. "I'm sorry. *What*?"

"I said *no*,"' Gareth shot back, his own fangs dropping and his eyes going from crystal blue to menacing green. "Venus will have no part of this."

The power dancing around the room was suffocating. The two brothers went toe-to-toe and for a moment I forgot Gareth was dying. His anger was terrifying.

"Whoa, whoa, whoa," Astrid squealed, jumping between the two men. "While undead testosterone is all kinds of smexy, you boys are being ridiculous. No one here wants me to get involved because there's a fine chance we'll lose a good portion of the compound. I'm quite good at ending violence, but I'm also wildly fucking adept at blowing out walls. SIT!" she yelled at the vibrating Vampyres.

Turning away in fury, Ethan went back behind his desk and punched a hole in it. "This is *my* territory. I am the undisputed leader here. Venus is my top general— deadlier than anyone else in my Dominion. I'm trying to save your goddamned life. Explain yourself now, or I'll put you out of my misery and call it a day," Ethan roared.

"I need to speak with you alone," Gareth ground out through clenched teeth to his equally fuming brother.

"Oh my hell," Astrid griped as Ethan nodded his head at his mate and me, clearly indicating that we should leave. "I call no motherhumpin' fair."

I wholeheartedly agreed with Astrid. Did the bastard think I wasn't qualified? My anger bubbled beneath the surface, but before being dismissed I needed a few more pieces of the puzzle.

"With all due respect, I deserve to know more about the plan. I'll follow your orders without question, but it's only fair that I know what I'm doing," I said, trying not to flinch at the litany of swear words coming from Gareth.

The man didn't own me. He had no say over what my Prince demanded of me. And if he kept cursing at me, I was going to go Rambo on his ass. I didn't care who was present.

"Enough, Gareth," Ethan shouted. "You will get your privacy with me momentarily. Venus is not out of line."

"Thank you, sire." I bowed my head to him, avoiding eye contact with Gareth at all costs.

"The plan is for you to get information from Juliette. We will then register you for the next pageant that the object of Vlad's obsession will be competing in. If the woman is agreeable, we'll use her as bait. If not, we go with plan B."

"That's the worst damn plan I ever heard," Gareth yelled and further defaced Ethan's office by putting his fist through the wall. "What the fuck is plan B? We invite him back to the house for tea and crumpets?"

"Plan B is to dismember him—arms and legs—so we can take him alive," Ethan went on ignoring the destruction to his office. "Actually, that's also part of plan A. It'll just be easier if we have a decoy."

The sound of lamps crashing and furniture being thrown was difficult to ignore—difficult but doable.

"I won't have Venus put at risk that way," Gareth said taking a short break from demolishing Ethan's office. "Not happening."

"Not your call," I shot back angrily, but baffled as to why he was throwing such a fit. It almost seemed like the jerk *cared*. Wishful thinking was going to get me in trouble. Not going there.

"Enough," Ethan said to Gareth. "Venus, are you agreeable?"

"I am," I said, accepting the flimsy proposal. "Do you have a likeness of this female Vamp from the pageant?"

"I do," Ethan said reaching into a stack of drawings and handing me one.

The ringing in my ears as I looked at the face of the woman blocked out Gareth's tantrum. However, it was her name printed below the likeness that was a deadly punch to my dead heart. The room spun and my gut burned like it had been knifed with silver. My body shook and I grabbed Astrid by the shoulder for purchase. How was this possible? There was a slight resemblance to Juliette, but not as much as I'd expected. I could never forget this particular face. Ever. It was burned into my memories.

"Are you all right?" Astrid was alarmed as she wrapped her arms around me.

"I am," I replied, but my voice seemed to come from somewhere far away. "No, I'm not."

"Talk to me," Astrid urged.

"May I have permission to end the woman after we capture Vlad?"

Ethan glanced at me sharply in confusion and surprise. "Why would you want to kill the Vamp? She has nothing to do with Vlad."

"Call it an old vendetta," I said tonelessly. I slipped gently from Astrid's embrace and stood on my own two feet. "She'll be the bait. I can guarantee it. She owes me a life—several, in fact. But I want to be granted full permission to end hers."

Gareth was now silent and I felt all eyes in the room boring into me.

"You ask for very little, Venus," Ethan said in a measured tone. "I know you wouldn't ask for a life without reason. I grant and support your request. However, as your Prince I have the right to know why."

Nodding my head and trying to find words instead of the scream that wanted to leave my lips took more effort than killing Trolls or Demons.

"Her name is Claudia. I had no idea she'd been turned or she'd be ash already. She was the wife of my *master*," I spat.

"Your master?" Gareth asked, not following.

It wasn't a surprise he didn't understand. Master could mean several things to a Vampyre—a sire, a leader... but that wasn't what I meant. Gareth didn't know my history. Honestly, I didn't want him to know my past. It was mine and I wanted no pity for it. I'd taken care of the man who'd murdered my mother, sisters and brothers in cold blood with a whip. The image of their broken bodies covered in bloody stripes where the whip had torn their skin away from the bone was branded into my brain for eternity.

I'd tried to end my own life after their deaths, but the memory of my family and my need for vengeance wouldn't allow me to do something so selfish. It took me many decades to let go of the guilt of not being with them when they died.

Much to my genuine surprise and serious shock, the wives' tale that had always terrified me as a child about the walking dead turned out to be very real. I'd been hiding in the woods and living like an animal for weeks when I happened upon the beautiful man whose sparkling green eyes and sharp teeth I would never forget. I begged him to make me like him. His ethereal skin was pale and he glowed like what I'd always imagined an Angel would look like.

Initially I was unsure if I was hallucinating from starvation or if I'd gone insane—it was neither of those things. He was very real and I was drawn to him like a moth to a flame. I'd expected him to spit on me—the only way I'd ever known whites to treat blacks—but he didn't. He told me he'd watched me for many years and it would be his honor to gift me the strength to do right by my family.

After I'd been turned, I saw my benefactor only once more. He stood and watched me destroy those that had destroyed me. Afterward, I'd pleaded with him to take me with him, but he told me that was impossible. He promised to watch over me when he could and urged me to find the Vampyre Prince named Ethan. It took me a few years, but I followed his orders. I eventually became one of Ethan's people—loved, cared for, and trained to be a killer. Often I'd searched for my undead guardian Angel, but no one knew of a Vampyre by his description. I thanked the man daily in my prayers and hoped to one day come across my savior again.

As for my *master*, I killed him. I killed the man whose name I would never utter again as brutally as he'd killed those I had loved. I'd also taken out the foreman, and everyone else who looked the other way, or enjoyed the horrifying death of my indentured family. The only one I'd missed was the wife. I had missed killing Claudia.

Somehow, she'd gotten away. But this time she wouldn't.

Maybe that's why I was still here when the rest of my family was long gone

The risks I'd taken with my undead life suddenly bothered me. I could have perished and Claudia would have gone on living—me never knowing she did. Although, the risks I'd taken had made me the killing machine I was today... so perhaps things had worked as they were meant to.

"Claudia was the wife of my master," I repeated flatly. "I was a slave during my human years. He's dead by my hand, and if I could kill him again, I would."

The silence in the room was as thick as the power still floating around.

"This might be a bad idea," Ethan said, staring at me and trying to gage my reactions. "This is too important to risk mixing it with vengeance. Perhaps it hits you too close to home."

"But..." I started, only to be halted by his hand.

"You have my blessing and permission to go after her. She's yours after we have Vlad. But you will have nothing to do with the mission."

"Finally some sense," Gareth snapped.

"Sire, you're wrong," I said, imploring Ethan with every cell in my body. "By Vampyre law, she owes me many lives for what she was complicit with in her human years. She *will* be our bait, but you need me to make that happen. She was, and I assume is still, a woman who is only out for herself. The only way to make her play is to play her... and I know how."

"Not liking this," Ethan said, pressing his temples and thinking it through.

"I'm your best bet and I want the job. While it's not something to brag about, if I catch Vlad from behind, I can take his arms and legs in a heartbeat."

"No, no, no," Gareth said, approaching me with narrowed eyes.

"Stop," I hissed, halting him with my glare. "You are not my Prince. You are a dying man, along with three of your siblings. If Vlad and an Angel were able to curse the four of you, they can curse more. Ending Vlad is the only way to stop his idea that he can kill off the entire Royal Family. And unless you have a better plan, I'd suggest you shut your overbearing, macho, jackass cakehole, and let some qualified people save your worthless damn life."

Again the silence was thick. Astrid's eyes were wide and Ethan's proud smile could not be contained. It was only Gareth who still fumed.

"Guess she told you," Astrid told Gareth with a solid poke to his ribs.

With a grunt, he moved right to his brother. "Fine. Venus goes, but I go with her. I know Vlad. I'll know him in disguise. She doesn't leave this compound unless I'm with her."

"You're dying. You're a liability," Ethan said bluntly. "Venus is safer alone than with you."

"Not if I get a little stay on my illness," Gareth countered.

"How in the ever loving hell are you going to do that?" Astrid demanded, with her hands on her slim hips.

It was a very good question.

"Funny you should mention *hell*," Gareth said with a devastating grin. "Can you get ahold of Satan?"

"Oh, hell to the no," I muttered, knowing for sure the Vampyre had lost his mind.

"You're joking," Ethan said, pressing the bridge of his nose and shuddering.

"Not one bit," Gareth assured him.

"You'll owe him a favor," Astrid warned.

"Bring it on," Gareth said, completely uncaring that he would be indebted to the King of the Underworld.

I didn't think this day could get any worse.

I was wrong.

Chapter 5

"Alrighty, watch out. This shit might get messy. Uncle Fucker occasionally gets pissy about being summoned by surprise," Astrid warned as she cleared some furniture out of the way.

"This is a very *bad* idea," Ethan grumbled as he helped his mate move the coffee table and armchairs.

"No duh, Sexy Pants," Astrid shot back. "It's never a good plan to invite Lucifer into your home after eleven, but a gal's gotta do what a gal's gotta do when a psychofuck like Vlad is still on the loose."

"I take full responsibility for the request of his presence," Gareth said, firmly. "All favors owed shall be mine."

"Damn right you will." Ethan shot his brother a glare that would have withered a lesser man.

"And if he steals anything, you have to replace it," Astrid added with a laugh.

"Steals?" I asked, confused.

"He's got a thing for office supplies," Astrid explained as if it were normal everyday conversation that the Devil liked staplers.

I simply nodded. Weird didn't even begin to cover that piece of news. I had to agree with Ethan on this one. Calling on the Devil should only be a last resort. I mean, I liked Satan—as much as one could say they liked a Demon from the Underworld. He was all kinds of tall, dark, gorgeous, and every kind of insane. He'd always been cordial to me, if not a little flirty.

"Back up," Astrid warned again. "Uncle Fucker's entrances tend to be a little fiery. Literally."

"Can't you just call him?" Gareth asked as he backed up and shielded my body with his.

"Dude, phones don't work so well from one plane to another," I told him, pushing him away. I didn't need his protection. "Verizon doesn't have a Hell plan."

"Right." He nodded curtly and moved right back into my personal space.

Whatever. There was no time to put Gareth in his place at the moment. If he needed to be an overprotective alpha-hole, so be it. If it made him feel better to think he was keeping me from harm, I'd let him believe the fallacy. However, a tiny voice in my head that I squashed with a vengeance kind of liked it. With a quick pinch to my arm, I reminded myself of my less than stellar taste in men.

An eerie silence fell over Ethan's office as Astrid closed her eyes and raised her hands high. A gentle breeze floated around the room and gave me a chill that skittered up my spine. I wrapped my arms around myself and pressed my body against the wall. Astrid was incredibly powerful, but occasionally her magic went wonky and things blew up unexpectedly. We'd all heal from any injury incurred from a blast, but it might not be in good form to receive Satan with missing body parts.

Astrid chanted in a long-dead language as she sparkled like a beacon. We watched in awe as she swayed to an ancient rhythm only she could hear. Ethan and Gareth's tension was palpable. My own fingernails bit into my arms. However, Satan adored his niece. The ramifications of Astrid summoning the Devil were far less dangerous than someone screwing around with a Ouija board. It wasn't without risk, but Astrid was one of the very few that had Beelzebub by the balls.

"For the love of everything vile and illegal, this had better be good," a familiar and ominous voice growled as Satan appeared in a blast of sparkling black glitter. The Devil was clad from head to toe in black Armani—both beautiful and scary. "And Astrid darling, the name is Satan, Prince of Darkness, Beelzebub, Lucifer or The Great Evil Handsome Devil. If you insist on calling me Uncle Fucker, I'll start spending every weekend at your abode."

"Fuck," Ethan groaned.

"Quiet," Astrid hissed under her breath. "He would never do that. Kentucky gets too cold for his fire loving ass."

"I can hear you," Satan said with an eye roll.

"It's the truth," Astrid argued in her defense. "You're a total weenie about the snow."

"*Weenie* resides in the same forbidden category as *Uncle Fucker*," Satan said, his eyes narrowing dangerously. "It's a good thing I enjoy your disrespect. Lesser beings wouldn't be breathing after a crack like that."

"That's kind of a moot threat since I don't breathe," Astrid pointed out with a wide grin as Ethan let his head fall back and bang against the wall.

"So it is," Satan agreed with a chuckle of pride at his niece's insolence. "You pulled me away from a *Hoarders* marathon. What do you need?" Satan asked, taking in the occupants in the room.

The Devil was a huge and imposing man. His very presence changed the atmosphere in the office from stressed to menacing.

"I need a stay on my illness so I can go after Vlad and have the curse removed," Gareth said stepping forward.

"Again?" Satan commanded.

"I need a stay on my illness so I can go after Vlad and have the curse removed," Gareth repeated in a voice so calm I was amazed.

I suppose if you had very little to lose, Satan wasn't all that scary. Either that or Gareth had a death wish.

"So, run this by me one more time," Satan said in a silky smooth voice. He made himself comfortable on the couch in Ethan's office grinning like a cat who'd eaten a pet store full of canaries.

"I know you're not deaf," Astrid grumbled. "Gareth repeated himself twice. Clearly you're older than dirt, but I was unaware that True Immortals could have hearing issues."

"Oh please, my beautiful, grumpy niece, I heard him perfectly. I just enjoy a bit of groveling."

I stayed quiet and watched in abject fascination. I'd been in the presence of Satan a good handful of times, but his otherworldly beauty was always something to behold—and fear. As Astrid had explained over and over, Satan wasn't evil personified like some referred to him. Evil existed because of free will—and God—Satan's brother—had created that little doozy. Satan didn't design sin. He simply punished those who chose that particular path. And he enjoyed his job. A lot.

"The favors I will owe you should negate the need for groveling," Gareth said with very little regard to Satan's position in the pecking order. "Tell me what you want and it will be yours, Devil. We've played this game before."

"Is he talking to *me*?" Satan asked Astrid as his fingers began to spark. "Because if he is, that tone will get him an ass smiting that will last an eternity."

"No, he was talking to the imaginary harbinger of evil sitting behind you," Astrid groused. "Look, you can either do it or you can't. If you can't, we'll call on someone else."

"For the love of everything dishonorable, disgusting and corrupt. Of course I can do it," Satan shouted, throwing a mini tantrum and setting the couch on fire. "Can't I have any fun? It's been boring in Hell lately."

With a flick of her fingers, Astrid put out the fire with magic and rolled her neck in preparation to handle the most dangerous man in the Universe.

"Here." Astrid shoved an electric pencil sharpener into his hands. "Play with this. I'm not in the mood for putting out fires tonight."

"Can I keep it?" he asked as he took the gadget and examined it with interest.

"Would it matter if I said no?" she asked with a laugh.

"Probably not," Satan replied with an answering laugh and then turned his attention to Gareth. "This will cost you—as you already know."

"The price is immaterial," Gareth replied.

"I'm quite sure you'll live to regret that statement," Satan purred.

"Possibly," Gareth agreed with a lopsided grin and a shrug. "However, if I live, it will be my great displeasure to pay you back."

"Holy Hell, you Vampyres are so much fun—balls and egos for days. Welcome back to the fold, Gareth. However, full disclosure, which mind you I'm not in the habit of doing because I'm not usually this *generous*, but you got me on a good day—there *is* another way."

"To reverse the curse?" I asked, before I knew I was even speaking aloud. And what dealings had Gareth had with the Devil?

"Ahhhh, Venus. You're a breathtaking sight for sore eyes," Satan said as his eyes lit up with sexual interest. "It would be my great pleasure to take you away from here—not to mention one of my fantasies. The things I'd like to do to you..."

Gareth's vicious growl made Satan bellow with laughter and prompted Ethan to step in front of his brother.

"Venus is under my Domain," Ethan said in a cool tone, eyeing the Devil warily. "Poaching is against immortal law—as is *kidnapping*."

"Your point?" Satan asked with a beguiling look of innocence on his face.

"Oh my Uncle God," Astrid snapped, smacking Satan in the back of the head. "You're an idiot, but I can solve this quickly."

Gareth, Ethan and I froze. Who in their right mind smacked Satan?

"Venus is a grown woman and can make her own decisions. Do you want to date the Devil?" Astrid asked me with a barely suppressed smile.

"Um... while I'm wildly flattered... I'm seeing someone else right now," I lied to Satan. Well, it wasn't all a lie. I *was* flattered.

"Your loss, you beautiful creature," Satan replied with a mischievous glint in his gaze. "No luck finding your *True Mate* yet?"

Staring at my feet, I shrugged and then raised my eyes to his. "No, and at this point I don't expect to."

Satan looked confused for a brief moment but covered it quickly. "Fascinating," he said, glancing over at the still growling Gareth. "The curse is well crafted. Who knew Vlad was so adept at screwing with the natural order of things?"

"What do you mean?" Ethan asked. "And it wasn't just Vlad. An Angel was involved."

Satan nodded thoughtfully, his focus still on Gareth. "Yes, I'll be expecting both of those despots in Hell eventually."

"Okay," Astrid said to her uncle, trying to get everyone back on topic. "You *can* do it. The question is *will* you do it?"

"Anticipation is so exciting, isn't it?" he shot back with a wink. He then furrowed his brow and feigned deep thought. "Yessssss. I can and I will. Gareth, I shall let you know the payment."

"When?" Gareth asked through clenched teeth, still trying to get himself under control.

"Eventually," Satan replied easily. "However, I want Vlad. When you're through with him, he's mine. I've been practicing my water boarding techniques—I think he'd enjoy helping me out."

"Our pleasure." Ethan gave Satan a curt nod. "Although before we go through with this, I believe you said there's another way."

"Yes, I did," Satan replied. "Gareth would you like to share what that might be?"

"No, Lucifer. I would not," Gareth shot back.

"That will cost you another favor," Satan said as he sauntered over to Ethan's desk and began going through the contents of the drawers.

"I expected as much," Gareth replied tightly.

"Hello," Astrid said in her outside voice. "Don't really like being left out of secrets."

"You already know the answer," Satan said staring hard at her. "I told you in the caves under Paris."

"So I'm the odd man out?" I questioned, confused by the cryptic banter.

"Gareth?" Astrid prompted, letting him decide. She clearly remembered the other way as did Ethan who looked pained.

Ignoring Astrid, Gareth approached the giddy Devil. Discord was delightful to Satan and the room was full of it.

"Give me a stay on my illness. I will pay you what you choose. The *other way* isn't possible. The curse has rendered that option moot—as you can plainly see."

"So be it. The other option might not work once I've done this," Satan replied as he stood to his full height and put his hand on Gareth's forehead.

"I understand," Gareth said.

"And there are a few caveats," Satan continued.

"Of course there are," Ethan muttered, which earned him a pissy glare from the Prince Of Darkness.

"The stay lasts a week. If you haven't accomplished your goal, the curse will resume. However, it will accelerate."

"Accelerate?" Gareth asked, looking far too calm at this new wrinkle.

The Devil nodded and gave him a tight-lipped smile. "To the point where you will be on real death's doorstep."

Wait. No.

What in the hell was Gareth thinking? We hadn't been able to track Vlad down for months. One week? He'd be dead in a week if we didn't find the evil bastard and reverse the curse. The chances of that happening were slim.

"No, it's too risky," I blurted out to the surprise of everyone including me.

Gareth's shoulders tensed and his hands fisted at his sides. Ethan and Astrid exchanged cryptic looks.

"Ahhh the exquisite one speaks. I didn't realize you *cared*," Satan said to me while staring at Gareth.

"I... don't," I lied once again in the presence of the Devil. "I mean, I... um, we might not apprehend Vlad in a week. And even if we do, it might take more time to reverse the curse. That's what I meant."

"So you *don't* care?" Satan pushed.

"No," I lied a third time and waited to be zapped by lightening. No such luck...

"This is even better than *Hoarders*," Satan said as he clapped his hands with glee. "Your turn, Gareth."

"I could die in a day," Gareth said tonelessly without sparing me a glance. "I have no idea how much longer I have. We have a lead. I have an option. It may be the only chance I have for myself and my siblings. Death comes in many forms. Immortality can be a very prolonged death. I'll take my chances."

What in the ever lovin' hell did he mean by *that*? If he wanted to be an ass with a death wish, it wasn't my problem. He wasn't *my* problem. I wasn't about to make him my problem. Shit, could this day get any worse?

"I actually might like you," Satan mused, tilting his head and narrowing his eyes at Gareth. "Of course that won't get you out of your payment."

"I wouldn't expect it to," Gareth replied flatly.

"I don't have all night," Satan said as he sighed dramatically and cracked his knuckles with an evil little smirk. "*Hoarders* waits for no one."

Speaking in a language similar to the one Astrid had used to summon him, the Devil closed his eyes. Magic filled the room and dulled my vision. The sound of Gareth's excruciating cry as he dropped to the ground with a sickening thud felt like it ripped part of my soul away. But that was ridiculous. He meant nothing to me. I certainly didn't want him to die, but...

"If you killed him, I will kick your ass," Astrid muttered as she squatted down next to the unconscious Gareth.

My legs moved without direction from my brain and I too found myself on the ground next to him. He looked dead—for real dead.

"Interesting," Satan said, watching me closely. "He should have waited a few days. The bastard might have gotten off scot-free."

"What are you talking about?" I hissed, pulling Gareth's arm out from beneath him so if he woke, he'd be comfortable.

"Nothing, darling," Satan said silkily, eyeing me like I was on the menu. "If you change your mind about a little night out, let me know."

On that note, he left in a blast of black and silver glitter—and with the pencil sharpener and a few other things he'd lifted off Ethan's desk. He was some piece of work.

"I think I might be dead," Gareth choked out with his eyes still closed.

"Nope," Ethan said, relaxed now that the Devil had gone and Gareth was awake. "You look and sound alive to me. As a matter of fact, you look like you did before the curse."

And he did. And something was wrong. Prickles of something I'd never experienced danced like needles beneath my skin and I felt faint. Standing was a chore as my body wanted to stay close to the mess of a man on the floor. All my instincts had gone haywire and the only sensible plan of action was to leave. I needed to get the hell out of the office before I did something wildly embarrassing and horribly inappropriate.

"Gotta go," I whispered hoarsely as I forced my legs to walk through the door. "Let me know when you want me in solitary. Need to… um, sleep or run or, um…"

"You okay?" Astrid asked with concern as she watched me with unabashed curiosity and a small smile pulling at her lips.

Strangely, my Prince had the same expression. It was only Gareth who looked as pained as I did.

"I'm just tired and hungry," I mumbled as I ran into the doorframe trying to make my escape.

WTH? I felt like I was drunk which was virtually impossible for a Vamp.

Leave. I needed to leave. Now.

"See you tomorrow," I called out as I picked up speed and ran down the long hallway.

"Oh shit," I heard Astrid say as I sped away. "This is going to be interesting."

"Understatement," Ethan added.

"Did Satan say the *other* way to break the curse *might* work or *won't* work?" Astrid asked.

"Might," Ethan replied.

"Thank Uncle God for that," she mumbled.

If I wasn't a massive bundle of weirdness, I would have turned around and demanded my friend and my Prince explain themselves.

However, I was pretty sure I didn't want to know what they meant.

Chapter 6

"I know I should be fucking enjoying this, but I feel really bad," Martha insisted as she purposely smacked herself in the head with the hilt of her sword.

"Ditto," Jane grunted as she too walloped Martha in the head.

They stood in the middle of the gym looking like they'd just found out Santa didn't exist.

The gals sported blinding lime-green rompers, brown socks and black sandals. However, the crowning jewels— pun intended—were their scabby heads. Apparently the staples went into the afros far more easily than they had come out. Without much hair of their own to begin with, the staple holes were very evident and unfortunate to look at.

Shaking my head and trying not to swear at the idiots, I put on my stern face. I'd gotten next to no sleep last night. Backtalk from fashion-free old ladies wasn't going to fly today. "Who's in charge here?"

"Um... you are?" Martha guessed, looking unsure.

"Yep." I crossed my arms over my chest and gave them a hard stare. "I'm teaching you how to fight. What I say goes, so do it. This chance comes along once in a lifetime—and we live for a very long time."

"You want us to use knives?" Martha whined.

"And our fists?" Jane asked with huge eyes and a shudder.

"And our titties?" Martha continued.

"No," I choked out on a gag. "No boobs. Boobs are not weapons."

"Yours are," Martha pointed out. "What are you? A perky 36C?"

"I'd call her a 34C or possibly D," Jane amended.

"Let's leave my girls out of this," I said, shaking my head.

This was not working the way I'd planned. I was due in solitary confinement in an hour and I needed to get beat up. Hoping to kill two birds with one stone, I was giving the ancient air bags a chance to really go at someone—me. Unfortunately, they weren't on the same page.

"So you're just gonna stand there and let us whack the living hell out of you?" Martha asked, still searching for the catch.

"Yes."

"While that sounds real mother humpin' appealing in theory, in practice it kinda sucks balls," Jane said while Martha nodded vigorously in agreement.

"For the love of God," I snapped. "I'm giving you a free pass. Take it."

"Why?" Martha questioned.

"Because I said so."

"Don't make much sense to me." Jane scratched her scabby head and looked mystified. "And as much as I won't admit it in public, I kinda like you. Seems wrong."

"When did you two grow morals?" I demanded with a huff of exasperation.

"Um... just now?" Jane offered.

"You're all kinds of mean, but you have a nice rack and not many would want to train us without removing our heads. Which wouldn't be such a bad idea right now considering they're itching like a motherfucker. Who in the hell knew staples would cause so much damage?" Martha griped.

This was not going to work. Self-inflicted wounds would look suspicious. I needed someone to go Rambo on my ass. At my age, I healed quickly so it needed to be violent.

"Listen to me," I growled. "While I can't give you the details, this is a direct order from Prince Ethan. Due to a... um... situation, I need to look like I've had my ass handed to me. This is for the safety of our people, so unless you want me to put staples where the *sun don't shine*, I'd suggest you two dingbats get to work."

"Well, in that case," Martha said with a shrug as she hurled a knife at me.

She completely missed. How in the hell were they still alive?

"Dang it," she shouted as she went to retrieve the dagger. "I should have nailed that one."

"What were you aiming for?" Jane asked, choking up on her sword in preparation to throw.

"Left boob, it's always the bigger one," she muttered as she squatted down and picked up her weapon.

Rolling my eyes, I stood there as Jane proceeded to toss three knives, two throwing stars and her sword at me. She missed every time. At this point it looked like self-inflicted wounds were going to have to suffice. I wasn't at liberty to explain the mission, so getting a normal Vamp to kick my ass was out of the question. Everyone in the compound was terrified of me.

Shit.

"Well, butter my butt and call me a biscuit," Jane squealed, pointing to the seating area on the other side of the complex. "I didn't know Billy Ray Cyrus was a Vampyre."

"He's not," I said as I looked in the direction Jane indicted.

A wide smile pulled at my lips as I spotted the country singer.

Jane was right... and she was wrong. Billy Ray Cyrus *was* sitting on the bleachers watching the shit show ensue. However, it wasn't Billy Ray Cyrus at all. It was The Kev. I almost cried with relief. If anyone could kick my ass in the nicest way possible, it was the two thousand year old Fairy.

The Kev took on the façade of different people—usually cheesy celebrities—because his natural form was so stunning, most couldn't look at him. He'd taught both Ethan and Astrid how to fight and was one of the most feared beings in the Universe. He was also one of my favorites—kind, wise, deadly and silly.

He was a goner for Gemma, who was his love and the soon-to-be Queen of the Fairies. Gemma was in my small circle of BFF's. I knew she wasn't looking forward to taking her rightful place amongst the crazy-ass Fairies, but fate was a bitch—and fate usually won.

"Howdy," The Kev drawled, sauntering over.

"Oh my Hell, did you paint those jeans on?" I asked with a bark of laughter and an amazed shake of my head.

"Nope," he replied with a smirk. "However, it wasn't easy. My man parts aren't pleased."

"I learned how to twerk by watching your daughter on TV, Mr. Billy Ray," Martha announced, all aflutter.

"Martha, it's The Kev," I told her quickly as she began to demonstrate her horrifying skill.

"Well, I'll be damned," Jane shouted. "You looked like Donny Osmond last time I saw ya! What in the hell do you really look like?"

"Venus, will you be needing the service of the gals today?" The Kev inquired with a sly smile.

"No, definitely not," I told him, turning away from what I knew he was going to do.

Thankfully the training facility was empty other than the four of us or what he was about to do would wreak havoc. A breezy magic filled the vast room and the scent of wild flowers and lemon permeated the air.

"Holy shit on fire," Jane screamed. "My goddang eyes are burning, but I can't look away. Those pecs. I wanna lick those pecs."

"Sweet baby Jesus in a mankini," Martha shrieked. "Look at the package! Gemma is one lucky gal. I'd like just ten seconds alone with that big ole..."

And then there was silence. Blessed silence.

"Is it safe to turn around?" I asked with a giggle.

"Yes, my friend, it is," The Kev replied. Thankfully he'd reverted back to the doppelgänger of Billy Ray Cyrus.

Martha and Jane were on the floor with enormous smiles on their unconscious faces. For a brief second, I'd been tempted to peek at The Kev in his true form, but I wasn't an idiot.

"They gonna be okay?" I asked, examining the passed out old fools.

"They'll come to in a few hours," he replied with a grin and a shrug. "What exactly were you trying to accomplish here?"

"Have you spoken to Astrid and Ethan?" I didn't want to have to go through the entire explanation again, but I knew it was safe for The Kev to know the particulars.

He nodded. "You'll be going to solitary and then after Vlad. I get that, but why would you let Martha and Jane—for lack of a better word—beat on you?"

"Juliette won't buy it if I go to solitary without a scratch on my body. I've been trying to train the idiots," I said referring to the lumps on the floor at our feet. "And I figured this would help them and help me. I was wrong."

"I see," The Kev said trying to suppress his smile.

He failed.

"It was a lame idea." I laughed and ran my hands through my hair. "However, I have a new proposal if you're up for it."

"And what would that be?"

"You go Rambo on my ass."

"Hmm..." The Kev tilted his head thoughtfully. "Not really my style. Plus if you just stand there and take it, it would be as obvious as self-inflicted wounds."

"This is true," I replied, realizing he was correct. Lack of sleep was making me sloppy—damn Gareth straight to hell and back. Even though Juliette didn't know me, I had to go on the assumption that she might know of my reputation as a warrior.

"Should I try and find a Troll real quick?" I winced at the thought.

Trolls smelled awful. I was fine with being a little bloody, but stinky was almost too much to take.

"No, not today," The Kev said. "I will fight you and you will fight back. Think of it as a training session with me—real and tremendously painful."

"You would do that for me?" I asked as I threw myself at him and hugged him tight.

"Of course I would," he said, giving me a peck on the top of my head. "You need your ass kicked? I'm your man."

"Not sure I can smack down on Billy Ray Cyrus," I slid out of his warm embrace and sized him up. It seemed kind of mean to kick Billy Ray's ass.

"How about this?"

He morphed before my eyes into Patrick Swayze.

"Ohmygod, no! I loved him in *Ghost*. That would be sacrilegious," I whispered, trying not to giggle.

"Hulk Hogan?" he inquired as he magically shifted into the famous wrestler.

"Nope. Can you go cheesier?"

In a hot second he was John Stamos.

"No. I loved *Full House*. I can't go Rambo on Uncle Jesse."

"You're not making this easy, little one." The Kev's tone was stern but his eyes were lit with amusement.

"Sorry," I mumbled with an apologetic smile.

The Kev paced while he further considered my request. "How about I take on the façade of someone you'd like to have a go at?" he suggested with a gleam in his eye.

"Someone I hate?" I asked, squinting back at him. That gleam made me a little nervous.

"Fine line between love and hate, my little friend. But for the purpose at hand, let's say yes."

It made sense. Needing to get it over with quickly before solitary, it might spike my adrenaline to feel like I was fighting a foe.

Wrinkling my nose in distaste, I suggested the very worst of the worst. "You want to take a crack at Vlad?"

"No, even I can't go that low," The Kev said with a shudder. "Let's just say I'll become someone that you're very angry at..."

"And who would that be?" I questioned, warily.

The Kev said nothing, but went from Hulk Hogan to the man I wanted to rip apart with my bare hands. I was unsure if I was angry with The Kev or my reaction to the man he'd just become. Deciphering that would take introspective thought and admitting things to myself that I had no intention of acknowledging—now or ever.

My fists clenched at my sides and my adrenaline spiked sky high. My face felt flushed and I was furious at The Kev for knowing my secret. I knew I was still with The Kev, but my reaction was anything but sane.

The Kev wanted to rile me up? He'd succeeded.

I was about to go hand to hand with Gareth.

Heaven help us all.

Chapter 7

"Oh my freakin' hell," I choked out, as I spit the blood that was filling my mouth. "I said hand me my ass, not rearrange my face."

We'd been brawling for twenty minutes—it felt like twenty years. The Kev was the toughest opponent I'd ever faced. I was just thankful it was a training session and not the real thing. I'd be dead on the floor if it was—for real dead.

"You calling it quits?" The Kev inquired as he expertly rolled and kicked my legs out from under me.

Jumping to my feet, I back-flipped and scissor kicked him in the head. The sound of his nose breaking was tremendously satisfying in a horrible way.

"I'm sorry," I apologized, and then grunted as he landed a fist in my stomach.

"No worries. It will heal." The Kev laughed with delight as he rang my bell with a solid right hook to my cheekbone. "No one has broken my nose in a fight in over seven hundred years. Congratulations."

"Thank you," I replied, and got in my own one-two punch to his jaw.

"I think it's interesting that Gareth evokes such passion in you," The Kev observed while landing an excruciating blow to my ribs.

"Don't think," I ground out, nailing an excellent jab to his lower back. "Thinking is overrated."

His bellow of laughter made me furious. He was correct about Gareth. However, so was I—thinking *was* overrated and I refused to do it. It would get me in trouble. I was in enough trouble at the moment trying to hold my own against a tsunami of fists.

"Enough," The Kev announced with great joy. "The mission has been accomplished."

Dropping to my knees, I knelt for a moment so my head would stop spinning. The Kev wasn't even breathing hard. Of course, I didn't breathe at all anymore, but if I did, I'd for certain be hyperventilating.

Beware of what you wish for was becoming my new motto. The Kev punched like a freight train that had derailed from the tracks and was hurtling toward Hell at warp speed. My lips were split and my arm was broken. I was fairly certain several of my ribs were cracked and my left eye was swollen shut. Not to mention every muscle in my body was on fire.

"You okay?" The Kev asked as he nursed a few wounds of his own and reset his nose with a click and a crunch.

"Absolutely not," I mumbled through my bloody lips. "I'm really sorry about your nose."

"Are you?" he inquired with a raised brow that was also bleeding.

"Um... no. Not really," I said with a giggle that sounded more like a wheeze.

His smile looked bizarre with all the blood pouring from his face. Thankfully he'd morphed back into Billy

Ray Cyrus. If he'd still been Gareth, I might have gone for another swipe at his head.

"I'm so proud of you, my little one." He squatted down and took my throbbing, bloody hands into his. "Not many in this world can give me a run for my money and live to brag about it. You are very special, Venus."

All the pain and agony I'd just gone through was now officially worth it. My aching body literally tingled at his praise. To be complimented by The Kev on my fighting skills was equal to a thousand Christmas mornings rolled into one.

Bowing my head in respect, I wanted to cry but I didn't. Big girls didn't cry. They kicked ass and took names. I was a big girl. I'd always had to be one.

"You humble me with your praise," I told him as I leaned into his comforting warmth. "I adore you."

"And I you," he replied as he carefully pushed my hair off of my wrecked face. "You look like Hell warmed over. You have accomplished your goal."

"Thank you."

"Welcome."

He stood and started to walk away then turned back and paused. "Venus, things are not always as they seem. You would be wise to take that to heart and listen to your instincts even if they don't tell you what you want to hear."

"Would you like to be more specific?" I went to put my hands on my hips, but my broken arm screamed in pain. Damn, he'd worked me over like a punching bag.

"Now what would be the fun in that?" he replied with a smile. "Be safe my little friend and know that you are exceptional—on the inside and on the outside."

And with that cryptic message, he left.

Glancing back at the still unconscious Martha and Jane, I checked my blood smeared watch and groaned. It felt like I'd spent hours with The Kev when in reality it was only a tremendously violent thirty minutes. I had about fifteen minutes before I had to go to solitary. I should find Astrid and demand an explanation about her secrecy last night, but healing was going to take all of my energy. The damage The Kev had inflicted would take the rest of the day to repair itself.

Energy for dealing with Astrid was energy I didn't have to spare at the moment.

***

Astrid clearly didn't get the *Venus doesn't want to talk* memo.

"What in the freakin' hell have you been up to?" Astrid demanded as she took in my sorry state with an expression of shock on her lovely face.

Five more minutes and I would have missed her but alas, luck wasn't on my side this afternoon. My bad day yesterday was now turning into a bad week.

"Got into a fight with the weed whacker," I deadpanned with a grin.

"Dude, seriously. What happened?"

We were standing outside the bolted doorway that led down to the area where solitary confinement was housed. It was heavily guarded with four outstanding and deadly Vampyres that I'd trained myself. I'd received a brief handwritten note from Ethan sketching out the plan, which I'd memorized and promptly burned. Paper trails were for amateurs.

"The Kev did me a little favor so Juliette will buy the fact I'm being thrown into solitary," I told her with a wince, glancing down at my blood-stained clothes. My pretty pink Lululemon workout outfit sported large red splotches.

"Brilliant," Astrid said with a wide grin of approval. "Did you get any good punches in? The Kev is a ball busting force of nature with a vicious left hook."

"He left bleeding, with a broken nose and a nice bruise on his jaw," I informed her proudly.

"Holy crapballs," she shouted and grabbed me in a hug that made me see stars. "You're my freakin' hero. Took me months to get a face shot on that wonderful son of a bitch."

"Ease up," I choked out as I felt my broken ribs shriek in horror. "Kind of a mess here."

"Sorry." She let go and then gently touched my face. "God, you look really bad. Is there anything you want to ask me before you go in?"

"Nothing about Juliette," I told her as I pondered that question and set the others I had aside. "The less I know the better. I can't slip up if I'm not aware of too many details. I'm just going to trash you people and hope she bites. Ethan got me up to speed on the plan. I know what I need to know, which is enough for now."

"Perfect. Your *execution* is scheduled for early evening, so work fast," Astrid said with a giggle and an eye roll. "You leave tonight for the pageant."

"Where am I going?" I asked, almost forgetting about the main part of the mission. Thirty minutes of getting pulverized by The Kev could make anyone forgetful.

"Oklahoma City. The armpit of the United States."

"Who gave it that nickname?" I asked with a grimace as I blotted away some oozing blood from my cheek with the back of my hand.

"I did," Gareth announced as he rounded the corner and froze when he spotted me.

The hallway became claustrophobic and I closed my eyes to escape. I'd pretended as a child that if I couldn't see what was happening it couldn't see me either. It hadn't worked then and it wasn't working now.

The shit I was in just kept getting deeper.

Gareth's blue eyes went green with fury and his lips compressed to a thin line. "Who did this to you?" he hissed as he put his hands on my shoulders and took in all my injuries. "I'll fucking kill them."

"Back off," I snapped and tried to get out of his hold. Not happening.

I was physically wrecked and he was screwing with my emotional wellbeing. There was only so much a Vampyre on the edge could take and I was at my limit.

"Who did this? Juliette?" he repeated in a tone that scared even me.

"I did this," I told him. "I needed to look beat up in solitary. I did it."

"Impossible," he snapped, looking me over. "You couldn't have done this. You will tell me who did this or I will put you over my knee until you can remember the name."

Astrid's snicker of amusement didn't go unnoticed, but was ignored by both of us.

"I'd like to see you try that," I growled, pushing down the little voice in my head that insisted that might be fun.

"Don't test me, Venus," he said in a voice that was as sexy as it was menacing.

I needed my head checked. I hated and wanted this insane Vampyre. He was causing me to feel things that I didn't understand. If I wasn't a bloody wreck, I'd do to him what I'd just done to The Kev.

"Drink from me," he insisted, pressing his wrist to my swollen lips.

"Nope, she can't," Astrid cut in quickly, saving me from a huge mistake. "She needs to look bad in solitary so Juliette won't suspect anything. She'll heal. The Kev just roughed her up, he'd never truly do Venus any damage."

"The Kev did this?" he demanded, his gaze boring into mine.

"Yes," I said wearily. "I asked him to. If you give him any grief about it, I will use all of my new found knowledge on you."

"Sounds intriguing," Gareth said as he tilted my chin up and further studied my face.

The hallway grew impossibly small and the guards were now watching the scene with far more interest than I was comfortable with. His hands on my battered face felt right. WTH? My instincts, which had clearly been broken along with my arm and my ribs, were telling me to accept his comfort.

"I don't like you," I whispered, trying to figure out why my insides were rioting.

He raised an eyebrow and tilted his head. A ghost of a smile pulled at his lips. "But I like you. A lot."

"That's a waste of your time," I shot back.

"Maybe. Maybe not."

"Um... guys?" Astrid cut in. "While I'm enjoying this a whole freakin' bunch, we have to shake it up here."

"Right," I mumbled in embarrassment as I wiggled out of Gareth's grasp and turned away. "Give me an hour at least. If I need more, I'll send Ethan a message."

"The transmitter on your watch still works?" Astrid asked, doubtfully checking out my blood-smeared timepiece.

I nodded and put more space between Gareth and myself. Spending time alone with him on the mission was going to be more complicated than I'd originally thought.

It sucked all kinds of butt that we were the only two going. Reminding myself of his reputation gave me strength. Reminding myself of my shit taste in men made my backbone stiffen with resolve.

I was doing my job. Gareth would not be a perk. Play me once? Shame on you. Play me twice? Shame on me. If we failed, he died. There was no time to dally with things that could possibly break my undead heart.

"An hour," I said, keeping my focus on Astrid. "Are there any hidden microphones down there?"

"Absolutely," she said. "We'll all be listening. We might understand things you'll miss."

"Then I'll apologize in advance," I told her with a grimace as I signaled to the guards to unbolt the door.

"For what?" Astrid asked.

"For all the shitty things I'm about to say."

Chapter 8

Solitary was dark, dank and depressing. The cells were small and each housed a cot and a chair. There were eight of them—four on the left and four on the right. A ten-foot aisle separated the row of cages. I shuddered at the feeling being locked up evoked in my gut, but quickly reminded myself that I was playing a game. Juliette was the only real prisoner inhabiting the bleak accommodations at the moment.

My guards, Gil and Sven, threw me into the cell violently and locked the door without speaking a word. Thankfully Sven's back was to Juliette because his expression of remorse at having to handle me so harshly would have blown the plan to Hell.

The two men were my good friends. We'd fought side by side through many battles. I'd trained them well. When I'd told them to handle me roughly, they took me at my word—no questions asked.

Juliette said nothing as I climbed painfully to my feet and ran my still bleeding hands over the thick stone wall at the back of the cage. Then I tested the lock chained to the bars of the cell.

"Forget it, Vampyre," she snapped with a laugh that sent a chill up my spine. "No way out."

I ignored her as I continued to case the tiny confines. Being nice and chatty wasn't going to get me anywhere. Juliette had responded to two people as far as I knew—her mother and Vlad. Both of those individuals were cruel and dismissive.

"Are you deaf or just stupid?" she demanded, watching me with interest.

"Shut it," I snarled. "Don't believe I asked you for advice."

"Whatever, bitch." She muttered a few other rude obscenities under her breath and then sat down on her cot to watch the show.

I could feel her eyes on me as I went over every inch of the cell with meticulous focus. However, it wasn't until I sat down that she finally spoke again.

"Told you," she said with a laugh that made me glance up at her.

It sounded a bit like Astrid's laugh, but she had nothing else of Astrid in her. They might have been born of the same evil woman, but that's where the similarities ended.

She was blonde where Astrid was a brunette. Juliette was every kind of vile sin personified and Astrid was the embodiment of every kind of goodness and light. The woman in the cell was insane and dangerous. I'd experienced first hand the deadly havoc she could wreak. Many of the Cressida House Vampyres had perished when she'd summoned Wraiths and brought Trolls to our compound. Juliette was batshit crazy and not in the somewhat sweet, politically incorrect way Martha and Jane were.

Martha and Jane—even with insulting afros—were harmless saints compared to the woman staring daggers at me. Juliette was simply horrifying.

"Why are you here?" she demanded.

Again, I ignored her.

She rattled the bars of her cage and hissed at me like an animal. "Fine. Don't speak, bitch."

"You. Will. Stop. Talking," I informed her as my eyes went green and my fangs dropped. "You are giving me a headache. Considering I just got pummeled by six Vamps, that's quite a feat."

"Ohhh," she purred. "I live for compliments."

"Doesn't look like you're living too well then," I shot back and gingerly set my broken arm. The snap, crackle, pop of the bones as they slid back into alignment was sickeningly satisfying. Even as long as I'd been undead, I was still amazed at my healing capacity.

"I'll be living large soon," she informed me snidely. "Too bad you won't."

"I call bullshit, Blondie. They'll probably remove your head along with mine later today. I hear they're vacating the compound," I lied going off one of the suggestions Ethan had made in his note.

"Really?" she asked, now rabidly interested. "Today is the day? This is so exciting. I've missed my family so. I can't wait to see my sister."

She paced her cell in tight small circles, pulling on her hair, and muttering to herself.

"Who's your sister?" I asked, closing my eyes and laying back on the cot.

"As if you didn't know..." Her voice was pure venom.

"Can't say I do," I replied easily lying through my teeth. I could only pray my indifference would spur her on.

"*Astrid*," she hissed and then cackled.

Juliette sounded like a witch from a fairytale nightmare. She really was truly stunning, but her looks belied the rotten core beneath.

"Again, I call bullshit." I barely glanced up. "If you're a royal, I'm a Troll."

"Take that back," Juliette yelled as she pressed her face against the bars. "You will show me the respect that I'm owed, Vampyre."

"Sure," I said with a laugh. "As soon as I take a little nap, I'll prostrate myself to your pathetic *royal* ass."

"You really don't know who I am?" she asked, clearly appalled.

"Nope. And I really don't care," I said, still refusing to acknowledge her with a glance.

"I'm *Juliette*," she shouted. "You will get down on your knees and beg my forgiveness, you insolent Vampyre. *Now*."

"Dude, dude, dude." My cavalier tone made her grind her fangs. So far she was quite easy to rile. "Juliette's dead. *Everyone* knows that. I don't know who the hell you are, but you're not Juliette. From the stories I've heard, Juliette was a looker. You? Not so much."

"I am beautiful," she growled.

"Yeah right. Why don't you just be beautiful with your mouth shut? I'd like to look my best when the real royal assholes remove my head in a few hours."

"I can prove it," she insisted frantically.

"That you're cray-cray?" I asked, sitting up and rolling my eyes. "No worries. You've already done that."

"If I wasn't in this cell, I'd behead you so fast," she threatened. "Save my brother the trouble."

"And your brother is?"

"Ethan," Juliette screamed. "You should know this, Vampyre."

"Lady, your delusions of grandeur would be amusing if your voice wasn't wearing on my soon to be ash last nerve. How about this?" I said, letting a wide disrespectful grin pull at my lips. "Just for shits and giggles, I'll pretend that you're *Juliette* and you can regale me with a bunch of lies. Might pass the time while I heal. I plan to take out few Vamps before they turn me to dust."

"Tell me your name, Vampyre," she demanded.

"Well, today my name can be... um... *Astrid*. Since we're playacting and all. I'll pick the most despicable of the royal shitshow."

"You hate them?" she asked, tilting her head and eyeing me with delight.

"About as much as I hate listening to you spout bullshit," I told her with a shrug of indifference.

She was silent as she digested my smack talk. However, I could see the deranged wheels in her head turning.

"You can't kill Astrid, she's unkillable," she informed me, still pacing like a lunatic. "However, there is a way to get her."

"You're almost as stupid as you are annoying."

"Do you want information or not?" she shrieked. "If you want to destroy the bitch, you'd better listen up, Vampyre."

Easing myself to a sitting position on the lone chair in my cell, I crossed my arms over my chest and waited. Did Astrid really have a weak spot or was Juliette just completely unbalanced?

"You have my attention," I said flatly.

"You will address me by my title," she said, clearly believing she now had the upper hand.

In a way she did, but not like she thought. Watching her shudder with delight as she waited to be addressed as a royal, I felt a fleeting pang of sympathy for her. She'd been hideously abused by both her mother and Vlad for hundreds of years, but the things she had done were so despicable, I was still surprised by my sympathetic reaction to her.

Shaking my head at the reckless direction of my thoughts, I focused on the fact she'd been responsible for turning many I loved to ash. At a certain point in our lives, we have the choice to leg go of wrongs done and take a different path. I had chosen to control my destiny. My tragic past shaped me, but I had opted to lead a mostly good life. It was the only real revenge I had.

Juliette, though, had clearly not taken the same route. She had chosen to let her hate control her.

"Fine," I said sarcastically. "I'll give you what you want, but you will tell me everything you know and prove that you own the title... my *Princess*."

Her eyes went unfocused and she danced around her cell, tripping over her cot and upending her chair. Landing in an ungraceful lump on the floor, she peered up at me like a lost soul. "Again. Say it again," she begged on her hands and knees.

"Make me believe you."

"My mother stole me away after my bastard father refused to turn her. She made a deal with the Demons and the rest is history," she babbled.

"You could have read that in the history books. I know that," I replied. "Who is your lover?"

"Vlad," she purred and ran her hands over her body suggestively. It was all I could do not to look away. "He loves me. He'll save me from this Hell."

"Yeah, right," I muttered and shook my head. "Good luck with that, *Princess*."

"He will," she snarled. "He comes to me in my dreams. He will rescue me and all will die who try and stop him."

This was certainly unwelcome news. Was Vlad a Dream Walker? As far as I knew, Baby Samuel was the only one of our kind who could do that. It was very dangerous and incredibly rare.

"You are so insane." I ran my now healed hands through my wild hair and narrowed my eyes at her. "No Vampyre can do that. Try again."

"He can," she informed me smugly. "You'll see."

"Umm… no, I won't," I reminded her. "About to lose my head in a few."

"Listen to me," she said, lowering her voice and crawling to the front of her cage. "If you can escape, you can come with me. Vlad will take care of you. Just kill Ethan. That's Astrid's weakness. She'll die without him."

"Right on, dumbass," I said with a rude middle finger salute. It was no secret that if a Vampyre mate was killed, the other would follow in death. However, Astrid was a True Immortal and I wasn't sure that applied to her. I was relieved that Juliette didn't have something real on Astrid. "Killing a Master Vampyre is a cinch."

"Vlad will rule the World and will be so grateful to you. We're systematically killing them off already." Juliette's excited laughter was sickening.

"Who?" I asked already knowing the answer.

Holy Hell, was the key to the problem here all along? Did Juliette know how to break the curse?

"My siblings… and we'll get my father too," she said with wide and crazed eyes.

"How?"

"A curse," she replied with a giggle that made me want to beat her senseless. "They're aging and dying. So simple. So brilliant."

"You created the curse?" I asked and prayed to God I sounded impressed.

"No, but I know who did."

So much for hoping she could break it... "Vlad? That dead dude can create curses?"

"Of course not. We caught an Angel not being very *angelic* and now we own his ass," Juliette informed me with pride.

"Your imagination is staggering," I shot back with a grunt of laughter as I moved back to my cot, laid down, and turned my back to her. "You're losing me here— getting bored with the fantasy land."

"I can prove it," she shouted.

"Sure you can," I muttered, still facing away from her. I wanted her answer more than I wanted to live a second longer.

"Promise not to tell?" she asked.

"Who in the Hell am I going to tell?" I snapped. "If what you're saying is even remotely true, then I applaud your crazy ass. If it's a lie, then you're more deranged than you seem."

"It's Rachmiel" she said so quietly that I sat up and faced her.

Was she serious? The Angel of Mercy was behind the curse? I hoped that Ethan and Astrid had heard her. Roberto needed this info immediately. Gareth only had a damn week. If we could get to the Angel, we might not have to go after Vlad at all.

My laughter sounded forced to my own ears, but Juliette bought it hook, line and sinker. What I wanted now was to get the Hell out of the cell and find the traitor

Angel, but I was certain I could get more from her. "Oh my God. You're hilarious. They should keep you alive just for the amusement of your whacked out stories."

"You think I'm funny?" she asked, delighted. "No one thinks I'm funny. I really am funny. Right?"

"Yes, you're a laugh freakin' riot. So let me get this straight. Vlad owns Rachmiel's ass and he made him put a curse on all the royal jackoffs?"

"Well, we could only get to a few, but he'll finish the job soon. When they're all dead I'll be the only living royal... and then Vlad and I will rule the world. I'd totally give you a post, Vampyre. You think I'm funny."

"I'd say thanks, but I'll be pretty dead by the time you're looking to fill your court."

"Vlad will be so grateful to you if you eliminate a few for us."

"It's all fine and dandy for Dracula to be grateful to me when I'm a pile of ash. If I kill the bastards, it's going to be for me, not Vlad. Sorry to bust on your *lover*, but he sounds like a lunatic asshole," I snapped, pressing my face to the bars and hissing at her. "And if you're *really* a royal, I'll come back and kill you too if I make it out of here alive. The only good royal is a dead one."

"God, you're fabulous," Juliette sang, jumping to her feet and smiling so wide I could see most of the teeth in her mouth. "Where were you when I needed a friend?"

"Pretty sure I just said I was going to kill you," I stated flatly. "With friends like that who needs enemies?"

"Let's do girl talk," she said, righting her chair, and pulling it to the front of her cell.

Again I had to push back my pity. She wanted my friendship because I threatened her life.

Shit. This Vampyre was all kinds of screwed up.

I had about ten more minutes. I probably had all the information I was going to get, but who knew at this point?

"I'll go first," she said with her hands clasped tightly. "Vlad is a wonderful lover. Do you have a lover?"

"The reason I'm down here is because I removed the fangs, arms, and legs of my last lover."

I watched her digest that little nugget. She clapped her hands gleefully and pulled on her hair.

"Did he cheat on you?"

"No, he bored me."

"Brilliant. Why didn't you finish the job?" she asked with huge blood-thirsty eyes and a throaty chuckle.

I was starting to feel ill, but it was very possible I could get something on Vlad. Swallowing back the bile in my throat, I continued to lie.

"They stopped me. He was a dignitary from the European Dominion. Total asshole. However, I'm fairly sure several died when they pulled me off of him."

"Vlad would love you," she assured me and then shook her head in confusion. "No, Vlad loves me. Right?"

"I have no clue," I answered her. "Did he tell you that?"

"Not in words," she whispered in confession. "In actions. He does love me, and if he stops, I'll kill him. I know his weakness too."

"He's a Master Vampyre. They don't have weaknesses," I said, hoping she'd bite.

"So little you know."

"Okay, since I'm about to die, and I have nothing better to do at the moment, I'll play. What's Vlad's weakness?"

If I had breath, I'd be holding it. It shouldn't be this easy.

"He despises imperfection and he's allergic to silver." Her head bobbed up and down with crazed excitement.

Well, so much for getting anything else useful out of the nut job. And as far as hating imperfection, the bastard must loathe himself.

"Umm... all Vampyres are allergic to silver," I told her. "You have nothing on him, my friend."

"Say that again," she insisted, reaching out to me through the bars of her cell.

"What?"

"My friend. Say my friend again."

Closing my eyes, I let my head fall to my chest. She was so unstable and pathetic.

"My friend," I said quietly. "Silver is not a secret. It harms us all."

"This is true, *my friend*," she said reverently, with bloody tears in her eyes as she smiled at me. "But you will only get burned if you touch it. He will die if it so much as touches his skin."

That stunned me to silence. How had the bastard lived for as long as he had? Silver was everywhere.

"Time to die," Sven growled as he and Gil reentered the chamber.

Unlocking the cell and grabbing me in a chokehold that I'd taught him myself, he punched me in the head so hard I saw stars. I knew we needed it to look realistic, but Sven was going to pay huge when I got out of here.

Juliette hissed and bared her fangs to the guards who studiously ignored her.

"Kill them all," she screeched as I was dragged down the hallway toward my death. "I will cherish you, my friend. Always."

God, I felt sick.

Sad and sick.

Chapter 9

It happened so fast I didn't see it coming. Sven dropped me in a heap as a raging force of nature threw him across the room and embedded his body violently into the wall. Crawling to my feet, I tried to assess what the hell was happening. I'd taken such a blow to my head when they dragged me out of the cell, maybe I was hallucinating.

I wasn't.

Holy shit.

"No," Ethan roared as he attempted to pull Gareth off of Sven.

Gareth was in full on killing machine mode as he yanked Sven to his feet, put his hands around his neck, and slammed him into the wall once again.

"Don't you ever lay a hand on her again, you fuck. I will kill you. Do you understand me?"

Sven's windpipe was being crushed and the words he tried to speak in his defense came out like garbled gibberish. Gareth was killing him and didn't seem to realize it.

"Stop him," Ethan commanded to the other guards who were so shocked by the violent turn of events they simply stood there.

No one had a chance against Gareth as unhinged as he was. Each man that approached was hurled just as violently across the room as Sven had been. This had to stop. Now.

Without a thought to how dangerous the enraged Vampyre was, I flew across the room and wrapped my arms around his waist. Laying my head against the tensely bunched muscles of his broad back, I followed my instincts—as broken as they might be. He wanted to kill Sven because he'd hit me, but Sven was only following my orders. He would not die for obeying me.

"I'm okay," I cried out as I clasped the furious man in my arms. "He didn't hurt me. You have to stop. Please. Sven is my friend. He's your friend. Gareth you have to stop. Let him go. Please."

The rigidity of Gareth's body slowly began to relax as he registered my words. He dropped Sven's body to the floor with a thud and Gareth's hands gently covered mine. He pressed his head against the cool wall and kept a tight grip on my hands at his waist.

"Take Sven to his quarters," Ethan ordered the stunned and silent men. "Now."

They other guards quickly and efficiently removed Sven and quietly exited the badly damaged corridor. Gareth stood motionless and rested his head against the wall. However, he held fast to me. The only three left were me, Gareth and Ethan.

"I'd ask you what the fuck that was about, but I think I know. Venus, you will come with me to my office. Gareth, you will cool down and meet us shortly," Ethan said tersely.

"Yes," Gareth mumbled as he reluctantly let go of me while staying in the same position.

"Come Venus. There's much to do before you leave."

I nodded to my Prince and moved away from Gareth. Everything was starting to make sense… yet it also wasn't making any sense at all.

***

"Penus!" Samuel squealed with delight as Ethan and I entered the office.

My favorite little boy in the world launched himself at me and covered my face in wet kisses. He was the miracle child born of two Vampyres. This was impossible. However, if the Vampyres in question were Astrid and Ethan, it clearly wasn't. There had been prophesy in our teachings that The Chosen One would come and save us. She would also, against all odds, bear a child.

The child would be one of unimaginable power and would encompass all the attributes of each of the True Immortals—a very heavy load to carry. The sturdy little man in question also had an adorable lisp and loved me hard.

"Hey, baby," I said, retuning his kisses and burying my nose in his soft blond curls.

Samuel was an anomaly in so many unimaginable ways. He was barely over a year old and had the intellect of an adult and the body size of a six year old. Thankfully his maturity level was still one of a little boy. He grew so quickly, I was always afraid a day would pass and he'd suddenly be a teenager.

"You wanna play wif me?" he asked with grin that made me think the world would somehow be okay.

"Maybe for a bit. I have a job to do." I held him tight and let his pure aura wash over me.

"Me know," he replied in a very serious tone for someone so small. "Me fix things up for you."

"No, no, baby." I looked him straight in his big blue eyes to make sure he knew this wasn't a game. "You don't need to worry about this. I've got it covered."

"Yessssssss!" he sang as he wiggled out of my arms and ran to tackle his father. "Me no go wif you. Me just fixed up Uncle Garif, so he be safe."

I nodded and glanced over at Astrid. With no clue what Samuel was talking about, I figured Astrid would be able to translate.

"Yes, about *that*," Ethan said as he swung a giggling Samuel up onto his shoulders then turned his focus on me. "I was quite surprised you recognized Gareth. Maybe it didn't take."

"It take, Daddy," Samuel assured him. The little man was making ponytails with his father's hair.

In my centuries of serving Prince Ethan, I never would have pictured him laughing like he did with his son. Astrid and Samuel had brought a very serious and hardened man back to life.

"But Venus recognized him," Ethan pointed out as he angled his head so Samuel had better access.

"Of course she do," Sammy said with an eye roll as his slid off his father's shoulders and hung off his neck. "Penus will always see the weal Garif. Always."

"So Venus doesn't see the blond haired, brown eyed man you glamoured Gareth into?" Astrid questioned, retrieving the little monkey from his father's neck.

Color me confused. What the Hell were they talking about? Gareth had black hair and blue eyes.

"Nooooooooo!" Samuel explained, cuddling close to Astrid as she sat down on the couch with him. "Penus see him cause…"

"Because she's very powerful," Gareth quickly interrupted his nephew, entering the room and keeping a fair amount of distance from me. "That's why she can see through the glamour you placed on me. Nothing more."

"You be Pinocchio," Samuel said, pointing a chubby finger at his uncle.

"And you're about to be Sleeping Beauty," Astrid said, tickling a laughing Samuel. "You want The Kev and Gemma to put you to bed tonight?"

"Ohhhhhhh, yes!" Samuel clapped his little hands and bounced in his mother's lap. "He do stowies wif lots of voices and faces. I wuv The Kev and my Gemma."

As if on cue The Kev and Gemma entered the office. If looks could kill, The Kev would have been a goner from the glare Gareth was sending his way. The Kev just waved and winked at him.

"Who you be today?" Samuel demanded as he marched over to The Kev and yanked on his shirt.

"Billy Ray Cyrus," The Kev answered as he scooped Samuel up into a hug. "Tonight I will sing for you."

"Heaven help us all," Gemma said with a wince and a laugh. "Does anyone have any ear plugs I could borrow?"

Gemma and Astrid had been best friends since childhood. When Astrid had been turned two years ago, Gemma had discovered she wasn't quite as human as she'd always believed. She was a Fairy just like The Kev and she was about to assume the throne in Zanthia.

Gemma was exquisite and while she didn't take on different faces like The Kev did, I knew she muted her looks with magic. I was the lucky third in the trio of women and I counted myself blessed to have such loyal and amazing best friends.

Her icy silver eyes grew wide with pleasure when she spotted me in the room.

"God, I've missed you." Gemma grabbed me and held me tight. Her fragrant scent of rain and orchids calmed my soul. "You will be very careful on this mission. If you die, I will yank your sorry ass out of wherever you land and drag you back."

Grinning and tucking a lock of curly golden blonde hair behind her ear, I rolled my eyes. "I'm already dead, dork. However, I have no plans of turning to dust in the near future."

"Roberto has been told the traitor is Rachmiel," Ethan said, bringing all of us back to the matter at hand.

"Did you hear everything Juliette said?" I asked.

Ethan's nod was curt. "The silver aspect is interesting. I'd highly doubt that a touch to his skin would kill Vlad, but he might perish if he were chained in it."

"Explain," The Kev said as he took a seat and cuddled the barely awake Samuel in his massive arms.

"Juliette said that Vlad was deathly allergic to silver—that a touch would kill him."

"A mere touch?" Gemma asked doubtfully.

Astrid closed her eyes and let her head fall back on the couch. "It's Juliette we're talking about here. She's not the most stable or reliable source."

"True." I nodded and pushed down the irrational pangs of sympathy I felt for her. "But she seemed sure."

Ethan stared at me for a long beat and then shrugged. "Best case scenario, it's correct. My guess would be that his allergy is more severe than most Vampyres. How would she know it could kill him? As far as I know the bastard is still alive."

"Not for long," Gareth muttered.

The Kev glanced over at Gemma and gave her a small nod.

Gemma reached out her hands to me and Gareth. "Come here."

We both approached warily while trying to keep as much distance between us as possible. It didn't go unnoticed by the occupants of the room. I ignored the snickers as did Gareth. He and I were going to have a serious talk. Soon.

"Give me your hands." Gemma's musical voice danced around the room and her eyes literally sparkled silver. "This will hurt like a bitch, but it's worth it."

"Like a bitch," Sammy mumbled right before he fell asleep.

"Whoops. Sorry," she apologized to Astrid and Ethan.

"Dude, relax," Astrid replied with a shrug and an embarrassed laugh. "My son's potty mouth is the least of my worries at the moment. What are you gonna do to them?"

"Just a little magic," she replied easily.

My Fairy friend was loaded with magic. I'd even seen her morph into a monster roughly the size of an SUV when seriously pissed—rather frightening, but very impressive. However, she was also a giver. Gemma hated that others weren't as safe as she was and was constantly handing out little extras to those she loved. The extras usually did hurt *like a bitch*, but that was the way life went.

Tilting her head to the side she stared at Gareth for a long beat. "You really look weird. I can tell it's you because of your aura, but it's still wonky."

"Thank you," Gareth said with a chuckle. "I'll choose to take that as a compliment."

"It's meant as one," she said as she glanced down at our hands and wrinkled her nose in thought. "Put your left hands in."

We did.

"No." Changing her mind, she her lips pursed and closed her eyes for a moment. "Take your left hand out. Put your right hand in."

"Should we shake it all about?" Gareth asked, bemused.

My giggle escaped before I could swallow it. I'd been thinking the exact same thing.

Glancing over at The Kev with concern, Gemma sighed loudly. "Wanna help me out here, babe?"

"Right hand," The Kev confirmed, seeming unconcerned that Gemma was about to do some kind of painful voodoo on us and wasn't quite sure which hand to use.

"Umm... dude," Astrid cut in. "Is this just gonna hurt or could you mistakenly blow their asses to Kingdom Come? Cause that would be all kinds of not good."

"Of course not," Gemma huffed, indignantly. "I would never risk the lives of those I love. It's just that one hand is silver and the other is gold."

"Should I?" Gareth asked, peeking over at me with a lopsided grin.

"Yep," I replied feeling giddy.

"Make new friends, but keep the old..." he sang, much to the confusion of all present except me.

"You done?" Gemma asked him.

"Depends on what else you say," Gareth quipped.

With an eye roll and a giggle, she took our hands and began to chant something melodic and beautiful. Tears pooled in my eyes and I felt like I was falling off the edge of a stunning cliff.

"Don't let go," she whispered in between the lyrics.

Peach and silver sparkles blew gently through the room as I felt my insides tickle and tingle. My head swam with vibrant colors and my body involuntarily swayed with the rhythm. Lost in a beautiful storm in my mind, I wondered why Gemma had said it would be painful.

And then I screamed.

Silver fire engulfed our hands that were clasped in Gemma's. The haunting melody continued, but my stomach now felt like burning knives ripped through my gut. Gareth didn't scream, but his displeasure was abundantly clear.

"Son of a bitch," he hissed, jaw clenched and body tense. "The result better be worth it."

I couldn't have agreed more. I'd been pummeled by The Kev, head-punched by Sven and now lit on fire by one of my best friends. It took everything I owned not to pull my flaming hand away from hers.

Swearing profusely, Gareth stayed as still as I did. He was a tough Vampyre—but then again, so was I.

"That's it," Gemma announced. The fire extinguished as quickly as it had started.

The sparkling mist remained and the melody she had sung still floated in my head. But thankfully the pain disappeared with the flames.

"What in the ever loving hell did you just do?" I asked, examining my hand. It was completely normal. No evidence that it had just been engulfed in silver fire.

Looking extremely proud of herself, Gemma preened and curtsied. "You're immune to silver."

"Completely?" Gareth asked, shocked.

"Sadly no," she replied. "Your right hands are. You can handle the metal and not burn."

"Forever?" I was truly amazed. Silver was our kryptonite. I'd barely touched it in over two hundred years.

"Again, sadly no. But it should last a month or two at least," Gemma said. "It's just a precautionary measure. If what Juliette said about Vlad and silver is true, this will make it easier for you to use it against him."

"You are so scarily brilliant and I am mother humpin' glad to be on your good side," Astrid said, checking out our hands with awe. "If only this could be permanent, we'd be in business."

"Working on it," Gemma said. "But I do have to say, it would probably suck big butts to be totally engulfed in flames."

I shuddered at the thought having just experienced only one hand on fire, but I'd go through it willingly if it meant silver wouldn't affect me.

"The little one is snoring," The Kev whispered, planting a kiss on Samuel's head. "Come Gemma. The Vampyres have plans to make and we have a child to cuddle with."

With hugs all around and a loving threat to be careful, Gemma and The Kev quietly left the office.

"All right, let's get down to business. Martha and Jane will be accompanying you," Ethan said. "You leave within the hour."

My laughter filled the office and Gareth joined in.

Astrid and Ethan were not laughing.

Oh. My. God. My Prince wasn't joking.

Chapter 10

"Call me *crazy*, but I have a theory," Jane said so seriously that I almost believed she had something worthwhile to say. Almost.

"Okay, I'll bite and raise you one. Motherfucking bat shit *crazy*," Astrid said without missing a beat.

Martha and Jane had joined us in the office and it was going downhill fast.

"I'm gonna ignore that, Chesty McBoobicles," Jane shot back. "We might be a smidge and a half off the old rocker, but we're good lookin' and extremely passive aggressive. That adds up to something."

"What?" Martha asked looking as confused as the rest of us.

Jane gave Martha an exasperated grunt. "Whose side are you on, hooker?"

"Yours?"

"Kill me now," I muttered, waiting to hear the theory. I was also secretly hoping Ethan would change his mind about them coming on the mission. It was abundantly clear that they were deranged.

Jane continued, but only after giving Martha a quick and painful looking noogie on her head. "So correct me if I'm wrong, but it's sounding to me like Venus is gonna be using her knockers as weapons."

"And *she* told us hooters weren't weapons," Martha announced to the room referring to our earlier discussion with her bony finger pointed at me. Apparently she was back on Jane's side.

"That's your damn theory?" I practically shouted.

Short of banging my head against the wall or removing theirs, I did all I could to keep my cool. There was no way in Hell I was going to let two old women wearing gauchos and sequined bras get the best of me. We had no time for this.

"Yes, that and I'd like to go on record stating that hooters are as deadly as throwing stars," Jane added.

"Can I hurt them?" I pleaded to Ethan.

"Sadly, no. Martha and Jane, Venus' *lady parts* have nothing to do with the mission."

"While I agree with my brother, *I'd* like to go on record and state that Venus does have a lethal pair," Gareth offered up only seconds before Astrid popped him in the head.

"Hear me out," Martha said, just winding up. "She's gonna parade them on the stage to catch the bad guy. So I say they're a weapon."

"You're gonna be working them 34C's like a dagger," Jane sang gleefully.

"34D's," Gareth added with a wink.

I shot him a glare that should have terrified the Master Vampyre. Of course he just gave me a lopsided grin that made my knees weak, but that weakness was something I was going to ignore.

Deciding not to grace Gareth's unnecessary, inappropriate, and entirely accurate knowledge of my cup size with a comment or a head punch, I closed my eyes and tried to figure out a logical reason to get out of the new mess that was being presented.

"I really don't see that bringing Martha and Jane to Oklahoma with us will be beneficial—*in any way*," I stated far more calmly than I felt.

Who was I kidding? It was a clusterfuck waiting to explode. The old farts were worthless in a fight and annoyed me almost as much as Gareth did. I couldn't begin to fathom why Astrid and Ethan thought this was a good idea.

"Normally, I would agree with you," Ethan said in a diplomatic tone. "However, Samuel insisted that they go."

"Why?" Gareth asked, still keeping his distance in case I lobbed something at him—like a knife. "Venus and I will work faster if we don't have any liabilities."

"Who in the Hell are *you*? You are one fine looking piece of man meat," Jane said, looking Gareth up and down with interest. "Pretty dang sure you just insulted my ass, but I'd wouldn't throw you outta bed for eatin' crackers."

"For the love of everything unholy," Astrid snapped and banged the old bag's heads together. "That's Gareth. Samuel glamoured him so Vlad won't recognize him."

"Offer still stands, Sexy Pants," Jane told him with a little shimmy than made her saggy bosom jiggle. She waggled her eyebrows and slid slowly into the splits while eyeing Gareth like he was dinner.

It was the first time I'd ever seen Gareth look terrified. He immediately moved closer to Ethan and stood slightly behind him. I bit back my laugh with effort.

"While I'm appallingly flattered. The answer is no. Never. Not once or at any time in eternity. Ever."

"Your loss," Jane grunted as she ungracefully got up from her *seduction split*.

"This is a very bad plan." I twisted an errant curl in my fingers and mentally catalogued all the things that could go wrong if Martha and Jane were involved. The list was endless.

Ethan shrugged and approached Martha and Jane who immediately zipped their lips and dropped to their knees in reverence.

"Possibly," Ethan agreed, looking down at the two old menaces. "But my son works in strange ways, and was adamant that Martha and Jane go."

"We've packed our bags, sire," Martha said, crawling over and kissing his shoe.

"And I burned them," Astrid chimed in. "You'll be taking the bags I packed for you. You'll look like respectable Vampyres from the Cressida House—Armani suits. Black. I did make a concession on the shoes. Instead of stilettos, I packed sensible low heeled pumps."

Martha and Jane took in the information with expressions that looked like they'd swallowed lemons. I tried to picture them in normal clothing and found that I couldn't. I was so used to sequins and ass bearing disasters.

"If I have to wear a suit, I'm definitely wearing a dickie," Jane announced.

"Enough. This is ridiculous," Gareth stated firmly, glaring at Ethan. "They stay here. We can't deal with insanity. The mission is life or death. While I believe Samuel to be a prophet, this is a mistake. I'm not dealing with crackpots who wear *dickies*. Unacceptable."

"Everyone has their... umm... quirks," Ethan said, trying like hell not to laugh or groan.

"Sweet Baby Jesus in a banana hammock, what in the hell do you think a dickie is?" Jane demanded.

No one spoke because no one knew.

"Um… some kind of strap on… um, male appendage?" I asked, with a wince of embarrassment.

"Hell to the no," Martha shouted with a bark of laughter. "A dickie is a false shirt front—also known as a detachable bosom."

Jane snickered at the word bosom and I rolled my eyes.

"It was designed to be worn with a tux, but I like a nice turtle neck dickie with a suit," Martha said.

Jane, not wanting to be left out, continued our education. "Back in the day some were made with elastic tabs that you could tuck into your pants so your dickie wouldn't flop around. A flopping dickie is a fucking disaster. I hated those dang straps. That elastic would get stuck in your hooha and you'd spend the entire day yanking it out."

"Damn straight," Martha said nodding and demonstrating the dickie elastic picking maneuver. "That's why when I wear a dickie around my neck, I use double sided stick tape or butt glue."

"What in the Hell is butt glue?" Astrid asked. Not a second later, she slapped her hand over her mouth in horror realizing she'd said something that would make them continue talking.

"It's mother humpin' awesome. Keeps my ass from fallin' out of my booty shorts," Jane explained. "I spray it on my money maker and then press my booty shorts into place. Voila! No extra badonkadonk."

"Used to use hairspray on my junk in the trunk until some wonderful bastard came up with spray on butt glue, but we still use hairspray to stop static cling and for deodorant in a pinch. And while we're sharing our morning routine, I always use a little Vaseline on my fangs to keep them from sticking to my lips when I smile," Martha rattled off.

"And Preparation H gets rid of puffiness under the eyes," Jane reminded Martha.

"Yep, I remember back in the day putting that stanky hemorrhoid elixir all over my body, wrapping myself in saran wrap and running ten miles so I'd look good in my skivvies for that cheating son of a bitch Herman. Found out he was popping Marge down the street so I tied his pecker in a knot."

"Really?" Astrid choked out on a strangled whisper.

I elbowed Astrid in the gut. She was making a nightmare-inducing situation worse by encouraging them to keep going.

"Nah," Martha said with a chuckle. "But I did bend it to the left and super glued it together. Heard it took months and two surgeries to get that beef thermometer straight again."

"Served that two timing son of a bitch right," Jane huffed. "I would have torn that giggle stick right off his skinny ass body and force fed it to Marge. You were kind."

Gareth and Ethan were pale and hunched over. I was wishing I could throw up, because my stomach was roiling. Astrid looked shell-shocked.

After that story, they had to realize that taking the gals was a huge mistake.

"Where did you learn all that stuff?" Astrid asked, smartly moving away from my active elbow.

"The gluing the meat popsicle part or the other part?" Jane asked.

"Other part," Astrid amended quickly.

"We were on the pageant circuit for years," Martha chimed in. "Watch this."

ROBYN PETERMAN

She pulled a tube of blood red lipstick from the pocket of her gauchos and applied it with an extremely heavy hand. Her partner in crime, Jane, held her pointer finger in the air to demonstrate something. What? I had no clue. Martha smiled and looked like she'd just fed. Her teeth were smeared with the red substance. Horrifying.

"Martha is a dumbass," Jane explained as if she was teaching a class of preschoolers. "She forgot rule number one of the Pageant Academy."

Jane then took a tube of hot pink lipstick from her sagging cleavage and applied with an even heavier hand. Baby Jane Hudson had come to life. She then took her pointer finger and popped it in her mouth like a popsicle— or something worse if one's mind was in the gutter—and pulled it out slowly. It was all kinds of wrong, yet morbidly fascinating. Jane grinned like an idiot—no lipstick on her teeth—or dentures. I wasn't sure what exactly was in her mouth.

"Suck the finger. Teeth will be spotless. Don't suck the finger. Teeth will be fucking gross."

"Did either of you ever win?" Astrid asked.

"Never, but our teeth were shiny and our keisters were always covered."

Her statement was met with silence. Everyone was busy trying to block visuals from their minds—at least I was.

"It makes sense," Astrid said much to my shock and everyone else's in the room. "I know why Samuel wants them to go."

"I'm still reeling from what I just witnessed," Gareth whispered as he fell into a chair and put his head in his hands.

I had to agree.

"How much do you know about being in a pageant?" Astrid questioned me.

100

Damn her logic.

"Nothing," I admitted, recognizing her train of thought.

She shrugged and laughed. "Bingo. The hazardous old dingbats know everything. Riddle solved."

Again there was silence while we digested the reality of what was to happen. Fine. They were going to go, but there were going to be rules.

"You will follow my orders with no questions asked." I crossed the room in a flash and planted myself in front of the now triumphant disasters.

Gareth was on my heels. "One wrong move could get all of us turned to ash. This is a one strike and you're out game. Do you understand?" His voice was soft, but his command was unmistakable.

The gals were no longer smirking. They were bobbing their heads in respect and a healthy amount of fear.

With the Vampyre version of a sigh, I gave the gals one last glance before I turned my attention back to Ethan. Time was ticking and we needed everything straight. "Has Roberto found Rachmiel?"

We might not have to leave at all if the Angel was captured. Dealing with the particulars ahead of us meant I didn't have to think about the confusing Gareth shit show and the alarming thoughts of how Martha and Jane could screw us up.

"No. Apparently Rachmiel's gone missing," Ethan replied with growl of disgust. "However, Roberto now knows he's the traitor. I'd say he'll be in custody shortly."

"He's aware he can't kill him yet," Gareth reminded his brother.

Ethan nodded. "Yes. And he said he wants Vlad alive."

"We can't guarantee that," I said, knowing taking Vlad alive would be difficult.

"Well, try," Ethan said. "Very hard. We need him alive as well."

"Leila, Nathan and Alexander have been apprised too," Astrid informed us. "They're on their way to the Cressida House now."

Gareth stood and began to pace in agitation. "I don't want my siblings as backup. They haven't made a deal with the Devil. They will stay here."

Ethan nodded in agreement. "Exactly my plan. They won't be pleased, but none of them are stupid."

"I'll need to pack." I stood and headed toward the door. Even though Martha and Jane knew the ins and outs of a pageant, I didn't want them choosing my attire— booty shorts and feathers were not going to fly.

"Already done," Astrid assured me. "Packed you myself. You have everything you need."

That made me a little nervous, but not as nervous as if the old dummies had packed for me. While Astrid's taste was impeccable, her idea of appropriate was a bit left of center. Whatever. She'd watched the Vampyre Network. Certainly she would know better than I would what was needed.

"Is Venus going to need a talent?" Jane brought up a question I hadn't even considered. "We can teach her a sexy little song and dance routine."

"What? I have to have a talent? I don't have any talent other than ass kicking."

"Then you'll be fine," Ethan assured me. "The talent in this particular pageant is a fight demonstration."

"Thank God," I muttered, getting more stressed by the second. "My focus will need to be on Claudia and Vlad."

"If he's there," Gareth added darkly.

"If he's not, you will leave immediately. We'll go after Rachmiel. Oklahoma is in my Dominion. I've gotten word out to those I've put in charge of the area and trust enough not to have to kill. They are to let me know if Vlad shows up," Ethan informed us.

Even though Ethan was the Prince of all of the North American Dominion, the sections were governed by Vamps who reported to him. It was a tenuous situation at best since we were a violent bunch, but Ethan had an outstanding grip on his people—or at the very least they feared him enough to stay in line.

"Who runs that section?" Astrid asked.

"Sheena," I replied with a small shudder. I didn't like her much, but she had shown herself to be loyal to Ethan over the decades.

"Difficult?" Gareth asked.

"Prickly," Ethan replied in a cold tone. "However, she owes me tremendously and she knows it. She won't cross you or she'll have to answer to me."

"Hear that, Jane? Shit's getting serious," Martha mumbled as she took Jane's gnarled hand in her own and stepped to my side. "We're gonna protect you and Spicy Boy there. You don't worry bout nothing."

Astrid groaned. Gareth swore and I rotated my neck to alleviate the tension building there.

Ethan kept whatever he was feeling to himself. "Pick a name, Gareth. Your identity has to be hidden. Keep it simple—something easily remembered."

"May I?" I requested with an evil little smirk on my lips. If we were walking into the face of possible death we may as well have a little fun.

"Be my guest," Gareth said, watching me with a raised brow that was all kinds of hot.

"Dickie."

I wasn't sure if he was going to be amused or pissed. However, I couldn't help myself.

He laughed.

Hard.

"Dickie, it is. However, you shall pay for that," he said easily with a sexy chuckle that made me get all squishy and uncomfortable—in a wildly inappropriate way.

Shrugging him off, I stood and bowed to Astrid and Ethan. "Anything else, my liege?"

"Your itineraries and all other info needed are packed with your things. You'll be driving. It will be the least conspicuous. You've been registered under your name and your hotel reservations put you on the same floor as Claudia. The pageant starts tomorrow evening."

"Claudia?" Jane asked. "Someone we need to beat?"

"In a manner of speaking," I replied coldly.

"Hot damn," Martha shouted. "This is gonna be frackin' fun."

Perhaps it depended on your definition, but I agreed somewhat. Taking names, kicking ass, and saving the world was right up my alley. I just hoped I lived to tell the story.

Chapter 11

"Are we there yet?" Jane grumbled from the back seat for the umpteenth time.

"No," Gareth snapped, gripping the wheel like he wanted to grip their necks. "And if you ask again, I will tie you to the roof of the car until we do get there."

The silver Mercedes SUV was sleek and powerful. Gareth handled it like he was meant to be behind the wheel. It was every kind of unnecessarily hot and stupid... and did I really just say it was hot? I was an idiot for letting my mind wander to forbidden and ridiculous scenarios.

"Can we listen to music?" Jane suggested.

"What kind?" Gareth asked, truly exasperated but trying tremendously hard.

"David Hasselhoff's greatest hits?"

"Absolutely not," he snapped, grinding his fangs.

We'd already been put through two hours of Air Supply's entire catalogue and some kind of ear splitting polka music. I had to agree that the Hoff's collection would end in bloodshed—theirs.

Flying would have been quicker, but it would have announced our arrival in a way that showed our hand. Flying was a skill that was rare. Not to mention the fact that Martha and Jane were novice flyers if you could even call what they did flying. It would have been awful and potentially very messy if they'd hit a telephone pole or a passing plane. The thought of having one of the old biddies strapped to my back all the way to Oklahoma was enough to make me love the long drive.

We were about seven hours into the ten-hour trip and the old pains in the ass had complained most of the way. I was actually impressed with myself and Gareth that they were still alive.

"So what's the plan anyway?" Martha asked leaning over the seat and popping her wrinkly head in between us.

"The plan is that you keep your mouth closed for the next three hours so I don't have to remove it," Gareth said tightly.

"Sounds reasonable," Martha agreed. "But I was talking about the actual mission—not the joy ride."

"We're winging it," I told her.

It was the truth. Not the best of plans, but we still weren't sure if Vlad would be there. If he was truly obsessed with Claudia, he would be in attendance. I needed to get to her first and twist her arm—or neck—into helping us. Hell, we didn't even know if she was aware of Vlad's obsession. It would be hell not to kill her on sight, but Gareth and his sibling's lives took precedent over my need for revenge. I would have my revenge, but not until she helped the man I... um, didn't like all that much.

What the hell was wrong with me? While the little needles under my skin that I'd felt right after Gareth had made the deal with Satan had calmed down, I still felt very left of center. I needed to get laid and *not* by Gareth. I was simply horny. That was all.

"But we're going for Vlad," Martha persisted. "We want to capture him and not kill him?"

"You will not be involved in that part," I informed her. As much as I wanted to decapitate both her and Jane, I wasn't going to let Vlad touch a sparse hair on their heads. I was beginning to understand Astrid's reluctant affection for the old dorks. "You will help me with the pageant and stay out of the way."

"Just want to put it out there that I bit a bad Fairy in the ass," Jane said with a not so humble shrug of pride. "I'd be happy to sink my fangs into that fucker's ass if it would help."

"Is this an alternate Universe?" Gareth asked with a helpless look of horror on his beautiful face. "They're going to get themselves killed."

"Listen to me, Dickie," Jane said, patting him on the shoulder. "We should have been dust about forty-seven times already. We're still here so that means we're supposed to be. We are fully willing to bite asses and strip if necessary."

"Stripping is never necessary," I hissed. "You will keep your clothing on or you're going home now."

"Fine," Jane huffed. "Don't say I didn't try to help."

There was blessed silence for about five minutes. I kept my eyes trained on the road ahead even though they wanted to stray to the Vampyre driving the powerful car. I never did get a satisfactory explanation from anyone as to why I could see through Gareth's glamour, but it didn't matter. It would make it easier for me to keep an eye on him.

It had been decided that he would pose as my guard and the old gals as my chaperone and coach. Apparently on the pageant circuit one travelled with an entourage of sorts. The more I learned about the undead beauty contests, the more disgusted I became. There was cage fighting, a barely there bathing suit competition, another in evening gowns, and an interview.

Nine times out of ten several contestants died—for real died—in the cage-fighting portion of the festivities. It was a sexist, barbaric, and royally screwed up form of entertainment.

"We're being followed," Gareth said calmly, checking the rear view mirror.

"Seriously?" I asked, glancing at the side view mirror.

"Yep, for about ten miles. I'm going to turn off at the next exit and see if our guests would like to chat."

"No one outside of us, Ethan, Astrid, The Kev, Gemma and Satan know what we're doing and only Astrid and Ethan know we're driving," I said, watching the sleek Porsche follow us through several lane changes.

Checking my weapons, I turned back to the wide-eyed and very excited Martha and Jane. "You will stay in the car and get low. Do not come out of the car unless I call for you. Understand?"

"Roger that," Martha said arming herself with everything that could pass for a weapon in the car.

Jane let her fangs drop and began to sharpen them with a metal file.

"What are you doing?" I asked, watching her go to town on her teeth.

"Sharpening up in case I need to bite some ass. I tell you, I'm really excellent at it."

"Me too," Martha said, revving up a hand held drill and having at her own fangs.

Speechless. They left me speechless. The only good thing was when they were sharpening their canines they couldn't talk.

"Open your window a bit and see if you can catch a scent," Gareth directed as he swerved across three lanes and took the exit.

Sure enough they followed.

"Angels," I said through clenched teeth. "Not my idea of a fun meet and greet."

"Chicken?" Gareth asked with amusement and a raised brow.

"Take that back." I laughed and punched him in the arm. "Very little scares me."

"I can think of something that scares you," he said so softly I leaned in.

Leaving that one alone, I turned back to the old gals again. "Angels are not the species to screw with. They make Trolls look like household pets. You will not bite them, lob weapons at them, or even make eye contact. Clear?"

"You're no fun at all," Jane griped.

"I beg to disagree," Gareth said. "And Venus is correct. If you make one false move with the heavenly bastards it will be your last."

"You think they work for Rachmiel?" I asked, feeling my adrenaline spike.

"I'd put my money on Roberto. Roberto is aware we're going after Vlad. They want Vlad alive for some reason. We're collateral damage. My guess is they could care less if we live or die."

"Not very Christian of them," Martha grunted.

"Excellent point," Gareth said flatly as he pulled into a deserted rest stop.

"Wait," I said, making a decision before I could really think it through. "Are you at full strength?"

Gareth paused and stared straight ahead. "No, but I can handle an Angel or two."

"No one can *handle* an Angel or two," I muttered with a humorless laugh. I rolled up my sleeve and pressed my wrist to his lips. "Drink."

"Are you hitting on me, Vampyre?" he asked as his eyes went green with desire.

"Absolutely not," I snapped. "Been there, done that. Not going back. Drink. I'm tough, but I've never gone up against an Angel. I need you at full strength for purely selfish reasons, *Vampyre*."

"Tis a pity." Gareth grinned and winked at me as he ran his talented tongue from the center of my palm to the veins in my wrist.

I'd fed him once before when we'd gone after a horrid and now very dead Vampyre named Spike. One of Gareth's gifts was that he could call and go to his siblings from millions of miles away. Spike had taken on Astrid's form and lured Ethan into a deadly trap. Gareth had transported a group of us to his brother. The effort it took left him close to death in his cursed state. And yes... I had fed him. I didn't regret it then and I wouldn't regret it now. I would do it for anyone who I was fighting along side with.

"Drink," I ordered.

"As you wish."

His fangs sunk easily into my offered wrist and a burst of color shot across my vision.

Oh my Hell. This wasn't like the last time *at all*.

Small shudders rocked my body as he drew blood from me. The needles beneath my skin returned with a vengeance and I grew wildly hot and uncomfortable. It didn't help that he kept his eyes glued to mine as he drank.

Shitty taste in men. Shitty taste in men. Shitty taste in men. I needed to remember I had shitty taste in men. It was just hard to commit to the mantra when Gareth was staring at me like he would die without me.

"Um… you guys want us to step out of the car?" Jane asked with waggling brows. "Gettin' a little smexy in here."

"I'll say," Martha agreed with a cackle. "I'm getting a woody and I'm not even involved."

"Women don't get woodies," I snarled, trying to cover my embarrassment and horniness with anger. Plus women *didn't* get woodies.

Gareth removed his fangs and licked my wrist to close the puncture holes. It was so appallingly intimate, I was certain I had a mini orgasm just watching… so again I covered my ridiculous reaction with indifference and anger.

"They're pulling up," I growled, refusing to make eye contact until I had a little more control. "Have you ever fought an Angel?"

"I have."

"Holy shitballs," Jane shouted. "And you lived?"

"Apparently," Gareth replied dryly.

"Any pointers?" I asked. I was as amazed as Jane, but not about to show it.

"Go for the eyes, it's where all the magic lives. Once you blind them it becomes somewhat of a fair fight. Not easy, mind you, but it levels the playing field a bit."

"And you know this how?" I inquired, checking my weapons one more time. I'd need short daggers and throwing stars if I wanted to take out an eye or two.

"I was trained to fight by an Angel," he replied smoothly as he too checked his weapons.

That was unheard of. No Vampyre was trained by an Angel. Fairies were deadly, but Angels were freakin' terrifying and none of them were partial to Vamps. Or at least I didn't think they were.

"I call bullshit," I said, gaping at him.

"Call whatever you want," he shot back with a shrug. "The truth is the truth whether you want to believe it or not."

The look in his eyes implied he was speaking of much more than the unbelievable fact that he was trained by an Angel. But this was not the time to press him for information I was certain I didn't want to hear.

"Who trained you?" I asked, still doubtful.

"The most powerful angelic ass of them all."

"Roberto?" I whispered, awed.

"The one and only. Shall we have a little celestial showdown?"

"You're not lying?" I was flabbergasted and impressed... and turned on.

Shitty taste in men. Shitty taste in men. Shitty taste in men.

"I never lie. Ready?" Gareth asked.

"I was born ready," I said as a small smile began to pull at my lips.

"That's my girl."

My stomach flipped at the endearment, but I quickly brushed it off. I liked it far better when he was being an ass to me.

"We will try and walk away from this without engaging. My guess is Roberto sent flunkies to keep an eye on what we're doing."

"Not very good flunkies if we spotted them," Martha pointed out.

"Trust me," Gareth said. "They wanted us to see them otherwise we wouldn't have. Oh, and don't call me Gareth. I don't know if they'll be able to see through the glamour, but it's best they not know who I am."

"Do you think they'll see through it?" I asked.

Gareth shrugged and then looked pensive. "Possibly. Can you keep a secret?"

"I can," Martha insisted. "I'll take it to the grave that Jane was born a hermaphrodite."

"Holy shit," Jane shouted, head butting Martha with an alarming battle cry. "You wanna play hard ball? Fine. Martha has four nipples."

"I'm gonna kick your ass, hooker," Martha grunted as she tackled Jane and they went to town in the back seat.

"Not sure they can, but I can," I told him with a grin.

"No worries," he said. "I'll wipe their minds later if I have to."

"What's the secret?"

Without a word, Gareth closed his eyes and shifted into the body of a gorgeous man with light brown hair and golden yellow eyes. It was instant and I sat slack jawed as I stared.

"What did you just do?" I asked loud enough to be heard over the ruckus in the back seat.

"One of my gifts," he replied easily. "While the Angels might be able to see through Samuel's glamour, I know for certain they can't see through this."

"Why did you let Samuel glamour you then?" I asked confused.

"This will only last a short while and takes a tremendous amount of power. I don't have that power at my disposal right now, but your blood helped."

"How long can you hold it?"

"Half hour—maybe a bit longer. So let's get this show on the road."

"What the ever lovin' hell?" Jane exclaimed in her outdoor voice as she came up for air and noticed Gareth's new appearance.

"Parlor trick," he said.

"Cool," Martha said as she too peered at him in fascination.

"My name is Dickie," Gareth said with a smirk. "Dickie the Vampyre."

"Understood." Biting back my laugh at his mention of the ridiculous name I gave him, I nodded and prayed this new version of Gareth would hold up long enough for us to get out alive.

There was only one way to find out.

Chapter 12

The Angels stepped out of their car at the same time we did. Tension was thick, but Gareth's body language was calm and composed. He leaned against the SUV and crossed his arms over his chest. I did my best to mimic his relaxed stance. I didn't believe for a second he wasn't as full of apprehension as I was.

The sky was filled with stars and no moon in sight. The eyes of the Angels burned as bright as the stars in the sky—eerily beautiful... and unsettling.

"Well, bless my undead soul if it's not *judgment* and *destruction*," Gareth said in a jovial tone, clapping his hands very slowly—and rudely.

Both were blond, built, and huge... and they were clad in all black—cargo pants, t-shirts, leather jackets and combat boots. They were dressed very similarly to us. I thought the color was an interesting choice, but what the hell did I know? The two men were ethereal and exquisite... and seriously confused.

"Forgive me, for I seem to be at a loss," the one on the left said in a melodically hypnotic voice. "You clearly know who I am, but I can't quite place you."

I wanted to cheer that they didn't recognize him, but I stayed silent next to Gareth and waited to see what he would do.

"You are forgiven, Azriel," Gareth replied smoothly, pushing himself away from the car and standing to his full height. He was as big and as powerful looking as the Angels. "However, I must say it's a bit odd that you don't know who you're trailing. I'd have to call that a jackhole move on your part."

Azriel's eyes flashed, but his casual smile remained in place. "Are you stupid or do you have a death wish?"

"Let me think," Gareth said, putting his middle finger to his mouth and grinning wide. "Neither. Just a little bored at the moment."

"Is he flipping me off?" the one named Azriel asked the other Angel with a surprised chuckle.

"I believe he is—very interesting. If I had to *guess*," the other Angel said, staring hard at us. "I'd say the insolent male is Gareth, but Gareth is cursed and this Vampyre isn't. And this imbecile looks nothing like the Gareth I remember."

"Aren't you the astute one, Azbogah." Gareth saluted and gave the Angel a mocking bow of respect.

I wanted to smack him. Hard.

My tension was building at an alarming rate. So much for not engaging... Gareth was pissing them off. I was shocked that he'd flipped an Angel off. But then again, he'd also smack talked Satan. He'd successfully pissed off Heaven and Hell within twenty-four hours. He was insane.

With the least bit of movement possible, I placed one hand on a dagger and one on a throwing star. I had no intention of dying at a rest stop in the middle of nowhere because Gareth was a grandstanding asshole.

"Your name, Vampyre," Azbogah demanded.

"All in good time," Gareth shot back. "Your reason for following us?"

"I believe I made my request *first*," Azbogah reminded him in a tone that sent a shiver down my spine.

"Your point?"

"Enough games," Azriel growled. "State your name, Vampyre. I shall not ask again."

"That tone will get you nowhere fast," Gareth replied with a chuckle. "Wouldn't *Roberto* enjoy knowing two of his top flunkies fucked up?"

"Excuse me?" Azbogah roared as he lit up like a lantern. The golden flames shot out bursts of silver glitter and hissed and cackled. He was completely on fire, but not getting burned at all.

The embers floated on the cool evening breeze and the air was scented with gardenia. It was beautifully terrifying. The Angel glowed like a deadly beacon in the night and his eyes blazed reddish gold.

"Come now," Gareth purred menacingly, stepping closer to the fire. "You can certainly do better than that. I've seen those beady little eyes go purple when you're pissy."

The flames subsided as quickly as they'd roared to life and Azbogah moved faster than my eyes could follow. He stood toe to toe with Gareth and hissed in his face. "You son of a bitch. I could have fried your undead ass to a crisp. You know far better than to mess with me."

"Damn it, man," Azriel said with a bark of laughter. "I knew it had to be you. How did you accomplish this, Gareth?"

"His name is Dickie," Martha yelled from the car. "Don't you touch him or I'll bite your ass so hard you won't sit for a year, fucker."

"Are those, um… ladies with you?" Azriel inquired, amused and confused by the threat.

"Unfortunately, yes," Gareth informed him.

Gareth glanced back at the cowering old gals with their heads poking out of the rear window and shook his head.

"Gimme the word, Dickie, and I'll go Rambo on his tight, sexy, bitable ass," Martha shouted and then ducked back down.

"No need," Gareth told her pinching the bridge of his nose and closing his eyes. "These ugly bastards are actually my friends."

"Friend is pushing it, Vampyre," Azriel said, still grinning. He turned his attention to me and assessed my stance with a raised brow. "Tell your mate to stand down. It would annoy me to be stabbed right now."

"I'm not his *mate*," I corrected the Angel, still keeping my hands on my weapons. The situation was beyond surreal and I wasn't taking any chances.

Azriel cocked his head to the right and gave me a quizzical look before turning away and focusing back on his *friend* Gareth. "Should I ask how you've broken the curse? You have an interesting track record for playing with fire."

"No, you shouldn't," Gareth replied.

"Is it permanent? Are you cured?"

"No and no. And to be quite honest I don't have the time or the inclination to play catch up with either of you—never liked you *that* much. Why are you following us?" Gareth got right to the point and showed no fear at all to the Angels who could smite all of us to ash with a well-placed flick of their fingers.

"You should really get a handle on your manners, Vampyre," Azriel suggested mildly as he strolled over and stopped in front of me.

I stood my ground and looked him in the eye. I said a quick prayer to his boss and hoped since they were friends, or at the very least friendly acquaintances of Gareth, I would live through the next few minutes.

"You do realize he'll take you to the dark side," Azriel said quietly, but loud enough for Gareth to hear. "I could show you a much better time, beautiful creature."

"I'm already on the dark side, Angel," I said. "And I like it."

"Back away from her. *Now*," Gareth growled as his eyes turned a brilliant green and his fangs dropped.

"Or?" Azriel asked.

"Or I'll do to you now what I did to you not so very long ago."

Azriel's laugh was wildly appealing and his power was immense, but he did nothing for me. I liked the asshole Vamp torturing him far better. God help me, but I did.

"I always seem to be a day late and a dollar short," Azriel said with a wink to me. "And you, Gareth, really need to let that *little episode* go. You were lucky."

"I'd rather be lucky than good any day." Gareth stepped between me and the Angel making his point very clear.

And for once I didn't mind.

"Am I allowed to speak?" Jane called out from the car.

"No," Gareth and I yelled together.

"Just checkin'," she replied grumpily.

"State your business and let us leave without bloodshed. I'd really hate to mess up your pretty face," Gareth said flatly. "I have places to be and things to kill."

"Yes, and we have orders to make sure you accomplish that without fucking up," Azbogah said walking back to his car.

"And you wanted us to know this, why?"

Azbogah tossed the keys to Azriel and paused for a moment. "Several reasons. I don't like surprises, and as I remember, neither do you. Meeting before the showdown is beneficial to all involved. I've been told coming upon an Angel without warning can be a rather unpleasant surprise."

"You can sure as hell say that again, flaming mother humper," Martha called out and then grunted when Jane slammed her head against the car door.

"I was also curious."

"About?" Gareth prompted, impatiently.

"To meet the woman who could bring the almighty Vampyre to his knees."

Gareth paused and glanced up at the star filled sky. "You've accomplished what you came for. Leave."

We stood our ground and waited. Gareth didn't set the Angels straight. He simply stared at them. Neither of us was about to turn our back on an Angel, no matter that the situation was stable at the moment. Of course, the statement Azriel had made was bullshit, but I wasn't about to correct him either.

"Have a nice drive," Azbogah said with a wave. "We'll see you there."

With a wave of his hand, the Porsche disappeared, and so did the Angels. I supposed driving was mundane for a species that could zap themselves wherever they wanted.

"Well, that was fucking bizarre," Jane said, hopping out of the car and stretching her old bones. "Waste of a good car if you ask me."

"I really wanted to sink my fangs into an ass—very bitable," Martha said sadly.

What I really wanted was a serious chat with Gareth, but not in front of Martha and Jane. Were my wonky feelings more than the need to get laid? Wasn't I supposed to at least *like* the Vampyre who was to be my mate? Was fate a big fat hairy bitch and playing a horrible joke on me? Did I have no say in my never-ending future? God, I needed Astrid right now, but that wasn't going to happen.

I had a mission. I would stick to that and deal with the rest later—maybe.

With a cautious glance over at Gareth, I was relieved that he wasn't staring back. If he was my fated partner in this very long undead life, he was going to have a tremendous amount of work to do to win me over. And if he wasn't, if everyone was mistaken, I would make sure he survived the curse... and then I would ensure our paths never crossed again. Hard, but doable.

"Let's go," he said tersely. "Everyone in the car. Martha and Jane if you speak, I will behead you. Am I clear?"

Both the gals nodded and gave him a thumbs up, clearly unsure when the talking ban went into effect. That was fine with me. I needed to try to sleep a bit before we arrived.

My emotions were scattered. I knew sleeping would be difficult, but I was going to fake it till I could make it happen for real. It was going to be the only way I would survive the next week—spiritually, emotionally, and physically.

Chapter 13

"Ohhhhhh my God," a nasally female voiced whined. "It's just not fair that you're soooooo gorgeous."

Rolling my eyes, I turned and expected to find Scary Voice hitting on Gareth—every busty female Vamp in attendance had eyed him hungrily. It pissed me off and made me wish I could knife a few without getting kicked out of the pageant. However, I was wrong this time. The fang grinding voice aimed her bitching at me.

The welcome cocktail hour was in full swing. My posse and I stood on the outskirts of the crowded room with our backs to the wall. I was doing my best not to engage with the Barbie Vamps, but this one was determined to move right into my space.

"Pardon me?" I asked politely, trying my damnedest not to wince at her voice.

She was a knockout, but her high-pitched squeak left a lot to be desired. My new *buddy* was a blonde haired, golden eyed, ridiculously booby annoyance. Why she had a problem with *me* was anyone's guess. She was lip-sticked and sprayed within an inch of her undead life. She was exactly the right type of gal for this bullshit.

"You're new," she pouted and examined my outfit with a critical eye.

When she found no fault, her pout grew more exaggerated.

I had no fault with my attire either—a red, low cut Prada halter dress and mile high stilettos. Astrid had done well in packing for me. Of course she'd neglected to put PJ's or any underwear whatsoever in my suitcase, but I would bet my undead life that the omission was on purpose.

She'd pay when I got home... if I got home.

"I am new." I gave the woman a curt nod and then looked away, clearly dismissing her. Didn't work.

"Where ya from?" she asked, shoving Martha and Jane out of the way and wedging herself next to me on the wall.

"Here and there," I answered, staying vague. I needed to keep my eye out for Claudia, not make small talk with someone whose voice made me want to head punch them.

"Me too," she said and rubbed her shoulder suggestively against mine.

Hold the Hell on a minute. Was Blondie hitting on me?

"What's your name?" she purred, with her heavily lined eyes glued to my cleavage.

Yep. She was making a move. I heard Gareth's chuckle, and I wanted to smack him, but first I needed to politely decline the absurd offer being presented.

"What's your name?" I asked, turning her question back on her.

"Tiara," she said with a totally straight face.

I gaped at her and bit back my laugh with enormous effort. "Seriously?"

"I know right?" she said with a shrill giggle that felt like a sharp stick shoved in my ear. "And it's real. My mother was a total bee-otch. Who in the hey-hey names their daughter after a fucking crown and expects her to be straight? For the love of God, I wanted to play football and she made me go to charm school."

"Wow," I mumbled, trying to figure out how to lose Tiara—fast.

"That's right, wow! I wore a strap on penis all four years of high school and she ignored it—never asked about it once. Talk about clueless. I went to prom in a tux. You'd think she'd catch on, but nooooooooooooo."

"Um... why are you here?" She wasn't an old Vamp but she wasn't very young either. I could tell by her scent and her mannerisms. I would guess her mother was long gone. She could live as a man free and clear now, yet she was competing in a beauty pageant—for women.

"Oh, right. It must seem odd."

She giggled again and I heard Gareth slam his hands over his ears. It was all I could do not to join him, but Tiara wasn't evil. She was just annoying—very annoying.

"A little odd," I agreed.

"A girl's gotta make a living. I keep getting kicked out of Vampyre Houses. I have no clue why. I'm a team player and I can kill shit while barely moving. Maybe that's it... jealousy. Ya think?" she asked in a pitch that brought to mind fornicating cats.

I would swear on my life that her voice would attract stray animals. It was no wonder Houses wouldn't accept her—eardrums were necessary.

"Probably."

"Anyhoo, it's next to impossible for a Vamp to have a sex change. My lower lady bits keep growing back along with my knockers. It's a bloody mess, let me tell you. Total bummer. So I decided to use my hooters to make some cash. If you can't beat 'em, you gotta join 'em."

Never in my centuries on Earth had I heard anything like this. Even Martha and Jane didn't have anything to add to Tiara's story. I stared at her for a long beat and tried to assess if she was full of it—she wasn't. I could scent lying and she was telling the truth. It was a God*awful* truth, but it was a truth nonetheless.

"I see." It was the only thing I could think to say besides something that might sound rude or insulting.

"So you busy after the party?"

"Tiara, while I'm flattered, I'm not interested," I told her as diplomatically as I could.

"Well, shit, I figured you batted for my team when I saw your lesbian handlers," she said with a nod to the now blustering Martha and Jane. "My peeps are gay like yours."

"What the holy fuck?" Martha grumbled. "I'm not a rug muncher. It was only one time and we laughed so hard it didn't count."

"It's the fucking suits." Jane snorted with disgust and glanced down at the classy Prada pants and blazer she was wearing. "No one mistakes us for muff divers when we're in assless chaps and boob tubes."

That certainly shut Tiara up for a brief moment. Gareth turned away and banged his head on the wall. I decided ignoring the dingbats was the best course of action.

"Um... Tiara, we could be friends or friendly acquaintances," I amended quickly lest she get the idea we were going to hang out. "But I like men."

"Too bad," she said sadly, shaking her head. "But I'll take you up on the friend offer. None of the bitches on the circuit will talk to me. *Everyone* is jealous of me. Drives me nuts."

With a smile that I hoped looked more sympathetic than pained, I nodded.

"I can size up the competition for you if ya want," she told me. "Of course, I'm gonna win, but you might come in first runner up. That is unless you have to go into the cage with me."

"Sizing up the competitors would be helpful, and what makes you so sure you can kick my ass?" I inquired, intrigued.

"Because I killed a Dark Fairy with my bare hands," she whispered. "Tore his head right off. He squealed like a piggy."

Holy shit on a stick. Maybe I'd written old Tiara off too quickly. Even Gareth quit laughing and took notice.

"I bit one of those Fairy fuckers in the ass once," Jane confided proudly.

"And I practically twisted his nuts off," Martha added, miming the appalling action with glee.

"My kind of people." Tiara gave a high five to the old bags. "So anyhoo, there are eight of us."

That surprised me since the room was full of people. The entourages must be huge.

"Me, you… wait. What the hell is your name?" Tiara asked.

"Her name's Venus," Martha said, taking command of her role as my handler. "I'm Martha. The ugly one is Jane, and that hunk right there is Dickie."

"Speak for yourself, hooker," Jane snapped. "You're uglier than I am."

"And how would you know that?" Martha demanded body-slamming Jane into the wall. "You ain't got no reflection."

"Neither do you," Jane said with a knee to Martha's gut.

"Stop it," I hissed. "You're both appalling. And if you keep this behavior up, you're going home."

"Sorry," Jane mumbled, flipping Martha the bird.

"I like those gnarly gals. I've been looking for some new blood for my entourage. You attached to them?" Tiara asked, sizing up the now nervous Martha and Jane.

I paused as Jane and Martha peered at me with childlike worry. They clearly didn't want to be given to someone who could make a Fairy squeal like a piggy—to be honest neither would I. It was so tempting to hand them off, but most other Vamps would behead them after five minutes in their company. The old idiots had grown on me... kind of like a fungus, but a non-deadly and slightly amusing fungus.

"No, they're mine and I'm keeping them," I told a disappointed Tiara. "Point out the competition."

"Yes ma'am. You got Dana, Deena, Deandra, Donna and Dodie—all blonde, mean and stacked."

"You're joking right?" I asked with a squint of disbelief.

"No, they're all at least 34DDD," she replied totally misunderstanding.

"No, I meant all their names start with D?"

"Oh that." Tiara rolled her eyes and laughed. "Those are stage names. I have no idea what the hell their real names are—could care less. Last bitch who won was named Desiree. All the numb-nuts took on names staring with D thinking it would give them an advantage."

"Seems they might be a little lacking in the brains department," I muttered.

"If ya took all seven of 'em and put their cerebral matter together, ya might come up with a quarter of a normal brain." Tiara laughed like a hyena at her analysis.

I smile-winced and plastered my hands to my sides so I wouldn't slap them over my ears or her mouth. I was getting somewhere with Tiara but I didn't want to piss her off. If she really tore the head from a Fairy, she was a badass. "But that only makes seven with me and you."

Maybe Tiara was missing a few cells as well.

"Right." She nodded and then leaned in close indicating we should all do the same. "One of the gals is on a date this evening with a Master Vampyre from Europe. The pageant director, Sunny who happens to be a wankin' bitchwad, made poor Claudia go with the skeevy bastard. Apparently, the pervert is the new underwriter for the pageants."

Poor Claudia, my ass. "Is the man her lover?"

"Hell no," Tiara grunted and threw her hands in the air. "*I'm* her lover, or at least I was. I got tired of dating a Vamp in the closet. She's as queer as a three-dollar bill, but too old school to admit it in public. Her loss."

"Umm... okay," I stuttered.

We'd hit a land mine of information. Too bad it was making our eardrums bleed.

"So this *Claudia* doesn't know the European Vamp?" I asked.

Gareth, Martha and Jane had closed all gaps around us to keep prying eyes and ears at bay.

"Nope. She didn't want to go, but Sunny insisted— said it would be good for her career. I called bullshit, but Claudia never listened to me when we were bumpin' uglies, so why would she listen to me now?"

"Claudia sounds like a whore," I said, only to get a discrete elbow in the back from Gareth.

"Aren't we all?" Tiara asked with an uncaring shrug. "We're all here—including you—trying to make a buck with our tits. If the stiletto fits..."

She had a point, but I wasn't here for the same reason she was. I had no intention of correcting her, but she was definitely going to be my new *friend*.

"Maybe we can hang out," I suggested, intending to pry more info from her about Claudia. "Sit next to each other in the dressing room."

"I would love that," she squealed, and I was sure I felt blood drip from my ear.

Tiara grabbed me in a wildly inappropriate hug, and if I wasn't mistaken—and I wasn't—she copped a quick feel of my ass.

"Alrighty then," I said, pushing her away. "Touch my ass again and I'll remove your hand."

"You homophobic, African Queen?" she asked with a raised brow and a ready to rumble gleam in her gold eyes.

"Nope, I'm an equal opportunity hand remover of those who touch my ass without permission. You racist?"

"Hell to the no. I'm an equal opportunity lesbian—don't give a shit about color, but I like big tits, and you, my friend have some perky puppies. You gonna pop hunky Dickie tonight? He's looking at you like he wants to eat you... the good way, not the cannibalistic way," Tiara clarified just in case I'd mistakenly taken her wildly alarming speech wrong.

"Um... no, but thanks for straightening that one out," I choked out, still taking in that she'd called my girls puppies and noticed that Gareth wanted to get in my panties.

"No worries, friend. I'm gonna go around and psych those bitches out. I find it helps. Want me to tell them there's a new girl in town—shake 'em up a little?" Tiara asked.

"No, but thanks. I'll do my own psyching out in the morning."

"Good on ya," Tiara said with a perfect pageant wave as she disappeared into the crowd of pretty people.

We stood in silence while we all digested what had just gone down. It was pure luck she'd wedged herself up next to me, but as Gareth said to the Angels... I'd rather be lucky than good any day.

We'd been fairly lucky so far. I just hoped it held up.

***

"Well, that was certainly informative," Gareth said dryly, taking my arm and leading us out of the party.

"Ya think?" I asked, stifling my giggle as we made out way through the dense crowd of bejeweled Vampyres.

"Holy Hell, that Tiara makes us look *normal*," Martha muttered, nodding at people as we passed.

"I wouldn't go that far," I said as I politely waved at a few smiling strangers.

"I'd just like to reiterate my theory," Jane said with a wide toothy smile. "Boobs *are* weapons."

I shook my head and laughed. The old bags might have a point after all.

"Martha and Jane you will go to your room. You will not destroy it and you will stay there until morning. Understood?" Gareth said as we approached the ornately carved elevator in the lobby.

"You gonna eat Venus?" Jane asked with a smirk and then hid behind Martha when I gave her a vicious glare.

"That remains to be seen," Gareth replied with a grin that would have made me blush if I'd had the ability.

Vamps couldn't blush, but Vamps could kick ass, and that was exactly what I was about to do when I got Gareth alone.

Chapter 14

"Start talking, Vampyre," I told Gareth while putting a healthy amount of distance between us. His quip in the elevator had ramped up my need for him to the point of embarrassingly unhealthy.

"You have absolutely no respect whatsoever for my title," Gareth commented with a delighted grin.

"Nope," I replied and placed myself behind a chair so I didn't tackle him to the ground and stick my tongue down his throat. His sexy smile made me stupid.

We had three adjoining suites. I was in the middle and the old gals' room was connected to mine by a door on the right. Gareth's suite was also connected to mine by a door on the left. I hadn't thought to ask about the arrangements before we left. I was both relieved and stupidly disappointed that we were in separate quarters.

He glanced curiously around my suite, and then made himself comfortable on the couch of my ornately decorated room. Not my taste, but it was perfect for the overly made up and pretentious pageant people.

Holy Hell he looked hot. Why did the asshole have to be so ungodly gorgeous? It was easy to forget the Vampyre was dying when he looked so healthy and beautiful and powerful and...

Shitty taste in men. Shitty taste in men. Shitty taste in men.

Gareth's large presence filled the room and made me nervous. His sheer beauty was ridiculous, but there was starting to be more of him... or was I simply seeing more of him because we were in constant close proximity? Or was it wishful thinking? Or had I lost it? The thought that there might be undiscovered parts to the man that was in my every waking thought made me happy yet terrified. His eyes glowed green with desire and a deep sadness that pulled at me. I knew those eyes. I'd dreamt of those green eyes for several lifetimes.

His scent was making me dizzy. I wanted to jump his bones or deck him—either would have been strangely satisfying. Either would have alleviated some of the tension and tangled emotions consuming me. I was totally off my game and I hated it. I never felt freakin' nervous. I made *other people* nervous, for the love of God.

Gareth stared at me for a long moment and then nodded slowly. For a brief unsettling beat I thought he was going to deny my request.

"It's time," he agreed.

My stomach flipped and the needles danced around under my skin. Gareth was correct. It was time. It was time to deal with whatever was happening between us. The conditions weren't ideal, but I needed clarification so I could concentrate on the real reason we were here.

"What would you like to know?"

Glancing around the room to avoid eye contact, I realized I couldn't ask the question I needed him answer. There were only two ways for him reply and I was unsure I could handle either response.

"You know what I want to know," I snapped, taking the coward's way out.

"I need you to ask."

Sitting down in a ridiculously embellished Queen Anne chair across the room from him, I put my elbows on my knees and let my head drop to my hands. Did I want him to confirm what I already believed and secretly wanted to be true?

Yes.

No.

Shit.

"Are you my True Mate?" I whispered, staring at the floor.

"I am."

My skin began to tingle and my stomach tightened into a knot. I felt faint and wildly unsure. This wasn't at all what I expected to feel when I found my True Mate.

"How long have you known?"

"Since before you were turned," he replied, quietly.

I glanced up sharply and a hollow laugh left my throat. "Right. I'm supposed to believe that?"

"You can believe what you want. The truth is the only thing that can't fuck you."

"If that's the truth, I'd have to say you're pretty *fucked*," I shot back, using a word I rarely spoke.

Gareth sat silently and watched me. Anger and confusion didn't even begin to describe what I was feeling.

"If you've always known, why haven't you come to me?"

He ran his hands through his hair and pressed his lips together. "Because you're far too good for a man like me," he replied.

"So you just screwed your way across the world to avoid me?" I spat, hating that fate had dealt me such horrid cards.

"That's one way to put it," he said flatly.

"Why can't I tell for sure you're my mate?" I demanded.

"The curse," he replied wearily. "However, you still recognize me even with the curse muting it, don't you?"

Nodding, I wanted to cry. I'd thought finding my mate would be wonderful—it would complete me and make the loneliness I'd always lived with go away. This was all wrong.

"This isn't the way it's supposed to be," I whispered.

His jaw worked rapidly and his hands clenched at his sides. Did he think I was good enough to bed, but not to mate?

"No, Venus it's not the way it's supposed to be."

"Why?" My voice sounded small childlike to my own ears. My weakness infuriated me, but I couldn't help it. It was all I could do to speak when I burned to touch him and discover who he might really be.

"I don't know."

"You told me you never *lie*," I hissed, finding the strong woman I'd momentarily lost. "You're lying right now. If you think I'm beneath the likes of you, say it. Trust me, being mated to a manwhore isn't exactly my idea of a happily ever after either."

"Omission isn't lying."

"You are one sadistic piece of work," I snarled and threw a vase at his head.

He caught it smoothly and placed it on the floor next to his feet. "This is true."

"You could die in a matter of days. If you do, then I'll never understand or know what the hell I did wrong to make you stay away from me for hundreds of years. I don't even like you, but I can't deny the uncontrollable need I have for you. You're an asshole and you're mean. I hate you."

Tears welled up in my eyes and the need to crawl out of my skin was overwhelming. The anguished expression on his face tore at my breaking non-beating heart. I would never have what Astrid and Ethan had—ever. Defeated, I let my tears fall freely and didn't try to hide my devastation.

"Fine," he growled and began to pace the room in agitation. "You want the whole truth, here it is... you're not going to like it. You've never done anything wrong. Ever. You are so far above the *likes of me* that it's absurd. You're everything to me. I knew you were fated for me when you were human and it killed me to leave after I turned you."

I froze and my blood chilled. What the hell was he talking about?

"I knew if I stayed that I would ruin you, like I've ruined everything else I've ever touched. I knew my brother Ethan would take good care of you and protect you. Watching over you all these years was easier since I knew where you were. It gave me comfort to watch you from afar and know what an incredible, loving, and deadly woman you'd become."

"Back up," I said, holding on to the arms of the chair so I didn't fall to the ground. I wanted to scream. Pain radiated through my body as I rocked back and forth in the chair like I did as a child when the injustices of having no control of my destiny tried to break my spirit.

"You were my savior? You were the man with green eyes who turned me? You were the man I begged to take me with you and you *left me*?"

He said nothing, simply nodded with an expression full of regret and pain.

"You were the one that gave me the gift to avenge my family," I whispered through my tears. "And then you left me—just like everyone else. You left me alone."

I knew his secret. He could shift into other facades. Was the man I knew now the real Gareth or was it the one I knew then?

"Why? I deserve to know why."

"Because I was stupid."

"Clearly," I said in a cold tone. "You owe me more than that."

"Because as a young Vampyre, I thought I was invincible. Because I was arrogant and vain enough to think I was stronger than a Demon. Because I made a deal with the Underworld that I lost and bringing you into that was not something I was willing to do."

"That should have been my decision to make, not yours," I said, watching his fury at himself with a sick feeling in my gut. "What happened and why did you chase me these last few months?"

"I made another deal," he said, walking over to the wall, cocking his fist back and then thinking better of it. "I told the old women that they couldn't destroy their suite. Do you mind if I punch a hole in yours?"

"Go right ahead," I told him, thinking it was an outstanding idea. "You'll have to explain the repair bill to your brother."

"Trust me, he'll understand."

Gareth violently put his left fist through the wall knocking a large painting to the floor with a crash. He picked the painting up, considered it for a second and then put his right fist though it.

"It was ugly," he said with a lopsided grin.

I had to agree, but I refused to smile at him. I was mad... I hated him... I wanted to hurt him... I wanted him to want me—to love me... I needed therapy. He was a stupid, stupid son of a bitch. What did that make me?

"The other deal?" I prompted.

"This time with the Angels—Roberto to be more specific. The best way to beat a Demon is to get into bed with his greatest enemy. So I did. I begged my Father to run the Asian Dominion for me and I trained with the Angels. My family had always known I was a fuck up and I didn't disappoint. The only one who believed in me was my sister Raquel."

"What happened with the Demon?"

"Demons," he corrected me.

"Demons," I amended.

"I killed him and then I killed his friend... and his friend... and then his friend—until all that thought they owned me were gone."

"Did Satan know?"

"Are you serious? He presided over it. He was wildly displeased I'd eliminated so many of his top boys. He promised to make my undead life a living Hell and he made good on his word."

I digested that silently. Now I understood some of the comments Satan had made about welcoming Gareth back into the fold.

"Which is another reason I'm tainted and don't deserve you."

He was correct. The Vampyre didn't deserve me... but he could. Gareth could deserve me, but he had to want it. I couldn't force that to happen. It had to be his decision. It had nothing to do with me and everything to do with him loving himself.

The self-destructive ways he'd adopted now made sense. It didn't excuse his appalling behavior, but I understood it. I'd been wildly self-destructive the first few decades after I'd died. My self-hatred for not dying with my family had led me to horrifying acts I wasn't at all proud of, but regret was a wasted emotion. I liked the woman I was now and I wouldn't be her without my past.

It was Prince Ethan who'd carefully drawn me out of my savage ways and taught me to love myself as I was. Personally, I would have kicked my insolent and wicked self to the curb, but Ethan had seen parts of me that I didn't know existed. Gareth, in his selfish bastard way, had sent me to the right person at least. I would have been ash centuries ago without Ethan's patience and care.

I stared at the man I'd prayed for every night for over two hundred years—the man I'd loved for centuries—and my tears welled back up. Emotions I'd kept locked away roared through my body. Putting the pieces of Gareth together with the man who'd saved me was difficult. Parts of the puzzle were still missing and if he died they could never be found.

"So you never really left me," I whispered brokenly.

"I never left you. You just didn't know I was near."

"Go on."

"Eventually Satan felt vindicated and left me be. However, the damage was done. So I did what was expected of a royal and I took back my post of the Asian Dominion. I was able to rectify some of my deplorable behavior to my family by taking over the European Dominion while Raquel was indisposed. I got my shit together and proved to my family that I was a good leader of our people, but..."

"But?"

"But I still wasn't good enough for you."

"According to whom?" I demanded harshly. Why was he such an ass?

"Me," he said.

"But you seduced me—slept with me—had sex with me," I accused, remembering every beautiful moment of something that meant the world to me, but apparently very little to him.

"No, Venus, I made love to you. You're the only woman I've ever made love to. Sex is a physical release. Making love is not."

"Am I supposed to be honored?" I snapped viciously, trying to hurt him the way he'd hurt me.

"No, but since I might be ash in a week, I want you to know—need you to believe me. It's just one more fucking selfish thing that I'm doing to you... but I can't help it. I touched you once and I can't get away from it. I don't want to. I want to deserve you."

That shut me up and an uncontrollable feeling of terror welled up inside me. I could defeat a physical enemy, but a curse was an invisible foe. A dagger wouldn't break a curse. And no weapon ever made would destroy Gareth's self-loathing.

The miserable, beautiful bastard had to live so he could make all of this shit up to me. It would take *decades* for him to do that—centuries even. Gareth simply wasn't allowed to die. I deserved to kick his sorry ass for years for what he'd done to us.

"You're a dick."

"Is that supposed to be a surprise to me?"

"Shut up, you asshole. When we slept together, it was perfect—for me. I let guards down that had been in place for over two hundred years. I thought you might be mine and then I saw you with other women."

"I thought it better for you to hate me."

"Too late, you shit. You should stop thinking—it's dangerous to idiots like you. Is this why I can see through the glamour?"

"Yes. Samuel knew we were fated. He can see things that most Vampyres many times his age can't."

I mulled this over and realized there was more. The Vampyre was no longer going to get away with omission. "What's the other way to break the curse?"

He silently walked over to the wall again and beat the hell out of it. I was surprised that security hadn't shown up, but maybe the hotel was run by Vamps and this was par for the course.

"The other way to break the curse is not going to happen."

"Fine," I said, frustrated. "But I want to know what it is. All of your plans thus far have sucked. I get a say in this."

"You don't."

"You are *not* the boss of me," I shouted. "I'm a grown woman with a past that's not pretty. You don't win for the worst choices in life. As far as I'm concerned, the evil playing field is fairly even. And you know it's equally as horrific for most of the undead, so that regret of yours is not gonna fly. You will answer me. You owe me that much."

"Can you stand up?" he asked.

"Why?"

"I need to break something else and that chair is ghastly," he replied.

I made an ungodly heroic attempt to hold my laughter back, but failed. Getting up from the chair, which I had to agree was unattractive, I backed away and let him have at it.

"Better?" I asked with a little smile pulling at my lips after he'd demolished it.

"Much." He nodded, took my hand and led me to the still pristine and intact couch.

Running his hands through his hair, he settled himself and stared off into the distance for a moment.

"If we had mated, it might have broken the curse."

"You're kidding," I said, wanted to punch his head like he'd punched the wall.

"I'm not. However, it's not proven. Such a curse has never existed until now and it's an educated guess that joining with my True Mate would break it."

"But it could," I said, watching him closely as the needles under my skin ramped up to something almost painful. "This is a no brainer. I want to mate with you. You'll have to earn my trust after the fact. It's going to be Hell for you, but as much as I hate your guts, I also love you. I always have. I just didn't know it was you."

"Venus." He took my face in his strong hands and pressed his lips to mine.

The feeling of being home was so very real. The kiss was full of promise and regret. It was so exquisitely gentle and loving my eyes welled with tears.

"The stay Satan gave me on my illness negates the effect that mating would have accomplished," he said quietly.

God, all the cryptic pieces were coming together.

"No," I said desperately, placing my hands over his. "I heard Satan say *might*. It *might* negate it. Please. Let's try."

"I don't deserve you," he growled. "The answer is no. The stay gave me a week. I'll die if we don't get Vlad and the Angel and break the curse. If we mate, you will follow me in death. It's the way our world works. So no. The only way I can accept my fate is to know that you'll go on."

"And you think I'll want to go on without you?" I demanded. My voice broke with the emotion spilling out of me. How could he be so stupid? "You're playing God. You're not God."

"You're correct. I'm not God. I'm a very bad Vampyre in love with a beautiful and good woman—a perfect treasure who I will not destroy. You have to understand me," he pled. "Please Venus. Very little would make my existence untenable. Knowing I was the cause of your death is that thing."

"There are many kinds of death," I said sadly, knowing I would honor his request. "You're killing me right now."

"Then help me get Vlad. It's the only way that we can win and you can put me through the ringer for the next decade."

"It's gonna take far more than a decade for you to make this shit right with me," I warned him, feeling a tiny flame of hope in my chest.

"A century?" he asked with a sexy little grin that made me tingle.

"At least. Will you stay with me tonight?" I asked in a small whisper.

"Yes. God knows I don't deserve you, but I can't stay away anymore." He smiled and touched my lips reverently with his finger. The relief that shot through me made my body sag into the couch. "You may think I'm your savior from long ago, but you're actually my savior, beautiful girl."

Leaning into him and resting my head on his chest felt scary and new. It also felt right.

"Can I trust you?" I asked.

"The question is can you forgive me?" he said. "My past is my past. I'm not proud of it, but I also can't change it. I'll give you no excuses because they're cheap, but I can tell you no one will ever love you like I can."

"I'm not interested in rehashing the past. It never gets anyone anywhere. I just want to be very clear that I don't share. If I commit to you, you're mine."

"Venus." He took my chin in his hands and raised my eyes to his. "Can I tell you a story?"

"Fiction or non-fiction?" I asked narrowing my eyes a little.

"Non-fiction."

"Happy ending?" I asked, feeling nervous. Was he going to tell me something that would be a deal breaker?

"The ending will be yours to choose," he replied, looking more vulnerable than I'd ever seen him.

"I like happily ever afters," I whispered, getting lost in his mesmerizing blue eyes.

Nodding and planting a sweet kiss on my lips, I watched him screw up his courage. It was strange and wonderful and somewhat disconcerting. Even if he shared some thing awful, maybe I could try to understand. Maybe.

"I trained with the Angels forty years ago. During that time I chose to take a vow of celibacy. I've kept that vow because I'd always used sex as a drug to numb my fucked up reality. I was dead inside. Roberto, as much of a pompous ass as he is—and trust me, he's a grandiose son of a bitch—saw through me unlike anyone ever had. I'll forever be indebted to him. The first time I broke my vow was with you."

I stared in shock and felt something lift from my soul. I was giddy and lightheaded.

"I beat myself up about it. I'm still not sure it's right you be involved with me, but…"

"But what," I asked, tangling my fingers in his hair and memorizing the feel of the silky strands. He was so mine.

"But, I'm in love with you. I've always been in love with you," he whispered, closing his eyes and enjoying my touch. "I'm a selfish man. I will always have a sordid past, but I left it behind."

"Your past is forgiven, Gareth," I said as his eyes snapped open and searched my face with wonder. "I haven't exactly been a saint. Can't say I was as hookery as you…"

"Thank God for that," he muttered. "Not that it would matter—much," he said with a grin as I punched his arm lightly. "Today matters."

"The past can live in the past. I want my future with the arrogant ass who makes me feel alive. I choose to end the story with a happily ever after—or rather start a new one."

"The arrogant ass is the luckiest man in the world."

"I'd rather be lucky than good any day," I said with a laugh as he pulled me to him and wrapped his arms tightly around my trembling body.

"Can we have sex tonight?" I asked with a giggle.

"We can make love," he correct me with a raised brow and a wide grin. "No biting though."

"Deal."

He reluctantly pulled back, but kept his hands on me. "I need to case the auditorium and the hotel. I'll be back within the hour. "Get naked."

I nodded, because words escaped me. I couldn't have his soul yet, but I needed his body like I needed blood. He was necessary to me. And I loved him.

"God, I feel strange," Gareth said, pausing at the doorway of my suite.

"You feel sicker?" I asked alarmed. Satan had promised us a week.

"No." He turned and stared at me in amazement. His smile was devastating and it undid me completely. "I believe I'm happy," he whispered. "You make me so happy."

On that wonderful note, he turned and left.

It wasn't even close to the mating fairytale I'd created in my mind. It was complicated and messy and potentially disastrous.

But it was mine—*he* was mine. And us being together was my version of perfect.

Chapter 15

The scratching on my door made me roll my eyes. Gareth had only just left and he'd taken a key so I knew he wasn't the culprit. Besides, I'd unlocked the door between our suites. I expected he'd use that in an hour.

Thankfully Tiara didn't know my room number, so she was out.

That left the dingbats. Why they were at the front door to my suite was a mystery since our rooms were connected. Back at the Cressida House they had a bad habit of playing Ding Dong Ditch. They'd been put in time out on numerous occasions for the juvenile game. Normally, I'd kick their ass for goofing around on a mission, but tonight was anything but normal.

Gareth wasn't the only one who was over the moon happy. I was stupidly giddy and counting down the minutes until he came back. Martha and Jane would get a stern talking to and then be sent back to bed.

Yanking open the door with eyebrows raised and lips compressed, I was surprised they weren't standing there giggling. They were notoriously bad at the Ditch part of the game. Getting busted was half the fun for the old dorks.

But it wasn't Martha and Jane at my door. On the floor at my feet, bleeding profusely and beaten within an inch of her life, was the woman I'd wanted dead by my own hand.

Claudia lay in a heap in the hallway, moaning and trying to crawl to her room.

"Holy shit," I muttered as I quickly looked both right and left to make sure she was alone.

She was. She was also so close to death it would take very little to end her.

The temptation was so intense that I stepped back and fisted my hands at my sides. Graphic images of my slain family blinded me to reason and I wanted to finish her. With Herculean effort, I stood as still as a statue, willing myself not to grab a weapon. My hands were as deadly as any dagger, but...

"Help me," she choked out through the blood gurgling in her throat. "Please."

She was face down and had no idea that the person she was begging for help wanted her dead more than any one else in the world. The irony wasn't lost on me. I had a choice. Win in the moment or win in the long run. The recent memory of the expression on Gareth's face as he realized he was happy was the only thing that kept me from taking her life. He was going to be my world and I needed the trash on the floor to ensure that I could have my happily ever after.

So I wasn't going to kill her yet, but being gentle and friendly was still out of the question.

"Well, what have we here?" I said coldly as I turned her over with my foot so she could see me. I wasn't rough, but the disrespect it showed was satisfying.

"Oh my God," she choked out. Her eyes grew wide and terrified with recognition. She made a feeble attempt to crawl away. Stepping on the obscenely short skirt she was wearing, I stopped her movement.

"No, no, no," she moaned as her body convulsed with shock and pain. "I'm dreaming."

"Nope. This is a living nightmare." I squatted down and flashed my fangs. "You're wide awake and I'm a very real monster."

She stared at me for a long moment and time seemed to freeze. The expression on her face chilled me to the bone—I'd seen it too many times in my human life not to place it. Claudia had the look in her eyes of a horribly abused woman—not just tonight—from centuries of abuse at the hands of others. Juliette had the very same beaten down look.

I stood and turned away. I had no idea what her life had really been like. For all I knew, she'd been living high on the hog for centuries since her turning. She would never have my sympathy. Ever.

The sound of the wood splintering as I punched the door in frustration was satisfying. My fury burned through my veins. The door was a poor excuse for her face, but her face had already been pummeled.

"Just do it," she begged. "Kill me."

Her voice was harsh and broken as if her undead life had been awful. I didn't care. I hoped it had been. She deserved it.

"Why would you think for a second that I would do anything for you that would make your existence easier?" I asked tonelessly, watching her bleed out before my eyes.

Wait. Why wasn't she healing? She was a Vampyre. Her wounds should be knitting together.

"Finish it. I don't want to live like this anymore."

"Tough shit," I snapped as I bent down and scooped the bloody monstrosity into my arms then carried her into my suite. "You owe me and you're going to agree to pay if I help you."

"You're not going to kill me?"

Claudia's body trembled and she was even slighter than I remembered. If it was Vlad who'd done this, he'd worked her over good.

"Not yet," I replied tightly, trying to block all feelings of compassion for her. She'd shown none to me or my people in my human life. I'd show none to her in her undead one.

"What happened to you?" I demanded as I put her down on the couch and backed away for her safety and my sanity.

She said nothing—simply watched me. Her blood was staining the couch, but with the demolished state of the room the blood fit right in.

"I asked you a question," I snapped. "You're in no position to defy me at the moment."

"Will you kill me if I do?" she asked in a hopeful voice.

What the Hell? She was offering me my revenge on a platter and I wasn't going to take it.

Gareth's face flashed in my mind—I needed her alive to keep him alive. If refraining from killing the woman I despised with every fiber of my being wasn't love, I didn't know the meaning of the word. Gareth was more important to me than seeking vengeance.

"No. You think you're in pain now? It's nothing compared to what I'll do to you if you don't answer me."

Her wince and gut-wrenching sob made me inwardly cringe with shame. Had I gone soft? My instincts were screwed up. The truth was that I should feel nothing for the horrid woman on my couch—absolutely nothing. I'd simply been an animal to her and her husband—never a human being. I wanted to treat her the same way they'd treated me and my family, but something felt wrong. The Kev's voice rang in my head with the cryptic message he'd

149

spoken... *Things are not always as they seem. You would be wise to take that to heart and listen to your instincts even if they don't tell you what you want to hear.*

Damn The Kev to Hell and back. There were too many puzzle pieces coming together in one night.

"Did Vlad do this to you?" I asked in what I hoped passed for a civil tone.

The look of fear on her face confirmed my assumption. She nodded slowly then closed her eyes. She was still bleeding out. What exactly had he done to her? She would do me no good as a pile of ash.

"Why?"

"Because I wouldn't have sex with him," she muttered and then choked out an ugly laugh. "He told me he wouldn't be denied next time and that this little punishment should be a warning."

God, he was a sick piece of shit.

"Why aren't you healing?"

"Why do you care?" she shot back weakly.

I ran my hands through my hair and considered her question. I hated her and everything she represented. I also needed her. My motives were not even close to pure. You can never get fucked for the truth according to Gareth.

"Honestly, I don't care. When I found out you were alive, my greatest desire was to kill you. I can't believe I missed you all those years ago. But I need you to help me get the bastard that did this to you. And you *will* help me."

Claudia opened her eyes and tried to focus on me. She was fading fast—she needed blood.

"You have to tell me why you're not healing. Now," I insisted, approaching her warily.

"My back," she moaned. "He carved something into my back with silver. I think there's still silver in there."

"He touched silver?" I asked, surprised. Juliette was incorrect about his *deadly aversion*.

"Gloves," Claudia whispered as her body jerked in agony. "Didn't touch it—wore gloves."

Gently turning her over and lifting her shirt, I gasped and felt the bile rise in my throat. She was correct there were bits of silver embedded in her skin. The sick son of a bitch had carved *Vlad's Whore* into her back and the silver ensured it would probably never fade.

"Hang on," I said as I sprinted to the door that connected my room to Martha and Jane's.

Throwing it open, I stopped dead in my tracks. Both of them had slathered on thick, goopy green facemasks and they were painting each other's toenails. The kicker was they were clad in Teenage Mutant Ninja Turtles nightgowns. It was beyond weird.

"I need you now," I said ignoring my need to ask about the nightwear. However, I remembered that Astrid had packed for them. Maybe this was her idea of a joke.

"You want your toenails done?" Martha asked, holding up a bottle of purple polish.

"No, pull up your sleeves. You're about to feed the enemy."

"Hot damn," Jane yelled jumping up and jogging over. "Whoa Nelly! What the hey-hey? We're gonna be blood donors for Vlad?"

"Absolutely not," I said, grabbing them and sprinting back to my room. "You're going to feed Claudia—the woman we need to help us trap Vlad."

"Sweet Jesus in a jockstrap." Martha whistled as she took in the destroyed walls and furniture. "You sure got a shitty room. I'd get my money back if I were you."

"You said it sister." Jane's head bobbled in agreement then she spotted Claudia on the couch. "What in the ever lovin' fuck is wrong with her?" she asked, yanking up her sleeve and squatting down in front of the dying Vampyre.

"Vlad did it. I have to remove the silver from her back while she feeds from you. As much as I've dreamt about her being a pile of ash, this is wrong."

"On it, Boss Lady," Martha said, carefully adjusting Claudia so I could work on her back while the gals took turns feeding her.

"Silver's gonna burn you," Jane told me with a shudder. "I can't even touch the shit. Goes right through my skin."

"I can touch it briefly if it hasn't been blessed," Martha said, pressing her wrist to Claudia's mouth. "Some of that Vampyre bull honkey from the movies is actually true."

"Not all of it," Jane grunted with disgust. "Wanted to see if I would sparkle in the sun so I ran outside in my birthday suit. Damn near burned my hooters clean off my body. The *Twilight* movie is fucking loaded with bullshit information. Just sayin'."

Holy Hell, how did they know things I didn't? Not the sparkling part—the blessed silver part... I'd been a Vampyre for over two hundred years. They'd been undead for less than two.

"Want me to do it so I get burned instead of you?" Martha asked.

"Your *nice* is showing," I told her as she grew on me even a little more. "But no thank you. Gemma did some voodoo and I can touch silver with my right hand for a while."

"Roger that," Jane said as she gently held Claudia's head so the blood wouldn't run out of her mouth.

Tearing the back of her shirt open I began to meticulously remove the slivers of silver from the horrifying message written in her skin. Putting the offending material in a vase, I muttered a quick and heartfelt thanks to Gemma. Thankfully the silver came out easily, but I stiffened in shock when I noticed something else.

Claudia had very faint scars all over her back—long and thin. Gently pulling the waistband of her skirt down a bit I saw that they covered her bottom and the upper part of her thighs. The need to scream or beat the hell out of someone boiled within me. Backing away quickly so I didn't accidentally hurt her more than she'd already been damaged, I tried to rein in my outrage. I recognized those marks. I had them myself.

However, I'd already beat on the man who'd left those marks on me—and I'd killed him. Now I'd bet my undead life it was the same man who left those scars on Claudia.

The silver was gone and to my astonishment, so was my hatred of the woman. Could one horrifying revelation erase centuries of loathing? Had she suffered like I had—felt the burning lash of a whip on her skin? Like my family had?

I knew the answer. Most of me wanted to deny the truth, but the evidence was forever branded on her skin. So many questions raced through my mind, but the words refused to leave my lips.

"Are you Vampyres?" Claudia asked Martha and Jane in a hoarse voice.

Her voice was stronger and the bleeding had slowed.

"You bet your fuckin' bippy we're Vampyres," Jane said, popping a fang to prove her undead status.

"But you're old," Claudia said in confusion.

"Speak for yourself," Martha snapped, insulted. "I'm in my mother humpin' eighties. How the Hell old are you?"

"In my two hundreds," Claudia admitted, gingerly sitting up and taking in her surroundings. "What happened to your room?"

"I was bored," I replied with a shrug, still trying to formulate my thoughts and tamp down my emotions. My room was none of her business. "I have some questions for you."

"I'm sure you do," she replied. "However, before you speak I need to know something."

Nodding, I got up and moved to the other side of the room. I still didn't completely trust myself with her. Seeing her brought back horrifying memories. If I was brutally honest, I had to admit that she was never part of the torture and humiliation. It was always the men—especially her husband. She was just the beautiful white woman we would see every now and then.

"Was it you? Did you kill him?" she asked with nothing to hint at how she felt about what she was asking.

Tilting my head and narrowing my eyes, I noticed Martha and Jane backing away. They recognized the look.

"And if I did?" I asked through clenched teeth.

"If you did, then I thank you," she replied, still watching me carefully. "I wanted to do it myself, but by the time I was able to make my way back, he'd already been butchered. It was apparently so grisly I assumed it was someone undead like me."

"It was no less grisly than the murders of my family by your husband's hand," I snarled, remembering far too much. It was seeing Claudia that broke the compartmental organization in my brain. It was all coming back—things I buried hundreds of years ago—all in vivid and heart breaking color.

Claudia lowered her head and clasped her hands together on her lap. "He deserved every second of what you did and more for all of his unspeakable atrocities. I hope the bastard is burning in the fires of Hell."

This was not happening at all like I'd thought it would go down when I came face to face with my foe. Was she for real or was she playing me to avoid my wrath? If it was an act, she deserved an Oscar, but the scars on her back were very real and had clearly been made by a whip.

God help me and her if she's lying. But my instincts were insisting she was telling the truth. I didn't like my damn instincts at that moment, but I was going to trust them.

"Want some more?" Jane offered her wrist to the healing Claudia. "If not, I gotta go get this mask off my face. It's itching like a motherfucker."

"I'm good. Thank you," Claudia said with a slightly bemused expression as she took in the entirety of Martha and Jane.

"You need us, Boss Lady?" Martha asked.

"No. Get some rest. Tomorrow is going to be a long one."

"Roger that," Martha said as Jane saluted and they made their way back to their own suite.

"Teenage Mutant Ninja Turtles?" Claudia asked with a soft laugh.

I wanted to join her, but it felt like a betrayal to my family to just jump in and be buddies. It was going to take some time for me to let go of the past—even if she wasn't directly involved.

"We need to talk about Vlad," I told her, ignoring her attempt to lighten the mood. I wasn't willing to go there with her—I might never be able to—but that had nothing to do with the here and now.

She was a person—a person I no longer hated—but she brought back memories that my worst nightmares were made of. Yet I realized with a sickening jolt of conscience that if I hadn't needed her to catch Vlad, I wouldn't have even bothered to find out anything about her before I killed her. Looking to the Heavens, I said a silent thank you to God for all of his blessings. The lesson sitting on the sofa was not lost on me.

"Yes, we need to discuss Vlad," she said as her eyes went slightly unfocused with fear. "We do. What did he carve into my back?"

Should I tell her? Shit, would she freak?

"Vlad's Whore," I said quietly. I'd want to know and there was no way to sugar coat it.

She was silent as she took it in. I was unsure if she realized it was probably always going to be there since he'd used silver. Her face held no hint of her feelings. I didn't see anger, embarrassment or fury. There was nothing. It was the same way my mother looked after she'd been inhumanly punished for no reason other than the color of her skin.

"You okay?" I asked quietly. My instinct was to comfort her, but my body wouldn't agree yet.

"I suppose we're all whores in on way or another," she said flatly. "I'll just wear it on my skin now."

"You sound like Tiara," I said.

She glanced up sharply. Her face immediately filled with pain and something I couldn't quite put my finger on. The fact that she was branded by a monster elicited nothing, but the mention of Tiara brought on a maelstrom of emotion.

"She can't know this happened to me," Claudia insisted frantically. "She'll go after him. He'll kill her. Oh God, oh God, oh God." She began to pace the room while wringing her hands in agitation. "Please swear not to tell her and I'll do anything you want me to."

She was in love with Tiara. I recognized it because I was in love too. I'd die for Gareth and it was very apparent that Claudia would do the same for Tiara.

"Why'd you leave her if you still love her?" I asked.

Claudia stopped, shook her head and smiled. "I see you've met her and she talked your ear off."

"You could say that," I replied, making no mention of Tiara's voice from Hell or the fact that she'd hit on me.

"It's better this way—for her. I'm not a prize. I carry horrible baggage and..."

"Shouldn't that be her decision to make?" I demanded getting annoyed at having just had a very similar conversation. "You love her?"

"Yes, but love isn't always enough."

"I call bullshit, but that's your problem, not mine. Who turned you?" I asked, hoping to Hell and back she wasn't about to tell me it was a beautiful man with green eyes.

"My lover—a woman. She died over a hundred years ago. She was a good person."

"You've always been gay?" I asked surprised. It wasn't common back when we were human or at least I wasn't aware of it.

"Have you always been black?" she asked making her point of my insensitivity very clear.

"I apologize," I said, duly and correctly chastised. "But you were married to him. I just thought..."

"In those days, it's what a woman did. My parents basically sold me to him for land. A good daughter married. She had children. She was the property of the man she married. She never complained and always did what she was told," Claudia said sounding more robot than human.

"Children?"

"No, thank God. I never conceived. It would have been a child born of rape if I had. He thought I was frigid. I let him believe the lie because it meant I could keep my true nature a secret. He hated me and let me know in many ways.

"He beat you," I said, sure I was correct about her marks.

"He did."

My anger welled back up inside me, but this time it was for Claudia, not for myself or my family. I'd always mourn their loss, but this Vampyre in front of me had some of the same history I had. We were from the same place. Not for a *second* did I believe her life had been as tragic than ours, but it was clear that she'd lived in her own form of Hell as well.

When I was human, I'd always assumed the whites had no worries. Claudia was making me have to rethink. Normally I hated rethinking, but today I was thankful for the chance.

"He suffered," I told her. "I made him suffer."

A ghost of a smile passed her lips and she nodded to me in thanks.

"I live with many ugly things," she said slowly. "The guilt of what he was doing to you and your family and others wasn't something I could stop. If I brought it up, I was beaten and starved the same way you were. I'm not proud of it, but I went into survival mode. Getting through each day was like living in Hell on Earth." She paused and pressed her temples. "Sorry is a paltry word for what I want to express to you, but it's all I have."

"Forgiven." The word left my mouth before I knew it was going to come out.

Claudia's eyes shot to mine in surprise and I shrugged. Giving her a small smile, I felt the weight of the world fall away from my shoulders.

"I don't know that we'll ever be friends, but we're no longer enemies," I told her. "Now I have to tell you what I need of you—if you're willing."

"I'm willing."

"You don't know what I'm going to ask."

"Doesn't matter," she replied. "If it has to do with eliminating Vlad or someone like him, I'm in."

"We have to take him alive," I explained. "He put a curse on my mate and several others. We need him to break the curse."

"Can I have him when you're through with him?" she asked as her eyes lit up for the first time this evening.

"You'll have to get in line. Satan already called dibs."

"I'm immortal. I'll wait my turn."

My laugh was genuine and I was seeing there was way more to many of the people around me—Martha, Jane, Gareth—and Claudia. "Watch out, I might actually end up liking you."

"I hope you do," she replied with a laugh of her own. "I really hope you do."

Chapter 16

"Wait—let me try to understand this. Brain's not working so well at the moment since all the blood has travelled to my dick. So I'm *not* getting laid?" Gareth asked in confusion. He was standing in the doorway connecting our rooms in nothing but his glorious birthday suit with one of my favorite parts of him standing up at attention.

Yanking the curtain from the rod at the window, I covered up his undisputable beauty. The room was already destroyed—what would a downed drapery matter? I was well aware that Claudia was gay, but this Vampyre was mine, and I didn't want anyone seeing him naked but me.

"We have a guest," I told him trying not to laugh at the disappointment on his face.

Honestly? I felt the same way, but we were getting closer to making sure we had a future together. It was painful, but I could wait for the sex—or making love—part. I hoped.

Glancing over my shoulder, he spotted Claudia. She'd politely turned her head. Gareth growled low in his throat and his fangs dropped. Putting my hand on his chest, I stopped him from his unnecessary need to defend me. It was strange and bizarre to have someone who wanted to have my back in all matters, but it kind of rocked at the same time. However, I had this one under control.

"She's with us now," I said quietly.

I was very aware Claudia could hear everything. Vampyre hearing was bionic no matter how quietly we spoke.

"Are you okay?" Gareth's eyes searched mine for a telltale sign that I might be in pain or upset.

Nodding and wanting to jump his sexy bones, I ran my fingers lightly over his muscled bare chest. "Put some clothes on and come back. We have plans to make, my love."

"Again," he demanded as his eyes went a brilliant green. "Say that again."

"My love," I repeated with a giggle and a shove, sending him falling happily back into his suite.

"Be back in a sec."

"Venus." Claudia stood and moved toward the door. "Let me give you privacy. I can go to my room and we can strategize later."

"No." I stopped her with a gentle hand on her arm. "I'm quite sure Vlad knows your room number. Was he specific as to when the *next time* would be?"

She paled—which was difficult for a Vamp—and sat back down on the blood stained couch. Worrying her bottom lip with her teeth, she white knuckled the edge of the couch.

"No. He wasn't specific."

"You'll stay here—with me," I said. I felt fine about it—good actually. Nowhere near as good as being naked with Gareth would have felt, but protecting her from Vlad was right.

"You're sure?" she asked. "I understand what I must represent to you. You don't have to protect me. I can be strong when I have to."

"You're not strong enough to take on Vlad by yourself. I'm not strong enough to do that either. Gareth might have a chance, but he's still under the influence of the curse. We need to do this as a team or we're screwed."

"Your man is ill? He looks... um, quite healthy," she said with a laugh.

I grinned and laughed in agreement. "Looks can be deceiving. Gareth made a little deal with the Devil. We have several more days to accomplish our mission."

"Or?"

"Or he dies and I'll no longer want to live in this world," I told her truthfully. "I've only just found him. He's an ass, but he's my ass. I need him to live so we can mate and he can make his idiocy up to me."

"So you haven't mated yet?" she asked.

"He won't. He knows he may die soon and won't bring me with him."

"I understand that." Claudia nodded thoughtfully and placed a few pillows over the worst of the bloodstains. "He loves you too much."

"It doesn't matter. If he bites it, I'll follow him. His logic is off, but we need to focus on the mission and the rest might be moot."

"And the plan you and Gareth have come up with?" she asked.

"Call me Dickie," Gareth announced as he reentered the suite and took in the blood-stained couch with a raised brow. Without any embarrassment, he took me into his arms and kissed me till my head spun. We were going to have to find a closet or something. My need for him was becoming seriously debilitating.

162

"Umm, that was nice," I said with a grin—somewhat embarrassed that was had an audience, but too giddy to care.

"There's more where that came from," he said, pulling on one of my errant curls. "Anyway," he said acknowledging Claudia and morphing from the man in love to the Vamp in charge on a dime. "As I said, call me Dickie. Won't do to have Vlad know who I am—could put a crimp in the festivities."

"But what if he sees you?" she asked what seemed like a logical question.

"You trust her?" Gareth asked, unconcerned that Claudia was present.

"I do."

He crossed the room with his power literally vibrating off of him. His badass Vampyre mode made my damn knees weak. He was every bit the Royal Prince and then some—and he was mine.

"What do you see when you look at me," he asked.

"Is this a trick question?" Claudia's eyes bounced with uncertainty from me to Gareth and then back to me. She cowered a bit, but kept her head high.

"No. Describe how he appears to you," I said.

"Blond hair, brown eyes, about six foot four—very handsome—very powerful," she said hesitantly. "Why? Am I not seeing him correctly?"

"Yes and no," I replied. Gareth could share the rest of the story if he felt compelled. Not my place.

"That's sufficient," he said, still watching Claudia with narrowed eyes.

"Gareth, short version of a long story — I don't want to take her life anymore," I told him.

His eyes shot to mine. If we were mated I could communicate with him telepathically, but we weren't mated... yet.

"You're sure?" His gaze bored into mine, looking for a sign that I was playing a game.

Clearly he found none and nodded slowly.

"I'm very sure. Claudia is willing to help us trap the bastard. He almost killed her tonight."

"He's in the hotel?" Gareth demanded. His fangs dropped and his body went taut.

Looking to the frightened woman on the couch, I indicated she should speak. Gareth clearly made her uncomfortable... or maybe all men did. Although Gareth could be very frightening when need be.

"No, he's not staying here. I was driven to a large home about a half hour south of here."

"By Vlad?" Gareth questioned, casually backing away from Claudia due to sensing the fear she felt in his presence.

Shaking her head no, she went on cautiously. "It was a Vampyre, but not him. The windows on the sedan were heavily tinted and I couldn't see where we were going. My sense of direction is good and I knew it was south, but that's all I can tell you about where I was."

"What about the ride back?" Gareth asked.

"I was in the trunk for the ride back," Claudia replied tonelessly. "Don't think they wanted blood on the upholstery."

That put a slight pause in the conversation.

"He's a sick fuck," Gareth muttered.

"Couldn't agree more." Claudia shuddered then wrapped her arms protectively around herself.

"Can you describe the house?" I asked, knowing it was a needle in a haystack since there was no other solid information.

"Large—manor like. No other homes I could see around it. It was very well manicured and had a moat, believe it or not," she described with a disgusted shake of her head.

"Interesting," Gareth said. "Shouldn't be too hard to find a castle with a moat in Oklahoma."

He pulled out his phone and began typing away.

"So do you actually have a plan?" Claudia asked a very fine question.

"No, but we're outstanding at winging it," I told her to her look of surprise. "Tiara said the pageant director made you go with Vlad. Is this right?"

Claudia nodded and let her head fall to her chest. "Yes. I owe her money. She promised to erase the debt if I entertained the Vampyre."

"Um... you mean have sex with him?" I asked bluntly.

"Sunny said sex wasn't part of the deal, but clearly Vlad wasn't informed of the finer intricacies of the contract."

"He raped you?" Gareth demanded in a clipped and furious tone.

"He tried," Claudia admitted, her eyes welling up. "I fought him and he seemed to enjoy it. However, he won the fight and told me that next time he wouldn't take no for an answer."

"Anything else you can tell us?" I asked, sitting down next to her and putting my arm around her shoulder for comfort. "Do you think Sunny the pageant director is involved with this?"

Placing her hand over mine, she gave me a small grateful smile. "Doubtful. She's all about the money. He

165

must have paid handsomely for her to forgive my ten thousand dollar debt. However, there was one odd thing," she said. "He kept calling me Juliette."

Bingo.

"I have a plan—kind of," I said aloud as I formed it in my head. "You will take a stage name. He'll be back or we'll go to him. Do you have it in you to seduce him?"

Claudia paled and then nodded yes. Her body trembled and I realized what she'd thought I'd just asked of her. The fact that she agreed without question made her lack of self worth very clear.

"You will *not* have to go through with it," I promised quickly. "We'll just need him focused on you until Gareth and I can take his arms and legs. Damn it, we need silver."

"Have it," Gareth said with a feral smile that turned me on. "A hundred feet of triple reinforced inch round silver. And start calling me Dickie—can't be slipping up in public."

"So what do we do now?" Claudia asked, giving us a look that conveyed how crazy she thought we were.

She was right, but I owned my crazy. I didn't even trust people who weren't at least a little bit crazy. Now of course Martha and Jane tipped the scale at batshit crazy, but I was beginning to be okay with that too. As long as there was underlying good with the insanity, it was fine with me.

"I believe there's an orientation meeting in an hour," I said checking my watch and realizing the night was gone and morning had arrived. "We go and act as if we're here to be in the pageant."

"And what's my stage name?" she asked.

"Juliette," Gareth said, taking the words from my mouth. "You will be Juliette. It will fuck with his head and we need all the extra weapons we can find.

"Juliette it is," Claudia said with her first real smile I'd seen since Gareth arrived. "Is she a real person? Do you know her?"

"Yep and yep. We'll fill you in as we go," I said, rifling through my suitcase looking for something to loan Claudia to wear. She was shorter and smaller in the bust.

"Do you think it's safe to go to my room and change?" Claudia asked.

I didn't know, but I was taking no chances. "Gar... I mean Dickie, will you get Claudia's stuff and bring it here?"

Again he raised his eyebrow and titled his head. "She'll stay with you?"

"Actually, I was thinking she could stay in my room and I could stay with *you*."

The Vampyre was gone so fast I didn't even see him leave the suite.

"That guy has it bad," Claudia said with huge smile.

I shook my head and gave her an answering grin. "And I have it even worse."

***

Fifteen minutes till we had to leave and we were gathering our little army in my destroyed suite. Thankfully Vamps didn't need to sleep regularly because Claudia, Gareth and I didn't get a minute of shuteye last night.

"You still have green goop on your face," I commented eyeing Martha with amusement.

A little green goop could be excused. At least she'd changed from her alarming nightclothes into her Prada suit. The Ninja Turtle Nightgown would have started off the day on a more unsettling foot.

167

"Fucking stuff won't come off," she grumbled. "Thank God I stole it and didn't pay for the crap."

Rolling my eyes, I tried not to groan. Served her right for having sticky fingers. The old bags had plenty of money, but seemed to enjoy the thrill of illegally lifting items. They'd apparently *procured* all the Christmas gifts they'd bought for Samuel through felonious means. Astrid'd had a fit.

"That Vampyre Beauty Network is bullshit," Jane chimed in with a disgusted grunt.

"You're correct there. Never buy *or* steal products from that network," Claudia informed her knowingly.

My foe-turned-friendly-acquaintance had changed into a gorgeous blue Chanel sheath. No one would ever know the shape she'd been in only hours ago.

"You tried that crap?" Martha asked, still scrubbing at her face.

"No, I used to own the network—left when hostile investors came in and insisted on subpar products," she replied.

Claudia was full of surprises. However, if she owned a Network why was she borrowing money from Sunny?

"I'm impressed you owned a network," I said, slipping into the Jimmy Choo stilettos that Astrid had expertly packed for me. Alice and Olivia on top and Jimmy Choo on the bottom. I was lookin' good and ready to kick some ass.

"Well, I had to make a living since we are notoriously long lived," she said easily and went to help the old coots remove the remnants of the facemasks gone wrong.

"Aren't you supported by your House?" I watched her expertly and gently peel the green flakes from Martha and Jane's skin.

Vampyre Houses were safe havens for the undead. Everyone was generously salaried and taken care of. It was necessary when we lived secret lives in public.

"Don't have a House," Claudia replied with a shrug and a small smile. "Never found one where I was comfortable."

"Cause you're a muff diver?" Martha asked in all seriousness, unaware of how truly hideously inappropriate she was.

What the hell did I expect? She'd stapled an afro to her head to impress me…

"Well, um… that's one way to put it," Claudia said with a bemused chuckle. "Does your House have a problem with *your* sexuality?" she asked Martha.

"It's the goddamned suit," she shouted. "I'm not a rug muncher. I mean, I have no problem with lesbos at all, or sissy boys for that matter. I enjoy ogling a nice rack as much as every heterosexual gal does. I don't get why everyone thinks I hump women."

"Wait one dang minute, does humping women mean I'm a dyke?" Jane asked, concerned.

"I'm done," I said sternly. "You two are so horrifyingly politically incorrect I can't believe you're still alive. I'm this close to putting both of you out of our misery—for real. Claudia is a lesbian—not a muff muncher."

"Muff diver," Jane corrected me.

The look I shot her made her drop and crawl for cover. "How about this? You try very, very hard not to be offensive, and I'll let you lose the blazer of the suit."

"No can do, Boss Mamma," Martha said. "I'm wearing a dickie with pasties underneath this ass ugly jacket. Don't think that sexy look is gonna fly here."

Speechless. The mental image alone was nightmare inducing, but the fact that I had to hear her utter the words dickie and pasty in one sentence was enough to make me behead them.

"Okay then," Claudia said pleasantly while trying not to laugh. "Keep the blazer on. I'm sorry I mistook your sexual orientation. Won't happen again."

"Better not, missy," Jane admonished. "Just 'cause I think Bette Midler is hot and Barbra Streisand has biteable hooters and I wouldn't mind locking lips with Cher… none of that means I bat for your team."

"Got it." Claudia turned away and had a coughing fit to hide her laughter.

Hell, even *I* was laughing. And again, I was mystified how Martha and Jane were still alive. Maybe they grew on everyone like a fungus.

"Are we ready?" Gareth asked, entering the suite sporting an Armani suit minus the tie with his shirt open at the neck.

It took everything I had not to fly across the room and tackle his sexy ass to the floor. All my girlie parts tingled and my stomach flip-flopped. His expression when he took in my outfit, my shoes, my hair, and finally my obscene amount of cleavage made the tingling ramp up. Holy Hell we really were going to need to find a closet or something. Our sexual tension was so intense I was certain everyone could feel it.

"You guys wanna screw real quick?" Jane asked as she picked up a satchel full of God only knew what.

"No," I said at the same time Gareth shouted, "Yes!"

Letting my chin drop to my chest to mask my ridiculous delight, I groaned. "We can't be late. I don't want any excess attention called to us."

"Venus is correct, sadly," Gareth said, turning his back to all to covertly rearrange his massive erection. "I'll be with you in a moment. My… um, zipper is stuck."

"That's a good one, Prince Dickie," Martha cackled and immediately zipped it when Gareth gave her a withering look.

"I thought…" Claudia started and then paused.

"You thought what?" I asked tucking a dagger into the elastic of my garter. I wanted my sword, but it might look a little conspicuous.

"I thought he might be a royal. I recognized the name Gareth."

"You thought right," I told her. "But please don't treat him as such. It will blow our cover."

"I'm just Dickie the blond haired, brown eyed, blue balled Vamp this week," he said in a pained voice as he turned back around.

He hadn't solved his *problem* at all, but everyone— even Martha and Jane—were polite or smart enough not to comment on his tented pants.

"All right, let's get the shitshow on the road," I said, slipping a few throwing stars into my smart little purse.

"We got some bad guys to kill," Jane crowed, doing a little jig that looked more like a seizure than a dance.

"Trap, not kill," Gareth reminded her. "And you will not be involved in that part. Clear?"

"As mud," Martha bitched. "We never get to do the fun shit."

"I wouldn't call dealing with a deranged, psychotic monster fun," Claudia said, checking her bag for her weapons. "Oh, and I don't want Tiara involved in this. This is not her fight."

"Got it," I said as Gareth gave me a curious glance. "She won't know a thing."

"She means too much to me," Claudia added quietly as she made her way to the door.

Her plea made perfect sense to me. If I could leave Gareth out of this, I would— *in a heartbeat,* and I was certain from the way he was staring at me, he felt the same.

Too bad, so sad. If we wanted a future together we were going to have to fight for it together.

And we would.

Chapter 17

Armed with a fairly decent attitude, two debatably heterosexual and certifiably insane old ladies, the woman I'd wanted to kill less than eight hours ago, and the newly realized love of my undead life was nothing I could have dreamed up. But it was real—very real. We were here and we were going to do this. Of course I had no clue what *this* was going to entail, but that had never stopped me before.

"You've got to be kidding me," I mumbled as we made our way into the auditorium and looked for seats to listen to the pageant director go over the itinerary.

The enormous room was filled with female Vamps in more sequins than I'd ever seen in my life. I was woefully underdressed even in my sexy little Alice and Olivia number with my killer stilettos. I suppose I'd missed the must have eye bleeding amounts of sparkle memo.

Even the handlers looked like contestants.

"Do you have handlers?" I asked Claudia.

"No, I can't afford them. Tiara's people help me out."

Claudia's money issues were a mystery that I was going to get to the bottom of very soon. I had more money than I knew what to do with in many lifetimes. I'd gotten bored over the years and had gone to college, earning both my Master's and Doctorate in business and finance. I'd invested brilliantly through my centuries and taught many of the Vamps in the Cressida House to do the same. If Claudia needed money, I could... Whatever. I'd deal with that later.

The sheer irony of having gone from wanting to kill Claudia to needing to make sure she was financially secure was mind-boggling. Analyzing my change of heart was useless. It was what it was and I felt peaceful with it. The Kev was far wiser than me, so I planned to take his damned advice and trust my instincts no matter how unbelievable my inclinations were.

On the stage, a severe looking but attractive woman in head to toe Gucci stood at a podium and adjusted her jeweled spectacles. It had to be the notoriously money hungry Sunny. I laughed. Vampyres had perfect vision. The glasses were a fashion statement. I wondered how much posturing there would be. If Sunny was any indication to go by, there would be plenty.

"Holy Hell on a piece of toast, I'm in Heaven," Martha said, eyeing all the sparkling gowns with delight.

"You just contradicted yourself," I muttered, giving the evil eye to a group of busty gals eyeing Gareth hungrily. He stood quietly at my side and ignored the flirtatious glances.

"What do you mean?" Martha asked, casing the competition and jotting down notes on a pad of paper.

"Nothing." I took a seat in the back of the auditorium. "Sit."

Gareth sat beside me and leaned in close to my ear. If I turned my head our lips would meet. I was so tempted. It would let the other Vamps in the room know he was taken—I mean technically he wasn't... yet. However dealing with advances from horny undead sequined hookers would hinder the mission—and piss me off royally.

"Exits are on the far left and right of the stage, and of course the doors we entered through. No exit from the backstage area, but there's a window with a fire escape. Dressing rooms off stage right and a few technical rooms and an office stage left."

"Got it," I said and looked to Martha, Jane and Claudia to make sure they'd heard.

Turning to Gareth while the pageant director droned on about good sportsmanship and no bloodshed, I leaned in and gave him a nice view of my girls.

"Are there any closets that lock in the backstage area?" I asked innocently.

With great difficulty he raised his gaze from my cleavage to my eyes before his face split into a panty-melting grin. It was all I could do not to throw myself at him.

"I should be pissed at you that my dick is as hard as a rock again."

"Sorry," I whispered, trying not to giggle. Glancing down, I was able to confirm that he was telling the very hard truth.

"*Are* you sorry?" he inquired with a lopsided grin that made my panties damp.

"Nope."

Trying to adjust himself covertly, he let his head fall back on the seat and muttered a few curses. "You do realize you'll have to pay, my beautiful girl."

"I certainly hope so."

"I see Tiara," Jane whispered and pointed to a woman sitting a few rows ahead of us.

Sure enough it was Tiara. She had a gaggle of very butch looking Vamps around her casing the competition and taking notes like Martha. Tiara spoke quietly to the gal on her left and patted her arm with praise. The woman

175

preened and bowed her head to Tiara. All the other women quickly followed suit with the respectful gesture.

Interesting.

"We'll meet up with her after the announcements." Claudia fluffed her perfect blonde hair and straightened her sheath nervously.

Hmmm, she had it bad for the loud-mouthed Tiara—I should know. I had it equally as bad for the beautiful Vamp seated next to me.

"There will be a half hour break then all the contestants must come back stage. Only women handlers will be permitted in the back stage and dressing room areas. All men will sit in the house," Sunny announced in a clipped tone with a practiced and cold smile on her face.

"Unacceptable," Gareth growled. "I'll be with you the entire time."

Claudia wrung her hands and then placed one hesitantly on Gareth's arm. "She'll go nuts on you if you go back there. I've seen her in action. It's not pretty."

"No worries," Gareth assured her, attempting to put Claudia at ease. "I'll kill her."

"Um… not the best plan, dude." I gave him a large and obnoxious eye roll. "We don't need any unnecessary casualties."

"You're not going anywhere without me." Gareth's eyes glowed green and his fangs peeked out from his lips.

"Your alpha-hole is showing," I hissed. "I've been defending myself for two hundred years. I'm pretty damned good at it. And if you're gonna be a dick, we're gonna have issues."

"Venus, issues mean fights. Fights mean make up sex. Make up sex is outstanding," he informed me in a tone that made me want to head butt him. "You and I will never stop clashing. It's the way we are and I find it painfully arousing," he said, referring his very noticeable problem. "If you don't believe me, you can check out my crotch—you will find rock hard proof. So that being said, you will go *nowhere* without me."

Jane raised her hand. When no one called on her she went ahead and added her own two cents. "What about the bathroom?"

"For the love of God," Gareth snapped. "We're Vampyres. We don't go to the bathroom."

"I always forget that," Jane said, smacking her forehead. "My bad."

Martha patted her cohort on the back. "Right there with ya. Every morning I sit on the crapper for at least twenty minutes before I remember my plumbing doesn't work anymore."

Ignoring the disturbing revelation, I considered fighting Gareth on his macho Vampyre bullshit. However, I realized my own protective tendencies were in overdrive concerning him. I didn't want him out of my sight either.

"There is a way for you to make this work," I said slowly. "But I think it would drain too much power."

Gareth knew exactly what I was speaking of—so did Martha and Jane. The only one out of the loop was Claudia and she looked confused.

"You're going to dress him up as a woman?" she asked. "Don't think you can get that past Sunny. Dickie's scent is very... um, male."

"Not exactly," I hedged, waiting to see if Gareth was in. I wasn't going to reveal his secret, but I couldn't think of another way he could stay with us and not cause a smack down with Sunny.

"You truly trust this woman?" Gareth asked, referring to Claudia.

"I do. You can take my blood, it will help like it did with the Angels."

Running his hands through his hair and mulling my offer over, he shook his head no. "Your blood did help, but you need it right now. I'll take my chances. I feel almost back to my old self—think it will be fine."

"I don't want to pry, but clearly I'm going to," Claudia said with a small chuckle. "Not sure what you're talking about and I don't want to be privy to anything I shouldn't, but Tiara's blood is rare and extremely powerful. I know she would let you drink if I asked her."

"If we do that, she's involved," I told her.

There was something odd going on with Tiara. She was deferred to like royalty by her handlers. And if she was truthful in her story about tearing the head off a Fairy, she was a mighty force of nature. Albeit one with a grating voice, but a badass nonetheless.

Claudia's focus strayed and landed on the back of Tiara's head. I watched the wheels turn in her head as she came to her decision.

"I don't want her in the battle, but she'll never forgive me if she could have helped, and I denied her—again. Follow me to the dressing rooms. We'll have privacy there for whatever you need to do. We'll grab Tiara and go."

The meeting was adjourned and people began to mill around. It was now or never if we were going to do this.

"You good with this plan?" I asked Gareth as I stood.

He shrugged. "If it gets me backstage without having to kill anyone, I'm in. You mean more to me than any secret I've ever kept. And since you've nixed any extraneous killing, I suppose I have to be happy with plan B. Just so you know, I don't usually follow orders this nicely, but you do have tremendous tits."

His grin made me want to laugh and his comment made me want to throat punch him.

If we made it out of here alive, we had *many years* of make up sex ahead of us.

***

"So let me get this straight," Tiara said while rolling up her sleeve in preparation to feed Gareth. "This is gonna give Dickie an extra boost to turn him into a woman? Why does he need to be a woman? And how in the Hell does a hot dude morph into a female?"

"This is so he doesn't have to kill Sunny," Jane said. "And he's got weird Vamp gifts."

Tiara took that in and then clapped her hands together with glee.

"But ripping Sunny's head off is a great idea," Tiara countered with enthusiasm. "Don't know why I never thought of that. Bitch deserves it."

Tiara had agreed to give Gareth blood even before she knew why we needed it. Her entire demeanor was sweeter and even her voice wasn't as heinous around Claudia. When Claudia wasn't looking Tiara stared at her with longing that was both sweet and sad.

What had happened here? Again, like Claudia's money woes, it wasn't my problem. But it clawed at me. Maybe because my own happiness was in reach so I wanted others to have it too.

"This shit is gonna give you a rush, Dickie," Tiara informed him cockily. "Might knock you on your ass for a while if you're not *man* enough."

She cackled at her own joke and I casually ran my hands through my hair so I could cover my ears. I was surprised the glass on the mirrors didn't shatter from the octave she laughed in. Jane and Martha had no qualms about being rude. They dug through the satchel they had brought and slapped ear plugs in their ears.

"He's powerful. He won't have a problem with your blood because…" Claudia said and then froze. She glanced with worry toward Gareth and me.

Gareth shrugged. "I'm assuming you can be trusted," he said to Tiara in a tone that confirmed his alpha hole, badass status.

She paused her preparation and stared at him with curiosity and a little fear. "What are you, Dickie? You a full Vamp?"

Odd question.

"First off, my name's not Dickie," he said, looking at her strangely.

He obviously though her question was unusual too.

"Well, thank God for that," Tiara laughed. "You don't really look like a Dickie. I mean you look like you could be a dick, but…"

"Um… Tiara, you might want to tamp that back," Claudia said, trying to stop her from inadvertently smack talking a Master Vampyre slash royal Prince slash someone *no one* would want to get on the bad side of.

"Why? Is he a bigwig Vamp or some bullshit like that?" she asked with an amused shake of her blonde curls.

"Actually, yes," Gareth said dryly.

"How big?" Tiara asked warily.

"Fucking huge," Martha piped in.

Tiara eyed Gareth suspiciously and then laughed. "Alrighty then, I'll make you a deal."

"State your terms," Gareth replied.

"Simple. I won't bust on you if you won't bust on me."

"For?" Gareth asked, intrigued.

"My lineage."

"Tiara," Claudia whispered, worried and unsure.

"It's okay, baby," Tiara promised her in a surprisingly soft tone. "Too many bastards are onto me and I need help from a bigwig. Of course it would be better if Dickie was a Prince or connected to The Chosen One."

"Why?" I asked, now more intrigued than Gareth and uncomfortably wary. "What does Astrid have to do with this?"

"That would be between me and her," Tiara replied.

"You carry a grudge?" Gareth inquired coldly.

Tiara laughed and rolled her eyes. "Um... no. I'd kiss that woman's ass if I ever got to be in her presence. You could say I have some family information she might be interested in."

"You know Juliette?" I asked.

"Who in the Hell is Juliette?" Tiara asked. "Can't say I know a Juliette."

The situation was getting stranger by the second. However, if she had something on Astrid we needed to know. Martha and Jane grew eerily silent and their eyes went green with aggression. It was going to be their final moments on Earth if they attacked Tiara, but their loyalty to Astrid was unbreakable. I actually kind of liked Tiara, but she was expendable if she posed any kind of threat.

Claudia could see the direction the situation was going and became frantic.

"Tell them now," she insisted to Tiara. "They can be trusted and I believe they can help."

Tiara sensed the change in the room as well. She backed herself up to the wall and pulled Claudia with her.

"If you take offense to what I have to say, you will not touch Claudia. Ever. She will be permitted to leave and I will take all of you on."

"I don't believe you're making the rules here," Gareth said so casually it made the hair on my arms stand up. His eyes glowed green and his fangs extended. "I'd suggest you speak truthfully and quickly—if not, it will be a very bad ending for you."

Tiara clearly didn't like his tone or his threat. She took a defensive stance. Her fangs dropped, but her eyes didn't turn green. Nope, one went red and one went silver.

What in the ever-loving Hell was she?

"Astrid is her sister," Claudia blurted out before the all the inhabitants of the room attacked. "They share the same father. She wants to thank Astrid for killing him. He made Tiara's life a living Hell. Please don't hurt her."

Well, that certainly gave us pause. Astrid's sister? The one red eye now made sense as she was part Demon, but the silver? And the fact she was also a Vamp? Tiara was a mass of contradictions.

"Claudia speaks the truth?" I demanded.

Tiara nodded, but still held her defensive position. She'd put Claudia behind her and was prepared to fight all of us. She was nuts, but I admired her insane spirit. She looked nothing like Astrid, but that didn't matter. She clearly had Astrid's balls.

Gareth relaxed slightly, but was still ready to attack if necessary. "My name is Gareth. I'm Prince of the Asian Dominion. Astrid is mated to my brother Ethan—Prince of the North American Dominion. If you want an audience, it shall be granted."

"No shit?" Tiara asked cautiously.

"Not even a squirt," Martha said, eyeing Tiara with great interest.

"Stop talking," I said to Martha. "Tiara, there's more and you will explain now. Your eyes are different colors and how is it you're a Vampyre?"

"Very perceptive," Tiara said easily. Her fangs retracted but her eyes still burned a mesmerizing red and silver. "I know your secret so I may as well tell mine. My father was the very same Demon that sired Astrid. My mother was a Fairy—and not a nice one."

"Is that why you can rip the head off one of those flying fuckers?" Jane asked, attempting to sound unimpressed. She failed.

Nodded tightly, Tiara continued. "I stupidly thought if I became undead I would find protection amongst the Vampyres from my Demon father. The Fairies never wanted anything to do with me and my mother hated me. I was a reminder of how low she'd stooped by having sex with a Demon."

"And..." I prompted her when she paused in thought.

"Well, the Vamps didn't want me either. I'm a goddamned Demon-Fairy-Vampyre who also happens to be a lesbian. Can't get more unusual than that combo," she said flatly.

"Word," Martha mumbled in agreement.

"And you think your sister would take you in?" I asked, knowing Astrid would do exactly that.

"No," she said in a weary voice. "I expect nothing of the sort. It would remove something from my fucked up bucket list to be able to thank her for killing the slimy bastard."

I wondered if Tiara's *baggage* was why Claudia wouldn't commit to her, but somehow I doubted it. Why? Not sure. But my *instincts* told me so.

"What will your blood do to me?" Gareth asked, approaching Tiara.

Sizing him up, she shrugged. "I can tell you're not in your true form right now. Can't see through whatever you have going on there, but you might want to drop it while we do this. Any extra magic on you could backfire."

"You can tell he's glamoured?" Her revelation stressed me out. If she could tell, would Vlad be able to as well?

"No, but I feel the magic due to my fucked up Fairy side. I just put two and two together and guessed. Clearly, I guessed correctly."

"You did," Gareth said letting the glamour drop and continuing across the dressing room to where Tiara stood. "You do realize you're directly related to Satan?"

Tiara blanched and let her head fall to her ample chest. "And the day gets fucking better," she muttered in disgust. "I thought I might be, but had always prayed I wasn't."

"You are," I confirmed. "But there is no reason for him to know if you don't want him to. You'll need to stay out of his presence. He's very smart. I'm quite sure he'd be able to tell."

"No problem staying away from the Devil—got enough on my plate without that shit. The last two years have been a relative Heaven on Earth since Astrid took care of old *Dad*."

"We don't have much time," Claudia reminded us. "If everyone is agreeable, we should do this now."

Tiara ran her hand gently down Claudia's cheek and kissed the top of her head. "My girl has always been very practical. She's right. Prince Gareth, my blood will enhance every gift you have." She paused a moment and stared hard at Gareth. "What's wrong with you? I sense something very off."

I glanced at Claudia and waited for her approval. I would tell Tiara the rest of the story even without

Claudia's blessing because Gareth's life was at stake, but I wanted to show some respect to Claudia. She hadn't wanted Tiara to be involved, but…

Claudia nodded and closed her eyes briefly. We'd gone way past the point of not involving Tiara and she knew it as well.

"Gareth, it's your story to tell," I said.

"I've been cursed by an Angel and the sorry excuse of a Vampyre called Vlad—as have several of my other siblings. Vlad's trying to dismantle the Royal Family and take over. Your Uncle Satan gave me a stay on my illness for a week. Vlad is here due to his obsession with Claudia and we plan to take him alive to break the curse. I'm not at full strength, and if I plan to shift to a woman, I need more power."

"Is that the Vampyre Sunny made you go out with?" Tiara demanded of a frightened Claudia.

"Yes."

"Did he hurt you?" Tiara ground out through clenched teeth.

After a brief pause, Claudia nodded. "Yes."

"Carved some awful shit into her back with silver. That's gonna leave a nasty scar," Martha volunteered.

"You will stop speaking or I will duct tape your mouth shut," I warned. "That is not your information to share."

Tiara turned and put her fist through the wall like it was made of butter. "If you had let me take care of you, this wouldn't have happen," she hissed at a teary Claudia.

"I'm beneath you. I'll bring you down."

Tiara proceeded to put her other fist through the wall and then attempted to regain her composure. "Our private life isn't the business of our new and somewhat friendly acquaintances. We will speak of this later," she growled.

"If you want my blood, take it now. It's on the edge of boiling like a Demon's and that would fucking kill you for sure."

"Seriously?" I asked, shocked.

"Very," she said tightly. "Give me a sec here and we'll do this."

After a minute of pacing the room like a mad woman, Tiara calmed herself enough to stand still.

"This Vlad... Is he the Impaler?" she asked.

"Yes," I replied.

"I want him after you're done with him."

"Satan's got dibs," Gareth said. "You'll have to get in line."

Tiara lifted her wrist to Gareth's mouth and smiled a dark smile. "Not if I get to know my uncle, I won't."

"Not sure you want to go there," I said trying to be diplomatic. She clearly had enough problems without adding Satan to her list.

"Ahhh," she replied with a hollow laugh. "You don't know me. You can fuck with me till the cows come home, but if you fuck with those I love, I will kill you so dead you'll wish you'd never been born. Owing Lucifer will be nothing compared to the satisfaction of making Vlad squeal like a pig being butchered with millions of tiny sharp knives."

"She's *definitely* Astrid's sister," Gareth commented as he sunk his fangs into Tiara's wrist.

I couldn't agree more. She had the potty mouth and the compulsion to defend those she loved. I'd have to say Astrid was slightly less violent, but she was also a Hell of a force of nature. Their first meeting was going to be very interesting.

Chapter 18

"Holy shit, that was intense," Gareth said as he grabbed my shoulder to keep his footing.

"Told ya," Tiara said, pulling the sleeve of her gorgeous Byron Lars dress back down over her wrist. "My blood's not for weenies."

"Make sure you call Satan a weenie," I said with a laugh. "He loves it when Astrid does it. Not."

"I'm sure I'll have a few choice words for my Uncle Fucker," she replied with a grin.

"*What* did you just call him?" I asked as my grin grew unbelievably wider.

"Uncle Fucker," she said. "Of course I won't really call the King of the Underworld that. I don't have a death wish, but ya gotta admit it's funny."

"She is *so* Astrid's sister," I marveled. Their potty mouths were scarily similar.

Gareth chuckled and walked around the small room to get used to the new surge of power he'd just ingested. "How long will this last?"

"A week or two," Tiara said. "Ya gonna to shift now? I'd love to watch."

"Shortly," he confirmed. "Venus and I need a few minutes alone to make a plan. Martha and Jane, you will stand guard at the door. Claudia and Tiara, it's best if we behave as if we don't know each other well. I don't expect Vlad back until the actual show, but I could be very wrong."

"Claudia won't leave my sight," Tiara said, giving Claudia a stern look that said she would brook no defiance on the matter. "And we've only got eighteen minutes before we're due backstage. I'd suggest ya make the *most* of it."

She winked and grinned broadly as she ushered the other gals from the room. If I could have blushed I would have, but my need for the insanely gorgeous Vampyre outweighed any embarrassment I felt for being outed.

The door closed firmly behind our crew and Gareth turned to me with a look that made my knees weak.

"Strip. I can make eighteen minutes work," he ordered, yanking at his clothes.

My dress flew over my head and I removed my weapons from my garters in a hot second. It wouldn't do to accidentally remove one of my favorite parts of him with a dagger. Of course it would grow back, but we only had eighteen minutes.

"This will take the edge off," he said as he cupped my breasts in his large hands and gently pinched at my hardened nipples.

"Really?" I asked on a gasp. I greedily ran my hands over his naked chest, loving the feel of the light sprinkling of dark hair that veed down to the area I adored.

"Probably not," he muttered as his lips replaced his hands and my knees buckled with desire.

My body felt hot, the need within me roared with an urgency I'd never experienced. My gums ached and my fangs slid out.

"I am so in love with you," he muttered almost unintelligibly as he worshiped my body.

I tried to repeat his sentiment, but my words came out like a garbled moan.

"No biting," Gareth insisted, frantically. His fangs had dropped too and he scrubbed his hands over his face in distress. "I will not bite you. You will not bite me. I will not bite you. You will not bite me."

"Are you talking to me or yourself?" I asked as I took the very hard evidence of his desire into my hands and stroked.

"Me... no, you. Shit, me and you, and me. Can't think with your hands on my dick," he said, tangling his fingers in my hair and slanting his mouth over mine.

I expected his kiss to be violent. I couldn't have been more wrong. It was gentle and loving and brought tears to my eyes. My entire body tingled and I suddenly felt shy and exposed. Gareth was right. Sex was a release. Making love was entirely different. I'd only really made love one other time in my life and it had been with him.

Picking me up and moving to the couch in the dressing room with Vampyre speed, he finally laid me down. His eyes roamed over every inch of my naked body like a predator sizing up his prey and I shuddered with delight. I'd never felt so beautiful or wanted. This man who drove me crazy also made me feel like more of a woman than I'd ever felt.

"I want you," I whispered, holding my arms out to him. My tears fell as my emotions overtook me. "Knowing you're truly mine makes this feel like the first time."

"The first of many," he promised. He eyes were hooded with lust, but his love for me shone through—clear and heartbreakingly honest.

I wanted to believe him. I needed to believe him. We had such a beautiful future ahead of us, *if* we could break the curse. Pushing my fear away I focused on the living reality in front of me. Living moment to moment was all we had now and I was going to treasure what I could get.

Gareth was gorgeous in his naked glory and I wanted him so badly it hurt—my breasts ached and a coil of need curled low in my belly. I wanted to mate with him— wanted to be completely his and needed him to be completely mine, but that would have to wait.

"Are you okay?" he asked as his large body blanketed my own making me feel safe and cherished. "Why are you crying?"

Lowering his mouth to mine, his tongue tickled the seam of my lips and I opened willingly to him. His taste was addictive and his body on top of mine felt so very right.

"It's a happy cry," I promised, tracing his full lips and high cheekbones with my finger and marveling that we'd finally found each other.

He ran his open mouth along my jaw and nibbled on my earlobe sending little shocks of pleasure through my body. He was careful not to pierce the skin, but God I wanted him to.

"You're my perfection. I've waited my entire life for you," he whispered huskily.

His voice went all through me, sending jolts of the purest pleasure I'd known right to my core. Wrapping my arms around him and holding on for dear life, I never wanted to let go. I pushed the ugly thoughts of him dying to the back of my mind and focused on the here and now.

We were together. It didn't matter that it was in a dressing room in Oklahoma or that Martha and Jane were right outside the door. All that was important was that we were in each other's arms and we belonged to each other. The pressure in my chest and the needles dancing beneath my skin verged on pain. I buried my face in his neck and tried to control my rioting emotions.

Love was far more complicated than lust.

"Tell me you're okay, baby. Tell me that you want this as much as I do." He took my face in his hands and searched my eyes.

The utter simplicity of the moment was more difficult to deal with than if we'd been all over each other and completely out of control. It was real and raw and all consuming. It was frighteningly perfect. I would fight to the death to have this again and again.

"I think I might love you too much," I said, running my hands over his beautiful face to memorize what it felt like to touch him.

"No such thing," he replied with a chuckle.

Gareth shifted his weight to his elbows, but still covered me completely. His lips followed the path of my tears from my eyes to my lips then to my neck. I felt too small to hold everything I was feeling for the man. My insides couldn't contain this much love and need.

"Gareth, I..." Words escaped me, but words couldn't begin to convey how I felt. Wrapping my legs around his strong body I arched into him and tried to tell him with my body what words were simply too inadequate to communicate.

"I want to go slow," he said with a pained expression, trying to hold back. "But we're under a little time crunch here."

"Slow is for weenies," I replied with a giggle, writhing under him like a wanton woman. "No foreplay this time," I gasped out, feeling his huge erection against my stomach. "Next time slow—this time, *now*."

I cried out as his body joined with mine, uncaring if the entire auditorium could hear. His control was insane. The slow pace was more erotic and soul baring than the first time we'd made love. Our eyes locked and our bodies moved in a rhythm as if they recognized each other—as if we were made for this perfect, uninhibited dance. We became one entity—sexually and spiritually. It was every kind of right. Two bodies with one glorious non-beating heart.

"Need to be closer," he said hoarsely as he increased the speed of our lovemaking.

I was in for the ride of my life as my body willingly met every deep thrust with joy. My eyes closed involuntarily as tingles shot through me and went straight to the tips of my fingers and toes. I clenched his thick and beautiful length within me and mini orgasms rocked me speechless.

"Open. Open your eyes," he insisted. "Need to see you—need you to see me."

His eyes were clouded with lust. The sound he made deep in his chest made me clamp my legs harder around him to try to stave off the huge orgasm that was building inside me at a rapid pace.

"So good," I muttered, trying to focus on him through my tears of joy. I felt every inch of him with every inch of me. Sight wasn't necessary. The magic we were making was branded into me for eternity. I was unsure where he began and I ended.

"Want to bite you," he ground out. "Want it so bad— not going to do it."

"Soon," I promised, needing it as desperately as he did. My fangs literally burned, but I wanted him forever. I would respect his request to wait. I didn't want to... but I would.

The air around us sizzled with heat and the base desire to mate burned within both of us. As our bodies merged in passion, we surged as close as two people could without crawling inside of each other. Gareth shifted his weight and ran one hand possessively over my breasts and hip. His body slid in and out of mine and we became a wild frenzy of sensual movement.

His mouth closed over mine and I sucked at his lips as he grew larger within me. We were done with slow and gentle. We were into the ferocious and deliciously violent part. I was sure I was losing brain cells as forming thought was difficult, but this would be a fine way to go.

His otherworldly beauty and powerful magic surrounding us sent me into liquid meltdown. Unable to hold even a fraction of myself back, I writhed beneath him giving as good as I was getting. Our eyes were locked on each other's and I felt more naked than I'd felt in my life— vulnerable and unable to hide. However, I didn't want to hide anymore. I wanted to live in full color with the man who made me feel.

"So fucking gorgeous. Love you so much," he growled as he plunged into my body with a recklessness he could no longer control.

My insides danced with abandon and contracted around his girth making all my most sensitive parts pulse frantically. I gave to him as freely as he gave to me and it was more perfect than anything I'd ever imagined.

"God, Venus," he growled. "You're mine. Mine. Need you so bad."

And then he bit me. It was quick, but it was very real.

I screamed as the massive orgasm rolled through me. Colors ripped across my vision and I watched his eyes go unfocused as an explosion of pleasure tore across his beautifully masculine features. We came together and we came hard. My ears were ringing and I floated down from the most intense sexual experience I'd ever had.

"Fuck," he muttered as his body still moved inside me. "I shouldn't have fucking done that. I lost control."

He had and it took an act of God for me not to bite him back. We were only halfway mated without my reciprocal bite. Dangerous, but okay.

The aftershocks of my orgasm rocked my body as Gareth's lips captured mine in a kiss that promised me the world.

His masculine grunt of satisfaction as my body continued to contract in mini orgasms made me smile.

"Um... you didn't follow your own rules," I whispered.

"I'm an ass. I'm sorry. I'm so fucking sorry."

"I'm not sorry," I whispered and touched the tender spot on my neck with awe. "However, I'd like to point out that I did follow the rules. That means I'm the winner."

"No, I'm the winner in this relationship—always. You're the one getting the bum deal. I'll never come close to deserving you. I'm a Master fucking Vampyre and I'm like a pubescent teenage boy in your arms," he said.

"I love you," I mumbled against his mouth. The words were not enough, but they were all I had.

"You're my everything," he whispered, peppering little kisses all over my face and neck. "I want to take you away and make love to you for hundreds of years. You make me a better man."

Nodding and trying not to cry as reality rushed back in, I held him tight.

"It will be okay, Venus," he promised.

"It will?"

"It has to be," he insisted, cradling me to him and smoothing my wild hair from my face. "I've never had more to live for."

And neither had I.

As much as I wanted to pretend the dressing room was a remote island in paradise, it wasn't. We had a mission, and if we failed, the island would be no more.

I didn't like to lose.

And I had no intention of losing.

I couldn't live without him.

Chapter 19

Gareth was a spectacular woman just as he was a spectacular man. However, it was definitely unsettling to leave the dressing room with Gareth as a girl, especially considering what we'd just done, but the life of a Vamp was nothing if it wasn't unconventional.

Martha and Jane were wildly impressed with his perky hooters and complimented him profusely. Gareth slash Dickie slash *Ginny* was beside himself with glee over his newly attached playthings. Thankfully there was a Diane von Furstenberg wrap dress in the dressing room that we *borrowed* or else he would have been naked.

We'd made it backstage with about a minute to spare. Post sex, I'd quickly pulled myself back together while my man switched sexes. All kinds of strange, but very fascinating.

The backstage area was packed, but I spotted Tiara and Claudia immediately. Tiara's mouth dropped open with she saw *Ginny*. Elbowing Claudia, they both gave Gareth a rousing thumbs up.

All of this praise was going directly to his coiffed head. I had to admit that with black wavy hair and icy blue eyes he was stunning, but come on. His ego was large to begin with... we didn't need it to knock out the back wall of the auditorium.

"You have got to stop feeling yourself up," I muttered, pulling his hands away from his breasts. "It's weird."

"Oh my God, I don't understand why you don't do this to yourself—all the fucking time. I would," he said squeezing his 36C's with great joy.

"Um... you are, and you're drawing alarmed looks. Either put your hands in your pockets or behind your back. Now."

"Can I fondle my ass?"

"Can you do it discreetly?" I asked with an eye roll. He was going to touch something—he couldn't seem to stop himself. It may as well be lower than higher on the body. Less noticeable.

"I think I can. You know, I thought I would miss my dick—and I do—but these boobs almost make up for it."

Glancing around to make sure no one had overheard, I elbowed him. Hard. "Okay that's more information than I would ever need in a hundred lifetimes. Go over there and stand against the wall. That way you can touch your ass and no one will be the wiser."

"Can I turn around, face the wall, and feel up my boobs?"

"No. No you can't."

Gareth followed my orders with out any backtalk. He was too involved in his new body parts—mainly his boobs—to fight me. God, never in a million years did I think I would put those words together in reference to my very masculine mate.

"All right ladies," Sunny yelled over the din of the crowd congregating in the wings. "Today you will practice speaking about your cause. You'll each have three minutes. You go even one second over and a tenth of a point will be deducted from your score. I'll have a stopwatch and a bullhorn during rehearsal today and don't think I won't use it."

The crowd tittered politely.

Was that supposed to be a joke? If old Sunny was trying to be funny, she'd just failed miserably. And what the Hell was she talking about? Glancing over at Martha and Jane, I felt a bit ill. They were frantically searching through the satchel. Did they have my 'cause' in there—whatever the Hell that was?

"You're new," Sunny snapped as she approached me, looking me up and down like I was a car in a lot. "You're a last minute entrant. I don't *ever* take last minute, but I had no choice. You'd better be all you were made out to be."

Before I could even get a word, or a head butt in, she turned on her ridiculously high heels and went to terrorize someone else. Awesome. Thankfully she'd saved me from committing an act of unnecessary bloodshed like I'd forbidden Gareth to do.

"What did she say to you?" Tiara asked as she and Claudia came over and flanked me.

"Something about a cause. What the heck is she talking about?"

"You don't have a cause?" Claudia asked with concern marring her lovely features.

I was so out of my comfort zone here. The worried expressions on Claudia and Tiara's faces made me feel like I was about to take a final exam in school that I hadn't studied for one little bit.

"I have a bathing suit and a damn glittery dress. I didn't know I was supposed to have a cause," I muttered frantically.

Gareth was too into his ass to even notice my mini freak out. He'd better get over fondling himself fast. We were going to have to take on Vlad and whoever else the bastard had with him. If Gareth kept massaging his boobs, we were going to be in huge trouble.

"Fuck a duck on a Slip-n-Slide." Martha came waddling up to us with a terrified look on her face. "You gotta come up with a fucking cause pronto."

"What do you mean *I*?" I hissed, wanting to wallop her. "You're my damned handler. You're supposed to have this shit under control."

"Didn't say nothing about a cause in the memo we got," Jane explained in a tizzy. "We can do this. Most causes are about a disease or some shit like that. Just pick one and go out there and say you care about it."

"We're Vampyres, you dumb ass, we don't get diseases." I was beginning to panic. Old Sunny would boot my ass if I wasn't up to snuff and I had to be here.

Damn it.

"Vampyres also don't go to the bathroom," Martha reminded everyone just in case we'd forgotten.

"What's your cause?" I asked Tiara. Maybe I could pick something similar.

"Advancement of the Gay and Lesbian Undead Society. It's not real popular, but I'm so good in the cage they overlook it," Tiara explained.

Hmm... I had nothing for that one.

"Claudia—now going by the stage name *Juliette*—please come to the stage," Sunny's snarky voice boomed over the sound system. "Your three minutes start NOW."

Claudia made a hasty exit and sprinted to the stage.

"What's her cause?" I asked, still racking my brain for something I could actually speak about and not sound like an idiot.

"NAACP," Tiara said with pride. "Claudia is from a dark time in history—just fucking awful. She lived on a slave plantation with a fucker that beat her almost to death on a daily basis. After she was turned, she searched out all the descendants of the slaves that had been on the plantation. She's been quietly funneling money to them over the years without them knowing where it comes from—you know, educational scholarships, home loans, medical bills that kind of shit. It's why she's always broke. I'm real proud of her—just wish she'd keep enough to keep her own head above water."

"What?" I choked out. I felt light headed and like I'd entered an alternate universe.

I'd had plans to kill her. Claudia was an Angel living on Earth and I'd been so close to having her blood on my hands. I could have taken the life of the woman who was supporting the great-great-grandchildren of those who had labored beside me in my former life. My knees gave out and I landed in a clump on the floor. Tears filled my eyes as I rocked back and forth like a child trying to comfort myself.

Shame, I felt shame—and so very small. I owed The Kev my sanity and my undying trust. I owed Claudia an apology. Vengeance had almost ruined me.

"What the ever lovin' Hell?" Martha cried out as she squatted down and wrapped her boney arms around me. "Don't you worry your pretty head," she murmured. "I'll think up a mother humpin' cause. I'm here for you, baby."

Gareth dashed over with fangs out ready to kill. "What's wrong? Who do I need to kill?" he demanded.

It sounded odd coming out of a woman, but the arrogance was all man.

"I'm okay," I said, taking his hands as he gently pulled me to my feet. "I just…"

"She doesn't have a cause," Jane said, still in a tizzy. "She needs a goddang cause. All the busty gals have something they support or have a passion for."

"Even better if it's something that pulls at the undead heart strings," Tiara added.

"Finance," Gareth said, brushing his hands over his boobs.

Clearly he was still obsessed—men were so easy. Ignoring his need to play with his new toys, I focused on what he'd said.

"What about finance?" I asked, thinking it was at least something I knew about.

"Talk about investing wisely," he said with a wink.

He really *had* kept tabs on me.

"And make a point of saying since we don't pay taxes, we owe something to the world since we live in it for such a long fucking time," Tiara suggested.

"Not sure she should actually say fucking," Martha pointed out.

Ironic coming from her, since her mouth belonged on a sailor.

"How about motherfucking?" Tiara inquired with a grin.

"God, you are so your sister's sister," I said getting excited. "Half the Vamp world wants her ass in a sling for making the undead tithe."

"Heard about that," Tiara said, sounding pissed. "If she needs someone taken out, all she has to do is ask. I owe her for offing *Daddy Dearest*. I'll have her back if she wants me to."

"She'll love you," I promised Tiara.

"You think?" Tiara asked shyly, clearly taken aback that anyone would like her.

"I know so. Okay, I have a cause," I said, relieved. Sunny wasn't going to kick my ass out just yet. "So Claudia gives all her money away?"

"Yeah, I try to give her cash all the time. I have freakin' millions. The Fairies basically buy my ass off so I stay away. I'm not exactly welcome in Zanthia with my colorful heritage. But my Claudia, she won't take a goddamned cent. Borrows money from that skank hole Sunny instead of taking what's freely offered."

"That's how she ended up having to go with Vlad," I commented and then regretted it instantly by the expression of rage on Tiara's face.

"Continue," she said through clenched teeth.

The Demon-Fairy-Vamp was close to losing it.

Shit," I muttered. "Tamp it back, dude. Not gonna help if you go all crazy right now."

With a terse nod, Tiara regained control. "Speak. Please."

"Sunny agreed to forgive a ten thousand dollar loan if Claudia entertained Vlad. Apparently he's bankrolling the pageant now. She was told by Sunny that Vlad was clear that the *date* didn't include sex and…"

"Sunny fucking lied," Tiara growled as her eyes went red and silver and her fangs appeared.

"Suck it up, sister," I ordered in a tone that I used in battle with my lieutenants. Tiara responded to it immediately. "Killing Sunny is going to get your ass kicked out or worse. We need you. Claudia needs you. Get ahold of yourself. Now.

She did. It took monumental effort, but she reined it in.

"Sunny dies."

"Dude, you do what you gotta do, but save it until after we have Vlad."

"Why Claudia?" Tiara demanded. "Why is he obsessed with my Claudia?"

"It's Juliette he's obsessed with," I replied, pulling her away from the crowd.

Gareth, Martha and Jane stayed close. I could hear Claudia talking in the background and had no clue if Tiara or I were next.

"Vlad is obsessed with Juliette. She one of the royals, but she's batshit crazy. Claudia looks like Juliette and he apparently transferred his dangerous obsession to her."

"Understatement," Gareth said flatly. "Juliette's my sister, but she doesn't rule. She's in a cell right now for trying to kill most of our family, including her sister Astrid."

"I am so fucking confused right now," Tiara said, squinting at all of us. "I thought she was *your* sister, Dickie."

"It's Ginny for the time being," he corrected her, adjusting his bosom. "My sister, for lack of a better word, shares the same father as me but has a different mother. Juliette and Astrid share the same mother."

Tiara still looked stymied. I didn't blame her.

"You're not related to Juliette," I told her quickly before her head went there. "There's tons more to the story, but you know everything you need to know right now."

"Claudia's in danger because she looks like someone else."

"Yes," I confirmed.

"And you're going to use this sick bastard's obsession to trap him with Claudia as bait?" she asked, very unhappy. "And she's going by the insane woman's name now?"

I nodded.

"I don't like this at all," Tiara growled.

"Neither do I, but Claudia's agreed to help. I won't let anything happen to her. I swear it."

"No. *I* won't let anything happen to her," Tiara corrected me. "I'm a goddang killing machine. You need me."

"He has to be taken alive," Gareth said. "As ash he's worthless. We need him and the Angel to break the curse. Alive. Not dead."

"Got it," Tiara said tightly. "Alive not dead. How about severely freakin' damaged?"

"That's fine. Just leave his head intact."

"Will do."

Chapter 20

"Did you come up with a cause?" Claudia asked as she approached.

Someone with a D name was out on stage droning on about high fashion. Was that actually a cause? Seemed pretty vapid to me. I mean I loved fashion as much as the next Vamp, but then again we were at a beauty pageant. What did I expect?

I nodded at Claudia and then went to my knees before her.

"No, no, no," she said frantically, pulling at me to stand. "Please don't do that. I don't deserve it. What did you tell her Tiara?"

"The truth," Tiara replied.

"You do deserve it and I honor you," I said quietly, still on my knees. "I also apologize to you."

Gareth glanced down at me on the floor, not quite sure what was happening but followed my lead and knelt beside me.

"Oh my God," Tiara whispered. "A prince is on his knees in front of you, my beautiful one. Don't you see how worthwhile you are?"

"No," she choked out. "Please stand. People are starting to stare."

We did, but I wasn't through. "I need to do something for you. First off, I understand pride, so I won't offer you money, but I want to show you how to invest. It will make your life better. I promise."

"I'll loan you the capital to start," Tiara insisted. "And don't start squawking about it or I'll sing my entire cause out there on that stage. You know when I sing stuff breaks and eardrums burst. So unless you want to be responsible for one ugly fucking mess, I'd suggest you take my money. And when you earn interest you can pay me back... or not," she added quietly with an enormous grin.

"Not sure why I was on my knees, but if my woman deems you worthy of such an honor, I will kneel beside her—always," Gareth said.

I loved him so much I was tempted to kiss him in his girly form.

"I understand neither of you has a House?" he asked.

Claudia was shaking and holding onto Tiara for purchase.

"Um... no," Tiara said. "We're a little difficult to place."

"Not anymore," Gareth whispered so as not to be heard by the Vamps still milling around backstage. "You are now part of my Asian Dominion—new members of the Guardian's House. It's is my main residence and you are now under my rule and my protection."

Both women were speechless. As they started to drop to their knees, Gareth and I grabbed their arms and kept them on their feet.

"No more kneeling," he said. "I'm pleased to have you join my fold."

"Where is the Guardian's House?" Claudia asked, her eyes sparkling with excitement and delight.

"Japan," I told her. "However, we now have to save your liege's life. Time's ticking."

"Alive not dead," Tiara reminded herself.

"But make sure you damage the turd knocker," Jane said.

"Not a problem," Tiara promised.

"I have an announcement," Sunny shrieked over the sound system. "Everyone on stage immediately. This is a disaster."

"Oh, shit. What now?" I asked falling into line with my group.

"Only one way to find out," Martha said. "Let's go hear what the bee-otch has to complain about now."

***

The stage was filled with confused contestants and panic-stricken handlers. We stayed toward the back so no one could come up behind us. Vlad wasn't expected until the actual show in two days, but none of us were taking chances.

"No more rehearsal," Sunny screamed over the mic.

The sounds of hands slapping over ears would have been almost humorous if the volume of her voice wasn't so painful. We were Vamps for God's sake. She didn't need the mic to start with.

"The new backer of the entire pageant system has insisted the show go on tonight."

"*What?*" one of the handlers screeched and then passed out cold on the floor.

Someone dragged her off the stage and threw her into the wings. Lovely.

"That's right," Sunny snapped, pulling on her hair so hard I was sure a clump was going to come out in her hand. "The motherfu... um, the gentleman is putting up millions to keep the tradition alive and kicking. It's totally not the way I run things, but matters have been taken out of my hands."

"Translation," Tiara whispered. "Vlad paid her a fortune under the table."

She was probably correct. What was the damn hurry?

"Surprised he's pushing the pageant up," Gareth murmured. "If this is about Claudia, why doesn't he just try to kidnap her?"

Interesting point. Wait. Maybe Vlad was aware that Rachmiel was outed as the Angel he'd worked with and he was running scared. He must want Claudia something awful to go to all this trouble.

"I was just thinking the same thing," I told him. "It has to be the pageant itself, along with Claudia. The intel Ethan had said he was addicted to beauty pageants."

"Everyone. And I mean *everyone* will bow down to our new benefactor," Sunny announced. "He will be arriving in four hours. I'd suggest all of you get ready. Immediately."

The busty D's were running around like headless chickens and freaking out. However, I couldn't even enjoy the ridiculous sight. My adrenaline had skyrocketed and I was ready to go.

"He wants the adoration," Gareth said with disgust. "He's a narcissist. Vlad wants his ass kissed before he takes Claudia and runs for his worthless life. Stupid."

"For him, not for us," I said. "If he believes Roberto is on to Rachmiel, he's gotten desperate. He'll be sloppy."

"True," Gareth agreed. "But I still say he's a fool."

"Gotta agree with you there, Dickie—I mean Ginny," Jane corrected her gender blunder. "That fucker is so stupid, I'll bet he thinks Taco Bell is a phone company."

She cackled at her joke. I had to admit I even smiled at that one. She was all kinds of whacked, but the old bag was funny.

Not to be left out, Martha had to add her two cents. "How bout this? He's so stupid that if the ball of stank worked for M&M's he'd get fired for throwing out the W's."

"Wait. I've got one," Tiara insisted, hopping up and down. "He's such a stupid buttsnatch that he's depriving a village of an idiot somewhere."

"Outstanding," Martha congratulated her.

"Can I play?" Claudia asked with a giggle.

"Go for it," Jane encouraged her.

"That son of a bitch is so stupid he cooks with Old Spice!"

"As pleasurable as it is to listen to you ladies blaspheme the bastard, we have plans to make," Gareth said with a chuckle.

"And we also have Angels watching," Martha whispered, nodding her head to the audience.

She was correct. Azriel and Azbogah were seated in the house watching the shitshow ensue with lazy smiles on their beautiful faces. They also were very obviously checking out the women—and not in an academic way.

"What in the ever livin' butt-brigade are Angels doing here?" Tiara demanded. "Are they after Claudia too?"

"No," I assured her quickly. "We're on the same side for the most part. They're watching us. They want Vlad as well."

"Fucker's quite the popular asshat," Tiara hissed.

I nodded and then stiffened with excitement. The timing was perfect. All the contestants were practicing their walks and strutting around the stage like their pants were on fire. Sunny was having verbal smackdowns with about thirty freaked out handlers down stage left. The chaos was to my advantage.

"Gar...Ginny, give me your bag," I said, developing the plan as I spoke.

Gareth handed me his big man-purse that didn't go with his Diane von Furstenberg dress even a little bit. I peeked inside and grinned.

"Tiara, Claudia, and Ginny, go to the edge of the stage and practice posing or do something pageant-y like that. I'm going out into the audience. Martha and Jane, go over by Sunny and see if she's saying anything worth hearing. I don't want you near Gareth right now—can't have any connection made. Gareth, you will not attack the Angels when I flirt with them. Am I clear?"

"No," he snapped as his eyes went green. "You're not."

"Do you love me?" I asked.

"You know I do."

"Do you trust me?"

"With my life."

"You want to get Vlad?"

"Redundant question," he said, squinting at me and trying to figure out what I was up to.

"Then don't attack. I need you to stand at the edge of the stage and look hot and hard to get."

"Holy shitballs, what the hell are you up to, Boss Lady?" Jane asked with a wide grin.

"I'm up to no good, but I'm pretty sure it will turn out exactly the way I want it to," I replied as I separated myself from the group and made my way into the audience.

At least I hoped it would.

Chapter 21

I approached from behind without them detecting me—so much for the Angels being the top of the food chain. I could have taken their heads without them ever knowing who did it, but the boys were busy. The Angels were far too occupied rating the women and talking about *bagging* them. They were celestial pigs and that was beyond fabulous with me.

"What a lovely surprise to see two such handsome, divine studs sitting in the audience," I whispered from behind them, making both of them jump in surprise. "Must be my lucky day."

Whipping their heads around, they relaxed when they recognized me. First dumb move on their part.

"Ahhh," Azriel purred as his eyes lit with sexual interest. "It's the gorgeous one. I was hoping to see you again without that tiresome Vamp in tow."

"Yes, well, here I am," I said, leaning forward so they got a nice view of the girls.

"So it appears the showdown will happen tonight," Azbogah said with his eyes glued to my cleavage.

"I know," I said with a vapid giggle. "I'm so excited."

I bounced in my chair and their heads bounced in rhythm with my jiggling breasts. Pig was too nice a description for these two Heavenly horn-dogs.

"I was hoping I could ask a favor from you," I said with another silly giggle. Inwardly I cringed at my stupid girl act, but the boys were buying it.

"Favors require payments," Azriel said with a smile that verged on a leer.

"Of course." I twisted a curl with my finger and ran my tongue over my lips. I had them right where I wanted them. "But I'd like to make it more *interesting*."

"Go on, pretty Vampyre," Azbogah said, indulging me with a condescending smile that made it clear he thought I was an idiot.

Second dumb move on their part...

"I'll bet you couldn't seduce one of the gals on stage and get a promise for a date after the show tonight," I challenged casually with a sexy little squeal thrown in for good measure.

"This is too easy," Azriel muttered under his breath with a covert glance to Azbogah. "And if I can? Do I get to seduce you too, my lovely thing?"

I was not his *thing*. I was no one's *thing*. However, I nodded and demurely let my chin drop to my chest. "Yes," I whispered in a sultry tone.

"I take it that it would turn you on to watch me with another first?" Azriel suggested, getting excited.

God, men were so easy. "Yes," I said softly. "It would make me, um... very aroused."

"And let's just say, for the purpose of the *game*, that I lose?" Azriel inquired cockily, clearly believing I was a pretty gal without a brain cell in my head.

"Then you will grant me a favor," I replied, running my hands down my body.

"Deal," he said, ignoring the calculated look Azbogah had thrown my way.

Azbogah was clearly the smarter one, but I only needed one oversexed idiot to get what I needed.

"Pick one," Azriel said, openly adjusting the large erection in his pants. "I can get any of them."

"Are you sure?" I asked, egging him on.

"Positive," he assured me with a smarmy wink.

"Azriel," Azbogah warned only to be ignored by his buddy.

"Do you like that one?" I asked pointing to Ginny-Gareth. "I think that one is *gorgeous*."

Azriel's overconfident laugh made me bite down on the inside of my cheek. "Had my eye on that one already. Two minutes," he promised. "I'll bag that beauty in two minutes."

"Do it," I squealed and let my girls bounce in agreement.

The Angel practically flew to the stage to conquer his prey. Holding back my laughter was difficult, but I was still seated with Azbogah.

"You just set the randy bastard up didn't you?" he accused with a put upon sigh, staring at me with admiration in his eyes.

"Yep," I said, letting go of the vapid girl persona I'd adopted.

"Are you sure there's no way in Hell he'll get that one?" Azbogah asked skeptically. "He is quite the ladies' man—and he is an Angel."

"It's the *ladies' man* part that will be a problem for him," I explained as I reached into Gareth's bag with my right hand and pulled out the rope of silver.

"Interesting," Azbogah said as we both watched Ginny knee the aggressive Angel in the balls and then land an outstanding punch to his nose. The blood spurted everywhere as Azriel grabbed his face and shrieked.

I was quite positive that Azriel wanted to smite Ginny-Gareth where he-she stood, but the room was crowded with Vamps who were now all freaking out over the melee on stage.

"Well, aren't you as crafty as you are beautiful," Azbogah commented as he watched his cohort get his ass handed to him.

"But wait... there's more. And in three... two... one," I said as Sunny fucking exploded in a rage and literally flew across the stage and attacked Azriel.

The Angel was now being pummeled by about thirty pissed off Vampyres. It was every kind of awesome. He had to lay there and take it or else reveal what he was. I knew there was no way in Hell he was allowed to show his wings. Roberto liked his Angels to work undercover and from the tales I'd heard the punishment for revealing oneself was horrifying.

Azbogah turned away from the beat-down of his partner on the stage and placed his laser sharp focus on me. Titling his head to the side, he grinned. "And what is it that you want?"

Lifting the silver up, I handed it to him. His look in his eyes was the only evidence he was shocked I could handle the metal—the rest of him stayed very still.

"Bless this. I need it."

"That's all you wanted?" he asked with a chuckle of disbelief. "You could have gotten this without humiliating Azriel. He won't take kindly to being made a fool of."

"Wasn't sure with you guys," I told him with a shrug of indifference and a sinking feeling in my gut. It wasn't a picnic to be on the bad side of an Angel, but that was the least of my problems right now. "Will you do it?"

"Don't seem to have much of a choice seeing as how we lost the *bet*," he replied, annoyed. "When do you need it?"

"Now."

"Pushy little Vamp, aren't you?"

"That's one way to put it."

"May I ask you a question?" Azbogah inquired.

"If you bless the silver now, yes you may," I shot back.

His laugh of appreciation at my tactics warmed me, but he was a dangerous being, and I knew it. Azbogah could end me with a flick of his fingers. We were on the same side this time luckily for me so I hoped I'd make it out of the conversation in one piece.

"I will." He nodded and glanced back at the commotion on the stage.

Sunny had Azriel by the ear and was marching him out of the auditorium swearing at him profusely. Gareth stood on the stage with his focus glued to me and Azbogah. He'd kept his word about not getting involved, but he was watching like a hawk.

"Why were you so sure that the female Vamp would deny Azriel?"

"She doesn't go for men," I replied easily.

"She's a lesbian?"

"No. Not at all. She's a man."

Azbogah's belly laugh drew a few stares, but most eyes were still cemented to the Sunny and Azriel show. He turned and stared at the stunning woman on the stage who was shooting daggers from her eyes. "It's Gareth," Azbogah whispered with a hard won respect in his voice. "That bastard will stop at nothing."

"First off, he's not a bastard," I informed him with a raised brow. "He's legitimate and he's mine."

"Lucky bas… man," Azbogah said with a grin, taking the silver into his large hands and closing his eyes.

He muttered quietly in a language that sounded a bit like Latin with a magically musical flair. He held the silver low to the floor and it glowed brilliantly as the words tumbled melodically from his lips. The air surrounding us crackled and sparked a bit, but the focus was thankfully not on us.

Azbogah's magic was mesmerizing and all-enveloping—warm and liquid soft. It would be incredibly easy to get lost in the enchantment of an Angel. I felt sad and empty when he finished. Handing me the silver and grabbing his cell at the same time. He quickly read the message and hissed out a curse.

"What's wrong?" I asked, alarmed.

He glanced at me in assessment for a beat and then smiled a vicious smile. "Roberto has located Rachmiel. Azriel and I are needed. I'd suggest you and your *girlfriend* get Vlad tonight. Rachmiel is a slippery one and holding onto him to break the curse will be a challenge."

My insides buzzed and I tucked the blessed silver back into the bag with care. This was very good news.

"Thank you," I told him as he stood to go. "And tell Azriel I'm sorry."

"Are you?" he asked with a lopsided grin that made the man breathtaking.

"Nope, but it sounds good, doesn't it?"

"Good luck little Vampyre. May God be with you."

On that note, he disappeared into thin air leaving only a small blast of glitter behind.

One thing down and a whole shitload more to go.

217

***

"I didn't like watching that one bit," Gareth growled. "It took all I had not to kill him."

"Which one?" I asked with an innocent grin. "Azriel or Azbogah?"

"Both," he muttered.

"Didn't it feel nice to rack an Angel?" I prodded him.

Shaking his head and laughing begrudgingly, he narrowed his eyes at me in fun. "Yes, it was very satisfying to place his testicles in his esophagus, but I saw them eyeing your chest. That's *my* chest. They are not allowed to ogle it. *Ever.*"

"Hush now, boy," Martha said. "You got your own titties. Venus got that dang silver blessed and that's gonna burn the mother humping Hell out of Vlad. I say she did some fine fucking work."

Gareth was speechless at being spoken to that way by Martha, but the old woman was correct—wildly disrespectful—but correct. I did do good work and Gareth did have his own set of temporary girls.

Biting back my smirk with tremendous effort I told him, "Azriel thought you were hot."

"And now I'm simply ill and appalled," Gareth griped. "My boobs don't even help."

Tiara and Claudia approached and moved our little group to the far side of the stage, away from the still panicky contestants and handlers. From the way the gals were practicing, you'd think the prize was for Queen of the World.

"Sunny wants Claudia to meet with Vlad before the pageant," Tiara said in a tight voice.

The Fairy-Demon-Vampyre was holding on by a thread. I admired her control, but knew it wouldn't take much for her to snap.

"Where?" Gareth demanded.

"In the Green Room," Claudia whispered.

"Green Room?" I asked. There were entirely too many terms I didn't understand.

"The waiting room," Jane explained. "It was the huge room with all the couches and a chandelier we passed on the way to the dressing room that you did the nasty with Gareth—I mean, Ginny—in."

"She did it with Gareth, not Ginny," Martha said. "Pretty sure Venus is straight."

We all ignored them. If we commented, they'd continue. We had no time for that.

"What time?" Gareth asked, checking the time on his phone.

"Six," Tiara confirmed. "Pageant is supposed to start at seven thirty."

"Will Sunny be there?" I asked, trying to get as much intel as possible.

Tiara shrugged. "She didn't say. I tried to volunteer to greet him as well and was told absolutely not. Claudia was to go alone."

"That sure as Hell won't be happening," Gareth said sharply. "Are there windows in the room?"

"Not sure," Jane said.

"Jane and Martha, come with me. We're going to case the room and all the exits. Venus, stay with Claudia and Tiara, and see if you can get anything else out of Sunny," Gareth directed as he began to cross the stage with the old coots on his heels.

219

"Dude's bossy," Tiara commented with a shadow of a smile.

"You have no idea," I replied. "Let's go bug Sunny."

"Umm… we have incoming," Claudia whispered, referring to all five of the D's approaching us menacingly. They were every kind of perfect in their glittery, figure-fitting, very short dresses. I almost laughed, but the expressions on their collectively beautiful faces implied that the D's meant business.

Help us all, I really didn't have time for this shit. "What the Hell now?" I said with a groan.

"We'd like a word with you, *new girl*," the D with the biggest rack snarled.

They all had big racks but this one defied gravity.

I rolled my eyes and didn't even try to disguise my laugh. This gal had no clue the can of whoop ass she'd just opened up. I was a ticking time bomb and this dumbass was carrying a lit match.

"I have a name," I said with a polite smile that didn't reach my eyes.

"Don't need to bother with niceties seeing as you aren't going to be around much longer," one of the D's boasted loudly to the amusement of her buddies.

"Why don't we go backstage for our little chat," I suggested flatly, trying not to stare as their breasts bounced in rhythm with their laughter.

"Very good idea," another D snapped and cracked her knuckles ominously.

"You need backup?" Tiara whispered, clearly in the mood to beat the hell out of someone.

"Nope, but I do like an audience," I said. "A little tension relief would be a good warm up for later."

"Damn," Claudia said so quietly I had to lean in. "I wish I had some popcorn. This is gonna be good."

"You can eat food?" I asked shocked and jealous.

"No, but popcorn would make me feel like I was at the movies."

"Move it, *new bitch*. We've got a message to give you," the apparent leader of the D's hissed.

"Can't wait," I said with a small smile that I hoped appeared scared.

It did. The vapid gals laughed and pushed me into the wings.

Chapter 22

The backstage area was deserted and I led our friendly little group to the very distant back right—as far away from Sunny as possible. Didn't need her butting in and grabbing ears. I could take care of this all by my lonesome and then some.

It was slightly dank and quite dark, but no one had any difficulty seeing. We were Vamps. Some of us were far smarter than others, but that wasn't my problem it was theirs.

"The odds are pretty bad here," I commented, cracking my neck and stretching my arms.

The walls were concrete block and the floor was cement. I stepped out of my stilettos and tested the slickness of the floor with my bare feet—wasn't slippery at all. This worked well for me. A nice hard floor and even harder walls.

"Tough titties," one of the D's hissed, flipping her blonde hair and pointing a very manicured nail at me. "You never should have shown up at *our* pageant."

"Didn't see your name on it," I shot back sarcastically. "My bad."

Tiara covered her grunt of laughter with a cough. Claudia just bounced lightly on her toes in anticipation.

"We're not pleased with more competition," another D growled while applying an extra coat of gloss to her already blindingly shiny lips.

"So we're just going to eliminate you a little early," the leader said with a shrill laugh as her fangs descended and her eyes glowed green with the excitement.

"Not our problem that your odds suck. You should've considered that before you moved in on our territory," big boobed D snapped.

"Actually," I said sounding as bored as possible. "I meant *your* odds."

"Come again?" the D on the far left of the group demanded with an unladylike grunt.

"*Your* odds suck—not mine." I spoke slowly and clearly as if English was their second language.

Turning on Tiara and Claudia, the leader of the D's got up in their faces. Tiara's frightening hiss of displeasure had the idiot taking a step back. However, proving that she was truly daft, she snarled at my girls and laid out her ground rules.

"You two will stay out of this if you value your lives," she hissed. "You should actually thank us for taking care of a *problem*."

"Wouldn't think of horning in on your demise," Tiara said much to the confusion of the all the D's.

"I'm just here to watch and learn," Claudia said with her hands up in surrender and her eyes alight with mischief.

"Damn right," a D said. "We'll show you losers how it should be done. You don't mess with the best because the best will take you out and then we'll…"

"Excuse me." I raised my hand interrupting her and rolled my eyes. "Are you done with your monologue yet? Getting bored here."

"Insolent bitch," the D growled as she came at me with her fangs bared. "I'll show you bored."

"Bring it, honey," I said as my grin grew wide. I really did need a tension release and the D's would suffice just fine.

Standing still and letting them come at me gave me the distinct advantage. They were pissed, sloppy and stupid—and about to go down.

The first D—or D#1 as she would hence be known—advanced like a bat out of Hell on steroids—she had to be running at sixty miles an hour. Impressive for her, even better for me. I simply stepped to my right and stuck my foot out. Her bloodcurdling shriek when she tripped and went flying like a tornado into the wall was music to my ears. The sickening thud she made as she hit the cinderblock wall was all kinds of unfortunately awesome. She was down for the count for a few minutes.

D#2 and D#3 screeched in shock and advanced at a somewhat more controlled pace. I checked my manicure and waited. This was far too easy. Of course the obvious slight of me examining my nails made them furious and they increased their speed. Shooting off the ground and into the air as they came for me confused them. Without giving them a second to recoup, I dropped back to the floor behind them and roundhouse kicked D#2 in the head, sending her into the heap with D#1. D#3 felt the wrath of my normally lethal scissor kick. I angled ever so slightly as not to break her neck, but I crushed her throat just for the fun of it.

D#4 and D#5 tried to sneak up behind me—not smart. Back flipping over their heads, I slammed my foot into D#4's back and broke it. Then I punched D#5 in the stomach so violently she doubled over with a scream of pain. Dropping to the ground and fanning my leg out, I expertly knocked the feet from beneath D#4. Quickly straddling her I landed a harsh left jab to her face. The crunch was sickening, but I couldn't even take a second to enjoy it as D#5 was still gunning for me—or so I thought.

D#5 was slowly backing away with a look of horror on her face. "What in the Hell kind of Vampyre are you?"

"A fucking awesome one," Tiara announced grandly and gave me a thumbs up.

"Are we done with our chat?" I asked the bloody crew.

They crawled back to their feet with effort.

"I have no front teeth," D#4 whimpered. "How can I smile with no teeth?"

"Guess you should have thought about that before you tried to teach the *new girl* a lesson," I said with a smile and a curtsey. "We have three hours till show time. Maybe they'll grow back."

"Orrrrrrrr," Tiara added with an evil smirk, casually leaning against the wall next to a happily impressed and wide-eyed Claudia. "You could knock out all of their teeth for showing you such disrespect."

"I could," I nodded in agreement, pretending to ponder the idea. "However, I can think of another way these wastes of space can make it up to me."

The head D, the one that hit the wall, stood and then lowered her head in a show of deference. "Don't know who you are or what you are, but not a hair is out of place on your head and we're all pretty messed up."

"Your point?" I demanded.

"My point is we will pay restitution to you for our misjudgment. You're definitely not one to screw with."

"I don't know. *Misjudgment* is a mild word for attacking a Royal Guard," Claudia said, tsking at the now very worried D's. "Venus has the ear and protection of the

Prince of the North American Dominion. I think he should be told about this disgraceful attack."

"We said we would pay," toothless D whined, throwing a vicious glare to her posse. "I told you bitches this was a bad idea."

"What do you want?" D#1 asked, dropping to her knees and bowing down.

The rest followed suit and I felt kind of bad for them—but not that bad. They were pathetic, but they were definitely violent. Brutal, stupid and ridiculously beautiful could come in handy.

"Do you have weapons?" I inquired.

"We do," they answered in unison like glossy little dolls. At that moment I realized how much alike they all looked—blonde, blue eyed and stacked within an inch of their undead lives.

"Do you know how to use them?" I asked narrowing my eyes and wondering if they were as inept as Martha and Jane.

They all nodded—again in unison.

"You will meet me in my suite at 4:45. You will be armed and you will follow orders. Am I clear?"

"May I ask why?" D#2 asked.

"You may," I said and then waited just to screw with her head.

"Umm... why?" she stammered.

"Because there's a threat to the crown by an abomination of a Vamp. I need the entourage of said bastard to be distracted while I take him down," I said.

"Alive," Tiara reminded me.

"Yes, the head son of a bitch has to be taken alive," I repeated.

"Can we kill the son of a bitch's entourage?" D#4 asked with a gap-toothed grin.

"Yes, but let me warn you, they'll probably be very old Master Vampyres. I think your assets," I said referring to their ample chests, "will probably do the trick. However, I want everyone armed."

D#3 raised her hand and waited to be called on.

"Yes?"

"Should we bring our handlers? They love killing assholes and since Sunny is off limits, I think it might be a healthy exercise for them. They would love to slaughter someone legally."

Glancing over at Tiara, she made a sour face and then nodded.

"Bring them," I instructed.

If it was going to be a shitshow, it may as well be a big one.

"Orders will be taken from me, Tiara, my guard Ginny, or possibly Dickie. Do you know who I'm speaking of?"

"The fuckable guy and the gorgeous gal that the idiot hit on?" D#5 asked.

"Correct, and if you say fuckable with Dickie's name in the same sentence again, it will be the last words you ever speak," I told her and let my eyes rove over the group so they were very clear that *Dickie* wasn't available. "I want you all dressed in the skimpiest outfit you have."

"We're using our tits as weapons?" D#1 asked with a delighted grin.

I was wildly happy Martha and Jane weren't present for what I was about to say. I'd never hear the end of it.

"Yes, your boobs will probably be the best weapon of distraction you have. I'd highly suggest not engaging physically with the Master Vampyres. If what you just showed me is a true display of your skills, you all suck."

Again D#3 raised her hand.

"Yes?" I asked, checking my watch.

"Do you give lessons?"

I looked up from my timepiece at her hopeful and flawless face and considered for only a brief second. "Yes. Yes, I do, and if we all live through this, I will happily train you. Fair warning… it will be ugly and painful."

"Works for me," D#2 said.

"So no daggers, just knockers," D#5 chimed in, clarifying.

Nodding and grinning at the irony of life, I repeated her mantra. "No daggers. Just knockers."

"No killing the son of a bitch, but his friends are fair game," D#1 said, making sure she had it straight. "Although you'd rather us smother them with our knockers."

I closed my eyes for a second and wondered if this was a mistake, but my gut said no. My brain said yes, but my gut was the one I was going with today. Instincts were my savior lately—I just hoped they held up.

"And we should be naked," D#4 finished off on a hideously mistaken note.

"Partially clothed would be better," I explained with a barely straight face.

"Got it," the said in unison.

"Alrighty then, 4:45 in suite 333. You're all excused," Claudia said, thankfully taking the lead. "I'd suggest wearing your swimsuit although if you happen to have some transparent lingerie at your disposal, that might be even better. And not a word of this to Sunny."

"You want our handlers in their skivvies too?" one asked making sure she had all the instructions.

"That will be fine," Tiara cut in before I slapped one of them. Hard.

They all skipped away babbling like the vapid gals they were. However, I would teach them to fight. They had raw skill, but very little finesse. Women should not count on anyone but themselves for defense. Having a man should be icing on the cake—not the cake itself.

"You know what you're doing?" Tiara asked, watching the D's flounce off.

"I'm winging it," I told her. "If my gut doesn't clench too badly when I make a plan, I go with it."

"And that works?" Tiara asked doubtfully.

"I'm still here."

"That you are, my friend. That you are."

***

"So what I'm getting from this is that knockers *are* weapons," Martha said nudging Jane and grinning from ear to ear.

My suite was filled to overflowing with very well endowed and practically naked female Vampyres. I had to hand it to Gareth. After the utter shock of seeing about forty mostly unclothed women, he never let his eyes drop below chin level of a single knockout in the room.

He was so getting a blowjob for that.

Letting my chin fall to my chest so the old idiots didn't see my grin, I grunted out a noise that sounded somewhat like the word yes. They were going to be more insufferable than usual, but credit had to be given where credit was due—even if it was painful and appalling.

Standing up in front of the group looking hotter than any man had a right to, Gareth slash Dickie cleared his throat and raised his hands. The chatter stopped instantly and all eyes were glued to my beautiful man. No one but our little posse knew he was a royal, but his command of the room was unmistakable—and hot.

"Thank you ladies for being here. I want to be very clear that what we're about to do is real and extremely dangerous—potentially deadly. The men we're going up against are Master Vampyres," Gareth explained in a no-nonsense tone. "If any of you feel uncomfortable with that, you may leave now with no repercussions."

Not one single D or one handler moved an inch.

"Dickie's correct. It's not a game. Some of us might not come out of this alive. We want to be upfront and truthful with you," I added.

Still not a body moved. They either didn't get it, they had a death wish, or they were insane. If I were a gambling gal, I'd go with insane—or possibly just in awe of *Dickie*. Holy Hell, wait until they saw the *real* Gareth... they were going to freak.

"We have nothing to lose," a striking, dark haired handler called out from the back of the group. "We're in."

"Explain," Gareth said, wanting to be sure they understood the ramifications.

With the Royal Army, missions were a no-brainer. This wasn't an army. It was a gaggle of beauty queens and their equally gorgeous handlers. Had any of them even seen battle? Had I made a huge mistake? Vampyres were very deadly by nature, but this group...

"We're like a traveling circus," she explained as others murmured in agreement. "A freak-show with lip gloss so to speak. As far as I know none of us have House affiliations. We just move from contest to contest—gig to gig."

"Vampyre gypsies," another called out.

How in the Hell was that possible? I wasn't aware so many Vampyres were on their own in our Dominion and I'd bet my undead life Ethan and Astrid weren't aware of the issue either.

"None of you have Houses?" Gareth asked, taken aback.

A chorus of no's filled the suite. Unbelievable. Sheena, the not so nice Vamp who ran this area was going to have some explaining to do.

Gareth ran his hands through his hair and shot me a glance. I knew what he was thinking and I loved him even more than I did five minutes ago. I shrugged and grinned. The Guardian's House wasn't going to know what hit them when the bevvy of beauties arrived in Japan.

"Without going into great detail, suffice it to say I'm at liberty to give you a home. It's in the Asian Dominion. You will be welcomed and protected there," Gareth said.

"Are you some kind of hot guy recruiter, Dickie?" D#1 asked.

"Something like that," he said, biting down on his full lips to hide his grin at what would be considered an offensive slight to someone of his royal bearing. "Welcome to the Guardian's House. The Prince will be delighted to take you in."

"Is he single?" D#4 asked, still missing her teeth.

"No, he's not," I said in a tone that made her take two steps back.

"He's definitely *not* single," Gareth backed me up with a wink. "However, if we don't take Vlad alive the Prince will die."

The gravity of the words he spoke, made my stomach knot up. It was easy to find humor in the ridiculous picture before us, but the truth was ugly.

231

"Is Vlad the cocksucker we're not allowed to kill?" another handler asked.

"Yes," Jane took over. Clearly hearing the word cocksucker inspired her. "You can't kill the cocksucker, but he has motherfuckers with him that you can go to town on."

"So leave the cocksucker alone and kill the motherfuckers with our tits?" someone questioned from the left side of the group.

"How in the ever loving Hell do you kill a motherfucker with your melons?" Martha demanded.

"Um... smother them?" another gal volunteered.

"No," I shouted over the chatter that had started over the techniques on how to murder with your melons. Running my hands through my hair, I was really starting to second-guess the plan. The brainpower in the room was seriously lacking. "These are *Master Vampyres* we're talking about. You will be used as a *distraction method* so Dickie and I can trap Vlad."

"The cocksucker is the *Impaler*?" D#2 asked with a shudder.

"Yep," Martha said. "You got it. Vlad the cocksucker Impaler is off limits. You do the booby bounce to distract his group of motherfuckers. Clear?"

They resembled a gathering of beautiful semi-nude bobble heads as their perfectly coiffed heads bounced in affirmation. Gareth glanced at me with a raised brow and I shrugged. As long as they kept the entourage at bay, we had a far better chance of taking Vlad alive—and an even better chance of coming out of this alive ourselves.

"Venus, give the specifics please," Gareth ordered.

I responded exactly like I was trained to do. The simple fact that he regarded me as highly as Ethan did in terms of battle, calmed my soul and made me want to make him proud.

Stepping forward, I eyed the crowd. "No one works alone. You will team up in groups of five. At 5:30, I want you with your unit. You will hide yourselves in the dressing rooms. As soon as Vlad is in the Green Room, the mission begins. You'll work as distraction—no engagement unless necessary."

"With our tits," D#1 added just in case anyone had missed the memo.

"It's kind of like an opening number of the show," D#5 announced to the room, breaking it down so it was more easily understood. "You stay in the wings until you hear the music and then you make your entrance—head high and bosom forward."

"Will there be music?" someone yelled.

"Music would really help—something with a sexy beat," a handler with light purple hair told me while demonstrating a move that belonged in a porn.

"Should we grease up?" D#4 asked.

"What does that even mean?" I asked, bewildered.

"Like body builders," she replied with an eye roll as if I should have known what the Hell she was talking about.

"Your choice," I told her, rolling my neck to relieve the tension they were causing.

"I think they should grease up," Jane chimed in. "If a motherfucker tries to grab 'em, they'll slip right out of their slimy hands."

"Okay," Martha shouted even though no one was talking. "No to the music and yes to the grease. If anyone needs baby oil, I've got ten family sized bottles in my room. Go ahead, Boss Lady."

"Mmm... kay. No music. Get greased up next door," I replied, gritting my teeth.

Why Martha had a family sized case of baby oil in her room was something I was never going to touch. Staring at the ceiling for a brief moment, I kept my cool and continued. I couldn't fix them, so I just needed to focus on their strengths. However, when this shit show was over I was going to train the handlers as well.

"Divide into eight units now."

They did—quickly and efficiently. Of course a few sashayed into place, but I wasn't sure some of them knew how to move in a regular manner. Overlooking their need to dance, I treated them as I would any unit—kind of.

"You will come out of hiding spaced two minutes apart."

"That's eight counts of eight," Jane said standing next to me like an interpreter for the dance-impaired.

Giving her a curt nod of thanks and trying not to laugh or scream, I went on. "Unit one will come out at 6:05 and so on and so on. The best strategy is to separate them and flirt like there's no tomorrow. Move them as far from the Green Room as possible."

"Should we do them?" a tiny red headed handler inquired with a hopeful expression.

"Um… no, that's not required," I said, trying hard to keep a straight face. Never in my history as a general had I fielded questions like these.

"What if they're hot?" she went on, gaining support from the interested troops.

"Probably a bad plan," I stated as diplomatically as I could.

"But if we get their pants down, we could do some real damage," the clearly undersexed red head insisted, miming removing a part of the male anatomy.

"I'm gonna leave that up to you. You're a warrior, not a hooker," I said firmly. "I'd also like to go on record saying everyone in this room could do far better than the scum we're about to encounter."

"Step over here," Tiara ordered our makeshift troops, and then conjured up some deliciously sweet smelling pink dust. Tossing it over the crowd, she smiled with satisfaction.

"What'd you do?" Martha asked.

"Covered their scent with a little Fairy dust. Wouldn't do to have Vlad and the boys know we're there."

Tiara was brilliant—loud, obnoxious and out there—but truly brilliant.

"Go with your unit and prepare for battle," I instructed as my bizarre army squealed with glee and moon walked out of my suite—in unison.

This was either the best plan I'd come up with or the worst.

It simply remained to be seen.

Chapter 23

"Do you think we're being smart taking him on here and not going to him? A surprise attack might be to our advantage," I told Gareth, still concerned about the plan that was in place.

The bare assed army had gone to prepare and it was time to take a step past winging it and put a loose plan together.

"It's a surprise no matter where we strike," he pointed out correctly. "Ironically, there are three large manors in the direction that Claudia was taken with *moats*." Gareth pressed the bridge of his nose and made a derisive noise. "Several of the Cressida House Vamps did a massive sweep and located them. At this point without more intel, we don't know which one Vlad's using. So no. But even if we narrowed it down, I'd rather not take him on his own turf. We stand a far better chance here. The likelihood is that he doesn't know this place as well as we do."

"Are the Cressida Vamps still in the area?" I asked, wondering which ones might be close.

"No, and it would be a bad plan to call in support. If Vlad catches wind of incoming, he'll run. As bizarre as using the gals to distract the entourage might be, it's brilliant."

His praise felt wonderful, but I was still worried for the girls.

"Are there windows in the Green Room?" I asked, taking a seat on my new couch in my suite.

Apparently the hotel was familiar with destruction and bloodshed. My suite had been repaired and the bloodstained and broken furniture replaced. Upon entering the suite with my friends, and my naked army, I thought I was in the wrong room, but my key had worked and my suitcases were untouched. Had to be run by Vamps, otherwise we'd have been bodily removed from the premises—by human cops.

"None," Jane confirmed. "No windows in the dressing rooms either. It's a Vamp owned hotel. Sunlight means crispy skin, pissed off dead people, and raw hooters."

"I'm sorry, raw *what*?" Gareth asked, closing his eyes in mental pain.

That was the old biddies best gift—death by words.

"Nothing," Jane said. "Just a little *Twilight* experiment I tried that went completely fucking wrong."

Ignoring the confusion Jane had caused with her comment, I nodded at what I'd already figured to be true. It made sense that a Vampyre beauty pageant would be held in a Vampyre run facility. This was excellent. Human casualties weren't something any of us wanted on our conscience.

I examined the meticulous map of the entire auditorium and backstage area that Gareth had drawn out freehand and marveled at the detail.

"This is amazing," I said, running my hand over the map. "You're really good at this."

Gareth winked and a slow sexy smile pulled at his lips. "I'm good at a lot of things."

"Get a room," Martha mumbled, with a smirk.

Gareth's raised brow made her zip it quick. He went from arrogant flirt to the Vamp in charge on a dime. It was all kinds of sexy, but I kept my game face on. There would be hundreds of years to flirt with him... and love him. I hoped.

"He'll have to enter here," Gareth said, pointing to the main entrance. "They'll come through the house to get to the Green Room and Claudia will be waiting."

"What about Sunny?" Jane asked. "Do we have anyone on her?"

"Outstanding point," Tiara said, slapping Jane on the back in congratulations and sending her flying halfway across the room. "This one's a keeper—mind like a steel trap and mouth like a sailor. I'd suggest putting Martha and Jane on the bitch to keep her occupied and away from the auditorium. She'll never know what hit her."

Jane crawled to her feet and preened like a peacock from Tiara's praise. I simply thanked God that we'd all found each other. Gareth's life and our future were on the line. I tried to push that to the back of my head so I could focus on the immediate, but it was impossible.

"You ladies up to distracting Sunny?" I asked.

"Can we maim her?" Jane questioned, waggling her eyebrows with excitement.

"Please do," Claudia said.

"Let's get changed, hooker," Martha said to Jane as she hopped up and started running toward her room. "Can't do it lookin' like this."

They were in their conservative Armani suits. What else did they have except for the Teenage Ninja Turtle nightgowns?

"Um... maybe you should just stick with the suits," I suggested.

"Can't fight no battle in this shit. Need my boob tube," Jane said as she too headed for their suite.

"You don't have boob tubes," I reminded them. "Astrid burned your suitcases."

"Yep, but she missed our backpacks," Jane informed me with a wicked little smirk that made her look kind of cute in a deranged old lady kind of way.

Martha paused in the doorway and grinned like a loon. "I never go anywhere without my assless chaps, black socks, sandals, and a nice sequined polyester stretch tube top."

"I gotta see this," Tiara said with a laugh. "You two freaks are a hoot."

"Finally, someone fucking appreciates us," Martha yelled over her shoulder before she disappeared into her room.

Gareth chuckled and went back to the map. Watching him study it, made my heart soar and ache at the same time. There were about a thousand ways this could go wrong and only several ways it could go right.

"So I'm going by Juliette?" Claudia asked, wringing her hands nervously. "Do you want me to pretend to be her?"

Pondering the question, I glanced over. She was very similar to Juliette, but lacked the brittle hardness. However, a little makeup and hair would definitely help.

"I suppose if we got you up to speed on a few things only Juliette would know, it might throw him enough to give us an opening. However, he knows you're not her, so if you drop anything, do it with caution," Gareth said.

"Would you mind if I fixed you up?" I asked Claudia.

"Why? Do I look bad?"

Shaking my head, I laughed. "Not even a little bit, but I need to harshen you up some if we want your appearance to confuse him."

"I'm in," she said nervously, clasping Tiara's hand for support.

"You're gonna be great," Tiara whispered, then hugged her and planted a sweet kiss on her head.

"Tiara, I don't want you in the Green Room. As much as I trust your abilities, I think it will be difficult for you to refrain from attacking to kill," Gareth said.

Tiara nodded tersely and kept Claudia close. "I'll run command in the hallway then. However, I'll stay close."

"Fine," Gareth replied and began to arm himself. "Venus, we'll cloak ourselves and be in the room with Claudia."

It was a plan with many deadly loopholes, but I couldn't think of a better one.

Right now nothing seemed real. Gareth looked healthy—not like a dying man. If I compartmentalized, I could even pretend for a brief moment that we were just on some bizarre trip with nothing hanging over our heads—like death.

"Claudia, if you can get Vlad to remove his clothes it will be easier to dismember him. We want his arms and legs. If we can do that before he knows what hit him, we can wrap him in the blessed silver and transport him back to the Cressida House," Gareth told her, checking that we were all armed.

"You need help transporting?" Tiara asked.

"You can transport groups to places you haven't been?" Gareth asked, surprised.

Gareth had that gift, but I was unaware others did.

"Dude… I mean my liege, I can transport a freakin' stadium of people. It might be a bumpy ride, but as long as I have an address I can do it."

"She a magical GPS," Claudia stated with a proud smile.

Gareth considered Tiara for a long moment and then nodded. "I can do it, but I don't know what shape I'll be in when we're through. So yes. I accept your offer, gratefully."

"One more thing," Tiara said, approaching me. "I want you to take my blood. It's superfuckingsonic and you'll be protecting the love of my life. If I can't be in the room, I need my blood to be there."

"What will it do to me?" I asked, not having had the time to really discuss with Gareth how he felt after ingesting the Vamp-Fairy-Demon blood.

"Enhance your gifts, give you more power and… I really don't fucking know. But I do know if I give it willingly, it will only be positive," she said, pulling up her sleeve and offering me her wrist.

"Do it," Gareth said. "I feel ridiculously strong— almost back to my old self. Far stronger than with just the stay Satan granted. Haven't tested what I can do to its limits, but I barely lifted my knee to Azriel's damn jewels and they lodged somewhere in his stomach."

"Well, that's certainly a rousing endorsement." I took the offered wrist and bowed my head in thanks.

"A few more things," Gareth said, watching me drink. "Vlad's over a thousand years old. He's a sick fuck and as dangerous as they come. He has magic, but he's a coward—usually lets others fight for him."

"You think we can do this?" Claudia asked, tucking her hair behind her ear in an attempt to appear calm.

"I think we have a fighting *chance* of doing it," Gareth replied honestly. "It's do or die for me, but not for you,

Claudia. I want you to call out to Tiara if everything goes south. Tiara, you will transport into the room and take Claudia to safety—if you come for Claudia, I also want you to take Venus."

"Absolutely not," I hissed, withdrawing my fangs from Tiara's wrist. "Your life is my life. You go down, I'm going with you."

Gareth crossed the room in a flash and grabbed me by the shoulders. He clearly forgot we weren't alone or he didn't care.

"Look at me," he demanded, harshly. "I can die if I know you will go on. Bottom line. The fact that you love me will be my dying thought—and I will be happy— something I never felt until you said you loved me. You shouldn't even be involved, and if something happens to you, I swear on my undead life I will come back and haunt the living fuck out of Ethan for allowing you to come."

"You don't want me here?" I hissed, hurt and angry.

"*Yes*, I want you here," he shouted. "I want you here because I'm a selfish bastard. You admitted you loved me here—best fucking day of my life. I bought the damn hotel earlier because I plan to bring you back here if we make it out alive. It's the location we had our first date."

"Date?" I asked with a small smile. Had he lost his mind—bought the hotel?

"Well, kind of," he admitted sheepishly realizing how utterly human he sounded.

"You bought this place?" I asked, wrinkling my nose. "Not a real sound investment."

"Call it a sentimental one. I'm going to have that damned dressing room replicated in my palace when we get out of here."

"God, that is so hot," Tiara chimed in. "You are one romantic son of a bitch, my liege."

"Thank you," he said, remembering we had an audience. "So Tiara, my order stands—you come for Claudia, you take Venus as well."

She nodded once and bowed. I said nothing.

She could come for Claudia, but it would take an act of God to pull me away. I had no plans to leave Gareth's side. Ever.

Not in this life and not in whatever came next.

Chapter 24

The air in the Green Room was thick with malice and the scent of fresh blood. Vlad now held a beaten-within-an-inch-of-her-life Sunny in his clutches. Her neck was partially severed and she was bleeding out fast. Her faint moans were the only evidence that she was still with us.

His entourage of Old Guard Master Vampyres surrounded him and couldn't have looked less interested if they'd tried. There were six of them and the sheer power in the room was suffocating. I lambasted myself silently for involving the pageant girls. These bastards unnerved me and I was a damn killing machine. I had no clue how the girls would react to the deadly, vicious Vampyres.

Gareth and I were positioned against the back wall. We were cloaked and Tiara had dusted us with the Fairy powder that removed our scent. I didn't like Sunny one bit, but she didn't deserve to be bludgeoned by a psychotic lunatic for being a bitch. Hell, if bitchiness were a punishable crime, Vampyres would be extinct.

However, at the moment my real worry was for Martha and Jane. Had the bastard killed the old ladies when he took Sunny? If he had, he was mine after the curse was broken. I didn't care that Satan had dibs. I'd fight the Devil himself for the bastard if we made it through the rest of the day.

"I brought you a gift," Vlad said casually as if he wasn't holding a half dead woman in his arms.

"Why?" Claudia asked.

She was seated on the couch. I'd done her up and her resemblance to Juliette was now uncanny. It had disturbed even Gareth. Claudia was dressed impeccably in a long diaphanous silver gown and was calmer than I'd ever seen her.

"To show you my devotion, my love," he told her, tilting his head and watching her every reaction. "I though it would be amusing to demonstrate what I would do to you if you insist on playing hard to get."

"I'm going by Juliette now," she purred and demurely let her chin fall to her chest.

Vlad's brittle laugh filled the room and made my skin crawl. His debased followers didn't blink an eye. They were expressionless robots gathered to do his dirty work. We needed them out of the room. If we had to go through them to get Vlad, he'd have time to transport out. If we could dismember him—even just a leg or arm—it would make his disappearing act impossible.

"You delight me. It warms my heart that you took your first warning seriously. It would be such a shame to have to tear something as exquisite as you apart."

"Neither of us has hearts," Claudia said with a small shrug that she somehow made look alluring. "Throw her in the hallway. I don't want that trash in the room when I give you my gift."

Smart move. If Tiara could get to Sunny, they might be able to save her.

"And what might that gift be?" Vlad inquired coolly as he passed off the dying Sunny to one of his men. He crossed his arms over his chest and eyed Claudia with interest. Technically he was a stunning man, but his insides were despicable. Dressed head to toe in black

Hugo Boss, he was covered in Sunny's blood but clearly thought nothing of it.

"Me. Your gift is me."

"Come." He held out a blood-spattered hand to Claudia as his eyes went bright green with desire. "Come with me. I will give you the world."

"I want it now," she whispered, lifting her eyes to him and bestowing him with a dazzling smile.

Vlad's hand dropped to his side and he stared at her with wonder. "Your wish is my command, my beauty."

"Not here," one of his entourage hissed viciously.

Without a word of warning, Vlad turned and struck the Vampyre so violently he crumpled to the ground with a thud. Vlad's roar of displeasure at being second guessed shook the walls and shattered every mirror in the Green Room. The fact that there were mirrors was bizarre since we had no reflection, but the nod to human beauty pageants was demolished. The chandelier detached from the ceiling and burst into thousands of sparkling pieces joining the shards of glass littering the floor.

"Get out," Vlad growled as sparks of fury bounced off of him and floated around the room singeing the furniture. "Take him with you. I will deal with his *lapse in judgment* later. No one tells me what to do."

Well, that wasn't quite what we were expecting, but it was going in a positive direction. We needed the henchmen gone and they'd helped us out. Of course the fact that Vlad's hands were flaming didn't bode particularly well, but...

"Lock it," Claudia said with a delighted laugh that would earn her an Oscar. "I don't like them."

Vlad's insolent stare at Claudia was jarring and a hideous smile spread across his thin lips. His weakness for Juliette slash Claudia was the key to the Kingdom. We just needed to make sure she stayed safe.

I could feel Gareth's presence. Even though I couldn't see him, he was next to me now. The show was about to start and I wanted us to take the final bow.

"My, my," Vlad said as he waved his hands and sealed the door with fire. "Such impatience."

"They won't interrupt us?" Claudia asked, raising her well-plucked brow and giving Vlad a pout.

"If they try, it will be the last thing they do," he assured coldly her as he crossed the room. "They can't reenter unless I break the spell."

"You're certain?" she asked.

"Quite," he replied and then paused. "Your turn around, while delightful, is somewhat curious to me. Why the change of heart?"

"As I already pointed out, we don't have hearts," Claudia said flatly with a small smile on her lips. "I did my research after our unfortunate little rendezvous. I realized the opportunity I might have missed by... playing coy with you."

"What do you want?" he asked in a calculated tone.

"Power... and you."

His resumed movement was slow—like a predator stalking his prey. His expression still registered his doubt, but he was a man obsessed.

The glass crunching beneath his handmade shoes was eerily similar to the sound of splintering bones. I centered myself and waited. Gareth would reveal himself first and I would follow.

The blood I'd taken from Tiara was in my system, but I felt no different. Maybe I was immune for some reason. Gareth had felt a surge of power and I was concerned that I felt none. When I'd shared my worry with Tiara, she'd shrugged and explained her power was in colors. She likened emotions to colors and said to draw on her magic she thought in vivid hues. It made little to no sense to me. I just prayed it might give me an extra boost.

"Disrobe," Vlad ordered as he seated himself in the chair across the couch from Claudia. "My tastes are particular, my sweet. You *will* submit to them."

"I might," she shot back smoothly. Her eyes glowed green with hatred, but clearly Vlad mistook it for lust. "However, I want to see what I'm getting. You've seen my naked body. You carved your name into my back. I want to make sure what's beneath those expensive clothes will satisfy me—my tastes are also out of the ordinary," she finished boldly.

She was telling the truth with that one and Vlad didn't have the plumbing to satisfy her. Vlad's eyes narrowed dangerously and then he laughed. Without taking his eyes from Claudia, he stood and removed his blood-stained coat and tossed it aside.

"I can guarantee you will be pleased."

"I'll be the judge of that," she replied rudely, much to his delight.

I felt Gareth drop his cloaking at the same time I did. We'd planned on revealing in a wave, but the timing was too perfect. Vlad was removing his shirt and he was at his most vulnerable.

Without a word or even a glance to each other, we went at him like a well-oiled killing machine. Gareth moved silently and with intent. He'd clearly dropped the Dickie façade, because the look on Vlad's face when he spotted him bordered on insanely humorous.

"Impossible," he roared as he expertly dodged Gareth's fist blow.

Vlad wasn't as lucky the second round.

"Need you to fix a little problem you created," Gareth snarled as he went at the Vampyre like a freakin' steam roller from Hell. The punches were so fast and violent, I could barely make out the movement of his hands. Vlad's shock at the surprise attack and the fury coming out of Gareth's every pore gave me the fraction of the second I needed.

The sound of Vlad's arm detaching from his body as I twisted it and wrenched it off with all of my might was the most beautiful sound I'd ever heard. The evil Vampyre's scream of rage wasn't and the fire that exploded in the room was going to be an issue.

"Get her out," Gareth growled at me in reference to Claudia.

Not sure how he wanted me to do that since we were effectively locked in, but I was going to try.

"No, she's mine," Vlad bellowed with wild eyes and gnashing fangs as he went at Gareth like a nightmare from the Underworld.

Which was exactly where he was going to end up. I hoped.

"Actually, she's not yours," Gareth said taunting him while dodging punches and blasts of magic. "She's a lesbian. She wasn't joking when she said her tastes were particular—your dick doesn't turn her on, dumbass."

"Royal scum," he ground out. "You should be dead. Why aren't you dead? I had you cursed."

"Too mean to die, you piece of shit. Oh, and Satan has dibs on you after I'm done."

Gareth took full advantage of the fleeting look of uncertainty on Vlad's face and he doubled his efforts. "This is for me," he said as he landed a remorseless strike to the stunned Vampyre's head. "And this one is for my family."

He continued to pummel him, but Vlad was giving back as good as he was getting.

ROBYN PETERMAN

They grappled in a match for their lives. Magic flew around the room with such force I had to duck both the sorcery and the fire to get to Claudia.

"Call Tiara," I shouted over the crackling of the blaze. "NOW."

Gareth threw vicious punch after punch, but Vlad—even with one arm gone—was a maniacal force of nature. The dark magic in the room blasted through my body in horrifying jolts and it was hard to make out Gareth and Vlad through the fire.

"Tiara," Claudia screamed, standing on the couch to stay out of reach from the licking flames.

In an explosion of silver and red magic that covered the room in a glittery haze, Tiara appeared and whisked Claudia into her arms. "You're not leaving, are you?" she asked me as I backed away and prepared to go at Vlad. Of course she already knew the answer.

"No, if he dies I'm going with him. Get her out and make sure the others don't enter," I shouted and dove back into the fray. "Help Sunny and find my old ladies."

"On it," Tiara said as she and Claudia transported out of the room that had turned into a fiery Hell on Earth.

I couldn't tell who was winning, but I wasn't taking chances. Vlad was a thousand years old and more powerful than both Gareth and I put together. However, he was fighting the losing fight of hatred and greed and we were fighting for love and justice.

"His legs," Gareth commanded.

I back flipped over both of them and landed in a crouched position about a foot from where they were tearing each other apart. Vlad's arm I'd torn off was already regenerating. Shit. Pulling my sword from the scabbard on my back, I waited to make eye contact with Gareth.

With a split second glance to me and then a horrifying left hook to Vlad's face, Gareth rolled away. Our timing was like a dance—a macabre dance—but beautifully executed. At the exact moment he was clear, I brought my sword down with such force if cut through Vlad's right leg taking the entire hip with it.

Of course, the bastard still had his left arm and got in a savage blow to my head that sent me reeling and praying for death. Staggering to my feet and smacking out the flames that were burning the clothing from my body, I sprinted back at him before he was at full strength.

Gareth was a mesmerizingly beautiful killing machine. There was no movement wasted as he and Vlad fought. Vlad might have hundreds of years on my man, but Gareth was his own deadly force to be reckoned with.

"Silver," Gareth shouted as he took a merciless blow to his throat by an unbelievably quickly regenerating Vlad.

Grabbing the bag we'd hidden by the door I took it in my right hand and calmly looked for an opening. Desperation and fear would get me nowhere fast. Too much was on the line to lose. Burying my emotions, I watched with cold-blooded laser focus and waited for a gap to move in.

They were exchanging blows with such inhuman speed I needed to make sure I lassoed the right Vampyre. Gareth was a more experienced and stronger fighter than me, but I was no slouch. I was fast, deadly and accurate. As long as I divorced myself from my attachment to Gareth, I could fight as emotionlessly as he did.

Vlad began to chant in a language that was foreign to me, but I knew exactly what he was doing.

A burst of red light splintered and hissed through the room. I put up my hand to shield my eyes from the intense heat. The door exploded into flames and then turned to ash. The fire in the room subsided, but we had bigger problems now. His men came at us fast and furious.

Pageant gals had attached themselves to the Master Vampyres and were tearing their hair out and clawing at their eyes.

Watching D#4 get thrown across the room like a rag doll made my stomach lurch, but it also gave me the opening I needed. Diving through the remnants of the fire I took head blow after head blow while I wrapped Vlad in the blessed silver. Gareth held him down and shoved a dagger into this throat so he couldn't call out more spells.

I used both hands, uncaring that the sliver was burning me to the bone. Both Gareth and I had already been burned badly. What did a little more singed skin mean at this point?

Nothing. It meant nothing if I could tie the bastard down.

"Finish," Gareth said as he jumped up and attacked a Master Vampyre that was gunning for me. I heard the noise and the gurgling sound as Gareth crushed the trachea of the advancing piece of shit.

Vlad thrashed wildly, but the silver was doing the trick. His skin mottled and melted as the metal touched it. Working as rapidly as I could, I removed his left arm and leg and then re-removed the stumps of regenerating appendages on his right side. With a speedy request to God that the silver would hinder his regeneration, I secured the Vampyre and threw myself into the fight.

"Out," Tiara commanded to the gals in a harsh voice.

They scrambled and ran. She bodily threw those that lagged behind through the blasted out doorway. It was me, Tiara, and Gareth against six Master Vampyres. Not the best odds, but not the worst either.

Tiara went like a maniac at two who advanced on her. Her battle scream hurt my ears and it was something that I was sure would revisit me in nightmares if I lived to dream.

Tearing my eyes from her, I scissor kicked the one coming for me. That meant Gareth had three on him. I couldn't take my eyes of my aggressor or it would be my final moment. I just hoped that Gareth in a weakened state could handle three.

The sound of fangs ripping though skin and the scent of blood permeated the air. Magic shot through the room like bullets and I dodged and danced around it. The lifeless stare of the Master Vampyre who wanted me dead bored into me. His smile and insulting chuckle made me see red.

"Get ready to die," he snarled.

I saw red. No—I *felt* the color. Now I understood Tiara meant. It was heady, frightening and almost uncontrollable.

Holy shit, if this is what Tiara lived with, I was damned glad I wasn't her.

Tiara's magic was definitely in me and my eyes glazed over. The entire room was bathed in red as was the Vampyre who had just made his final statement. I was normally a one-woman fighting machine. I was now a one-woman entire *army* with strength and power no one person should possess.

Something frightening and unfamiliar roared through my veins. I grabbed the surprised Vampyre by his neck and screamed like I was burning in the Basement of Hell. I didn't know where I was or what was happening, I just knew I had to kill. He fought back, but was no match for what was boiling in my blood.

I ripped his head from his shoulders and threw it at the new Vampyre that was fast approaching. His fangs were out and he carried silver stakes in each hand.

I could do this. I would do this. I was not going down when we were so close.

I was going to get my happily ever after.

"Venus," Gareth shouted as he dodged in front of me to take on the silver-wielding Vamp. "Move."

It was all happening so fast. In a frenzied whirlwind of violence and blood, we fought like our lives depended on it. And they did.

Tiara was truly frightening. She had sprouted horns and looked half Demon-half human. She tore through the Vamps and left them in pieces on the floor.

"To your right," she bellowed as I took on the last of the two still alive.

Gareth had the one with the stakes and I was going to obliterate the bastard coming at me like a freight train. He shot deadly magic from his fingertips and hit me several times before I was too close for him to aim.

"Got your back," Tiara grunted as she came in like an avenging Angel and tore through his body like a hot knife through butter. He didn't even know what hit him and his detached head showed the shock on his face.

"Gareth," I muttered to Tiara as I turned and time went into slow motion.

The Master Vampyre had him cornered and held a stake to his heart. Gareth stood motionless and I watched as the bastard destroyed my happily ever after.

The stake slid into the love of my life. All my hope and dreams died as Gareth's eyes closed in shock. An inhuman wail of pain came from the bottom of my shattered soul and left my lips as the man I loved slumped and fell to the floor. There was a ringing in my ears and I fought to keep control. I was a trained killing machine and I was going to prove it.

We had Vlad now. At least, Lelia, Alexander and Nathan could be cured. There was nothing left for me with Gareth dead, so I was going to take the bastard out, and then do what I should have done yesterday.

I didn't feel the pain on my outer body. The multiple bleeding wounds and my burnt skin were nothing compared to the feeling of my heart being shredded. I had been so close—so very close.

The Master Vampyre looked over his shoulder at me and smiled. The smile didn't reach his eyes—they were cold and evil. However, I was going to wipe that smile off his face for eternity.

With a cry that sounded foreign to my own ears, I launched myself at the destroyer of my dreams and pierced his neck with my sword. Pulling violently to the left, I severed it halfway off. Tossing the sword aside, I gripped his head and whispered in his ear.

"This is for my mate. I hope you enjoy Hell, Satan has a special place for fucks like you."

With a violent pull, I ripped the rest of his head from his body and then collapsed next to Gareth on the floor.

He was still and the stake protruded from his chest. His beautiful eyes were open in death and I knew I didn't have long before he turned to ash. Letting my fangs drop, I leaned over him and gently kissed his lips.

"Venus, the weapon hasn't been turned," Tiara said, squatting down next to me and examining Gareth.

"What?" I asked, confused.

"The stake. There's a chance I can still remove it."

"How can you tell?" I asked.

"Look at his skin. If it had been twisted, the skin would be torn."

She was correct, but Gareth was gone.

"Let me try," she begged. "Let me try to save him."

Nodding but not believing it would help, I gently touched Tiara's cheek. "Transport Vlad to the Cressida House quickly. There's a chance that the silver could kill

255

him and we can't have that. The bastard can help save Gareth's siblings. Astrid will take all of you in. I promise. Tell Astrid that I love her, but I can't go on without him."

Tiara's face was grim and her lips had compressed to a thin line.

"What are you going to do?" she asked. "Please don't ask me to kill you. I can't do it."

I laughed, but it sounded hollow and sad. "No, I wouldn't do that to you, my friend. Gareth and I are halfway mated. I'm going to finish the ritual and go with him."

"May God be with you," she whispered as tears filled her pretty blue eyes.

She carefully withdrew the stake, but just as I'd thought nothing changed. With one last kiss to his lips, I bit him. The feeling of finally being complete consumed me and I smiled dreamily. It was the first time in the two hundred years I'd been undead that I felt true peace. Wherever Gareth was going, I was always going to be at his side. Always.

I vaguely noticed the D's and Claudia surrounding Gareth and me, but they grew distant and the Green Room grew dark. Their sorrow and tears were more than I could take. I realized I'd forgotten to ask about Martha and Jane, but my lips couldn't form words anymore. A heaviness washed over me and my eyes closed involuntarily. Death wasn't scary. It was warm and tranquil.

If Vlad had killed Martha and Jane, I would just find them in the afterlife and take care of them. It would make my afterlife a bit Hellish, but it's what I would do. With Gareth finally at my side I could do anything—even look after Martha and Jane.

Chapter 25

If this was Heaven, it was seriously weird.

Astrid, Ethan, Gemma, The Kev, Tiara, Claudia, Pam and the King all hovered over me with terrified expressions on their faces. Was I in limbo? Had I screwed something up? I thought Heaven would be unfamiliar and beautiful. It sure as hell looked a lot like Kentucky. Who knew?

And where was Gareth?

Maybe I'd been sent back to be a Guardian Angel. That would be an odd choice on God's part. Maybe he thought I'd make a good Angel. The thought of that amused me, but I had no recollection of conversing with God.

"Hey, she's awake," Astrid shouted, causing me to close my eyes and wince. "Don't you dare go back into that fucked up sleep you were in Venus. I will kick your undead ass. You took freakin' years off my life which doesn't really matter since I'm immortal, but still..." she warned.

"Move," I heard Gareth snap.

The feeling of his hands on my face made me smile. Now I was in Heaven. I sure as Hell hoped all my friends hadn't died. Were we all in Heaven? That would be so strange.

"Oh my God," Gareth said as he ran his hands over my face and buried his head in my neck.

His scent made me happy and a wildly inappropriate feeling of lust consumed me. I wanted him and I wanted him *now*. I didn't care that everyone was standing around staring. Heaven was just as suffocating as being stuck in a car with Martha and Jane had been. I wasn't sure I liked it at all.

Astrid had always mentioned that Hell was pretty awesome. I liked it when I was at her wedding. Maybe I could have a chat with Satan and get a transfer. All I wanted was to be alone with Gareth. And I wanted it badly.

"Does someone want to explain why you're all in Heaven, or possibly Purgatory, with me?" I asked weakly as I tried to sit up.

"What in the ever lovin' Hell?" Astrid shouted with a laugh. "You're not in Purgatory. They have freakin' elevator music in Purgatory. You would hate it. And for your information, Heaven is mostly marble and shit—not your taste at all."

"Where am I?" I asked, touching Gareth's thick black hair and getting unfortunately hornier by the second.

"Dude, you're home," Astrid said as Gareth pulled me even closer and held on like he was never going to let go.

"Someone explain," I croaked out, crossing my legs to curb my sexual mini-crisis and happily noticed I was covered with a blanket.

"You're in trouble," Gareth chastised, giving me the alpha-hole stink eye. "You should have never done what you did."

"Shut your obnoxious cakehole," Astrid snapped and slapped him in the back of the head. "Honestly, I'm not even sure why she likes you. You're alive because she bit your sorry ass—or neck, if you want me to be anatomically correct—*and* because my awesome brand-fucking-new sister doped you up with her amazeballs blood. So you just swallow that bullshit, Gareth."

"Umm... can someone else help me out here?" I asked, mostly following what Astrid said, but there were a lot of holes in the story. "Where's Vlad. Where's Rachmiel?"

"Hell," Gareth said, pressing his lips to my forehead and continuing to run his hands over me as if he was convincing himself I was real. "They're getting acquainted with Satan and their new home."

As nice as his touch felt, it was making me very hot and bothered.

"Tiara transported all of us here. After the confusion of about fifty mostly naked Vamps and Vlad arriving subsided, apparently Astrid took over," he said with a grin and shake of his head.

"You bet your ass she did," Tiara said proudly, with one arm around Astrid and the other around Claudia. "She called on Roberto with some magic that yanked his Angel ass here so fast he was sweating. He had that fucker Rachmiel with him. Between Astrid, Roberto, and the most excellently profane Pam, the sons of bitches were convinced to break the curse."

"Convinced?" I asked, doubtfully.

"More like coerced with some wondrous violence thrown in for fun," Claudia said with a warm smile. "You scared us."

"How did they do it?" I asked, still trying to piece it together.

"Vlad caught Rachmiel in some very compromising positions with the Demons. He threatened to go to God with Rachmiel's *indiscretions*. Since that's an irreparable fall from grace, he was able to blackmail the Angel into placing the curse in return for keeping his mouth shut," Ethan told me.

"Angels and Demons?" I asked with a humorless laugh.

"And one very bad Vamp," Astrid affirmed. "Soon to be living *un*happily ever after in the Basement of Hell. And PS… you really did scare us."

"I tell you what," Pam bellowed at her usual volume. Astrid's Guardian Angel and mate to our King was a piece of work and then some—and really loud. "Damn near lost my shit when Gareth woke up and you didn't. And I'm serious. Occasionally livin' on the edge gives me gas. You, Little Missy, gave me major gas."

For such a beautiful woman, Pam was totally disgusting.

Astrid stood slightly behind Pam rolling her eyes and holding her nose.

"I can see you, Asshead," she grumbled at Astrid who immediately quit goofing around. Pam had a wicked left hook and wasn't afraid to use it.

"Sorry for the, um… gas," I mumbled, trying not to laugh.

"I'm just glad you missed out on that part," Astrid said and quickly ducked as Pam turned to backhand her.

"How do you feel?" Ethan asked, bravely stepping between Astrid and Pam.

"I feel… um," I stuttered, not really wanting to share that I wanted to jump Gareth's bones more than I wanted to live at the moment.

Gareth was feeling the same way. His eyes were hooded and he was gripping me like I would fly away if he didn't hold on. Maybe we could…

"Wait," I yelled. It came out like a croak, but I didn't care. "Martha and Jane? Are they okay?"

"Fine," Tiara confirmed quickly, aware of my impending freak out. "When they went to find Sunny, Vlad has already taken her. Her room was a bloody shit show, so Martha and Jane were searching for her when everything went down."

If I could sigh in relief, I would have. I didn't have that luxury, so I cried.

"Where are they?" I whispered, wiping at my tears.

Astrid's grin was wide and she barked out a laugh. "You love those obnoxious fashion disasters too. They really get under your skin like a disease. But once they invade, you can't shake them. Trust me. It's all kinds of awful, but it happens to the best of us."

She was correct. I had the Martha and Jane fungus and I was perfectly okay with it.

"They're with the D's and the handlers making sure everyone has temporary quarters," Ethan said, running his hands through his hair. "Some will stay and some will go to Japan."

"And Sunny?" I asked.

Tiara shook her head. "We tried to save her, but she was too far gone."

I was quiet for a moment as I took that in. I didn't like Sunny at all, but I felt saddened by the news of her death. This hadn't been her fight and she was a sad casualty.

"All the D's and the handlers?"

"All fine," Claudia confirmed. "A little worse for the wear, but alive."

"And booby," Pam added for good measure. "Never seen so many bare hooters since I took part in the Gay Pride Parade in San Francisco back in the 70's."

That gave everyone a moment of pause, but the King grinned widely next to his nut bag mate and kissed her cheek.

"Pam supports everything and everyone," he said with pride. "We're marching for undead women's rights next week."

"Where?" Tiara asked, clearly interested.

"In Hell," he replied. "Satan has offered up the venue."

"Well, that's the fucking weirdest thing I've ever heard," Tiara said, bemused. "You want some company? Claudia and I have wanted to see Hell for a while now."

"You sure you're ready to meet Uncle Fucker?" Astrid inquired with a raised brow.

"Yep, and I was hoping to get to see my buddy *Vlad*. I've got a little something I want to carve into his back."

As wonderful as it was to be alive with Gareth by my side and my friends surrounding me, I *really* wanted them to leave. I was seconds away from tearing Gareth's clothes from his beautiful body and have my nasty way with him. I didn't want it to be a performance, but I was very close to not caring.

"Umm… guys," I said, doing my damnedest not to writhe around on the couch. Glancing around, I realized I was in my own suite at the Cressida House.

Perfect, except it was still far too crowded.

"OUT," Gareth commanded, bodily removing everyone from the room. "Venus needs…"

"Sex?" Astrid squealed as she sprinted away from a near manic Gareth. "You guys are gonna be busy for a few hours—or days. Mating sex *rocks*. Welcome to the family, Venus. They're a bunch of pushy alpha-holes, but great in the sack."

"GET OUT," Gareth bellowed as he began ripping at his clothes uncaring that the last of the crew was still exiting. "Close the door behind you. NOW."

"Well, that was kind of rude," I said with a giggle when we were finally alone.

He turned and gave me a smoldering look that rocked my world and made my girly parts tingle with anticipation. Backing himself up to the far wall across the room, he held onto his composure by a thread.

"Are you okay? Do you want this?" he asked.

I knew it took everything he had to hold himself back. It was against every instinct we had and we were ruled by our instincts. My insides danced and my need for him was painful.

"More than I've ever wanted anything in my life," I promised, as I kicked off the blanket and pulled my shirt over my head.

I wasn't sure who dressed me, but they did a good job. My clothing was loose and came off easily.

"I love you to the point of unhealthy," I said, kicking my pants off.

"I'd have to agree with you there. You following me in death wasn't your best move," he stated as he tore off the rest of his clothing.

"Like you wouldn't have done the same?" I said as I stood and began to stalk him.

"True, but I'm insane. You're perfect."

"How about we're both perfectly insane and made for each other?" I suggested as I eyed my love in all of his flawless naked glory.

"I'll go with that."

He took me in his arms and kissed me senseless. I knew I'd always wanted this man, but that was nothing compared to the raw desperate desire I felt now.

"I'm so in love with you," he muttered against my lips. "I'll love you for eternity."

"Back at you," I swore as I ran my hands greedily over his body. "Need you now. Please."

"You sure you're ready for this? No going back now," he teased with a sexy lopsided smile that sent my insides into liquid meltdown.

"You better stop talking and get to work or I'm gonna find someone who can satisfy my needs," I shot back with a giggle and wrapped my legs around his strong body.

"No need. I'm the Vampyre for the job. You're stuck with me."

He flew—literally—into my bedroom and we dropped onto the bed in a tangle of kisses and touches.

"You're my everything," I whispered. "My savior, my love and my life."

Gareth closed his eyes and smiled. "You are my happiness."

"Your happiness wants you to make love to her until she can't walk."

His laugh filled the room and I knew I'd be at home with this man wherever life took us.

"Your wish is my command. Always."

And it was.

And he did.

And I couldn't walk for three days.

It. Was. Awesome.

Epilogue

The Grand Ballroom of the Cressida House looked like a strip club right down to the massive mirror balls that spun from the vaulted ceiling and dotted the enormous room in glittering spots of bouncing light.

There were stripper poles strategically placed around the room and the Baby Demons were handing out dollar bills to *enhance* the festivities. I truly couldn't believe this was actually happening.

I was certain Gareth would want my ass in a sling, but nope. He was all for it.

Or so he said. Payback was a bitch and I was positive I would pay for this. Big time.

"There you are," Tiara shouted as she and Claudia trapped me in a bear hug that might have crushed a rib or two.

I still had Tiara's blood in my veins and I'd been extra careful while training the D's and the handlers. My strength was staggering, but with focus, I could control it. The last thing I wanted to do was kill one of my new friends.

Yes. Friends. The conversations were vapid and occasionally bored me to tears, but the D's and their posses were all actually nice women—most with very sad and tragic backstories. They'd been lost souls wandering around for far too long. The fact that they hadn't gone rogue with no protection spoke to their characters. The *conversation* Ethan'd had with Sheena, who was supposedly in charge of the area that the gals were in was ugly, violent, and very satisfying. Sheena was on probation and Vampyre probation was not even remotely pleasant.

Most of the gals would be coming to Japan with Gareth and me, but a few had elected to stay here in Kentucky.

Ethan had given his blessing on my mating to Gareth. It was odd getting a blessing from the brother of my mate, but Ethan was as close to a father figure as I'd ever had. It made me cry to think of leaving the Cressida House, but my place was with the sexy insane man that called me his happiness. I'd follow Gareth to Hell and back if he wanted me to. I knew he'd do the same if our roles were reversed.

"My sister is fucking fabulous," Tiara said, referring to Astrid with so much pride I giggled. "And The Kev and Gemma are talking to me about taking a little trip to Zanthia with them."

"Will you go?" I asked, knowing how she felt about the Fairies—or rather how they felt about her. "I don't think Demons can survive there."

"I'm a mutt, I can survive anywhere."

"Like a cockroach?" I asked with a grin.

"Exactly, but a really good looking one with a fabulous rack and incredible hair. Anyhoo, if I go, it will only be for a nice short, somewhat violent visit with my mom. It'll send her uppity ass into a shitfit. Lookin' forward to it," she said with a wicked grin. "Plus I could be some good muscle to protect Gemma when she takes the throne."

"Gemma should be so lucky," I said picturing the three of them knocking Zanthia on its butt.

"Right?" Tiara demanded with a high-pitched giggle that made me wince—but only a little.

Getting used to Tiara's voice was a tremendous challenge, but I was always up for a challenge. I adored the freak just as everyone at the Cressida House did—especially Astrid. They'd been inseparable for the last week. Samuel hung on Tiara like she was monkey bars at the best park in the world.

"Are you feeling well now?" Claudia asked. Her kindness constantly reminded me of what I'd almost done to her. It was a lesson I'd take with me always.

"I am," I replied. "I've never been better. Um, but… Claudia, I'd like to…" I started, but she put her finger gently to my lips.

"Come with me, I will answer all your questions in private," she said, smiling.

"Go on with your bad selves," Tiara said, giving Claudia a quick and sweet peck on the lips. "I do believe I've spotted my illustrious Uncle Fucker. I'm gonna go up and introduce myself."

"Good luck with that. He's a crafty bastard," I said.

"No worries, so am I."

And on that note she was off.

Walking with Claudia to the far side of the ballroom, I marveled at the fact that we were in each other's lives in a way that I never could have foreseen. It was a blessing and I would keep tabs on her for the rest of my days. I'd already started teaching her how to invest and we were going to continue online. God bless modern technology.

It was quieter on this side of the room, but suddenly I was tongue-tied and unsure.

"I'm all yours," she said kindly.

"Can I ask you a question?"

She nodded and waited patiently.

"Do I have any… um," This was stupid. I'd be sad if she answered negatively and sad if she didn't. I should leave it alone, but… "I was wondering if I… Actually, never mind."

Claudia stopped me from walking away with a firm hand. Pulling me over to a settee and gently pushing me down, she seated herself next to me.

"Your oldest sister had a daughter that survived. The baby was taken from her at birth and raised in the main house to eventually become a maid."

My stomach lurched and a shudder of regret rocked me to the core. "I didn't know," I whispered. "I remember she had a child, but I was only a child myself… and then the baby was gone."

Claudia nodded and wrapped her arms around me. She held me until I stopped shaking and then left her hand lightly on my arm.

"What was her name?" I asked.

"She went by Baby until the day she died. She was a strong and wonderful woman. I loved her. She got married and had six children."

"Did she live as a slave?"

"No, she didn't. After the bastard died by your hand, I made sure all of the slaves on the plantation were freed. She settled with her family in Alabama."

"Do I…"

"You do. And they are a varied and loving bunch. You have a great-great-grandniece who's a doctor. Two great-great-grandnephews who are lawyers specializing in social work. Most still reside in the Alabama area—they're good people. They would make you proud."

"I want to see them," I said as a terrified excitement stole over me. I felt light headed and like I was in a dream.

Claudia smiled and touched my cheek. "That can be arranged. They know me as a human rights activist. I've been able to interact on a limited basis over the years that way. As long as you can hold yourself together, you can come with me next time."

I needed to absorb the information so I didn't lose my mind when I saw them. There was no way they could understand our connection. No way in Hell.

"I would like that," I said quietly, still trying to grasp the concept that I had living family. "Claudia, I'd like to be the one to support them."

"Your family is doing very well. Your line hasn't needed much financial support from me in ages, but there are others who do."

"It would be my honor to take some of that burden away."

"I assure you it's not a burden," she said. "But I would be happy to share the privilege with you."

Hugging her tight, I laid my head on her shoulder. "I'm so sorry."

"I'm sorry too, but the past is what it is. It's the past. It's the future that matters. Right?"

Pulling back I stared at her lovely features. "Right. Will your future include the loud mouthed woman who adores you?"

She laughed and let her head fall back on her shoulders. "Yes. Yes it will. Tiara has convinced me that I won't bring her down, and honestly I don't want to live without her."

"Good. That makes me happy."

"And you'll be going to Japan?"

"In a month." I nodded and glanced around the garish ballroom with a grin. "I need to train the girls, and then Gareth and I will go."

"And in a few minutes he's really going to... um," she stumbled over the term for what Gareth was about to do because it was so outlandish.

"Yep. He most certainly is. Come on," I said, pulling her to her feet. "We do not want to miss this."

***

Mother Nature's entrance was all I expected it to be and more.

A glittery peach haze erupted from of the ceiling and rained down on the surprised Vampyres in the ballroom. Several of the floor to ceiling windows blew out and I heard Ethan cursing up a storm. The D's and handlers bunched together in fear, but the rest of us simply rolled our eyes and waited for more. There was always more.

Mother Nature didn't like to disappoint. And she wasn't going to start this evening.

I hopped to my left as a massive flowering tree exploded out of the floor and yanked Claudia to safety as a flock of wildly colorful birds zipped through the room dive bombing all in their path. The beginning notes of Queen's *We Will Rock You* echoed through the vast ballroom and I scrubbed my hands over my eyes to make sure I was seeing what I thought I was seeing.

I was. Oh my God, I was.

"I thought he was dead," Tiara gasped out, pointing and jumping around like a teenager at a rock concert.

"He a Vampyre," I shouted over the music. It was so loud I could feel the drums reverberating through my body. "The whole band is!"

Freddy Mercury was in rare form in a sparkling blue unitard with enormous white sunglasses and stiletto boots that made me jealous. The band descended from the ceiling on a magical cloud of in the shape of a guitar. It shimmered and winked as it landed softly in the middle of the array of stripper poles. This was going to be a bitch to clean up.

Satan let out a girly scream and tried to hide his massive frame behind his newly discovered niece. "No one told me she was coming," he said looking terrified.

"Who are you talking about?" Tiara asked him, beginning to look frightened herself.

I mean who wouldn't? If someone scared the Devil, they must be pretty horrifying.

"Uh oh," Astrid said, sneaking up behind us and walloping Satan in the back of the head. "Looks like someone might have forgotten his Sunday call to his mother."

"This isn't funny," he hissed. "She's horrible and mean. And I haven't called her in a month. This is very dangerous."

"Pot, kettle, black," Astrid said with a laugh. "She's coming and you're staying."

"Who is he talking about?" Tiara whispered to me.

"Mother Nature—his mom," I whispered back.

"I'm calling in a favor," Satan insisted, while trying to make his large frame smaller.

Impossible.

"Fine," Astrid groused with an eye roll. "What do you want?"

"I want you to protect me from her," he said. "You owe me."

"That will cost you three favors," she bargained with a delighted clap of her hands.

"Damn it," he swore. "How many do you owe me?"

"I owe you three as you very well know," she replied knowing she had him by the balls.

"I call bullshit," he hissed. "You're taking advantage of me."

"I learned from the best." She shrugged and grinned. "What's it gonna be, Uncle Lucifer? Favors or the wrath of your mommy?"

"You win," he snapped, but with a smile of admiration at her besting him on his face. "But I won't forget this."

"I wouldn't expect you to," she shot back as Tiara and Claudia watched the exchange with mouths agape.

"Apropos of nothing, do you know how to write?" he inquired. "You're constantly reading all those trashy romance novels."

"Okay, that was kind of random and they're not *trashy*," Astrid informed him with an eye roll. "They're fun and why in the Hell would you think I can write? Because I can read?"

"Well, yes," he shot back defensively. "I'm looking for a ghost writer."

"For?" she asked with narrowed eyes.

"For my autobiography. There's so much misinformation out there on me. I thought I'd straighten the masses out, by letting them know my point of view on my favorite subject."

"And that would be you?" Tiara chimed in with a smirk.

"But of course," he replied with a devastating grin. "I'm the most interesting person I know. Astrid, we shall discuss this later."

"How about we discuss it when Hell freezes over?" she suggested.

"It's getting a bit chilly down under," he told her with a wink. "May I hide in Ethan's office? I promise not to *borrow* anything."

Astrid brows were raised and she couldn't disguise her grin. "And I'm supposed to believe that bullshit?"

"Of course not, darling niece. See you soon."

With that, he disappeared in a blast of black glitter.

"You're so screwed," I told Astrid with a laugh. "Completely screwed."

"Tell me something I don't know. Can you believe that idiot wants me to write his *autobiography*? He's going to be so sorry."

"Is that even allowed?" I asked imagining the reaction of the human world—not that they'd believe it was real, but...

"I'm sure it's not, but I'll deal with that later. Uncle God will have a freakin' hissy fit. Forget about that," Astrid said, punching my arm with glee. "You ready to see your man take on a pole?"

I laughed at the sheer ridiculousness of what was about to go down. "I can't believe you were able to force him to do this." I marveled at my best friend's ability to get people to do what she wanted.

"A deal's a deal, and I still owe you a shopping spree, but I didn't have to force him. By the way, it's basically impossible to force Gareth to do anything he doesn't want to do—just in case you didn't already know. All I had to say was that you wanted him to pole dance and he was in. That man has it really bad. Ethan thinks he's nuts."

"He is," I agreed. "And he's mine."

Never did I think I would say those words in reference to Gareth, but it completed my soul to be able to say it and know in my heart it was true. I was going to have my happily ever after. Of course he had a tremendous amount of penance to pay, but I looked forward to that too—make up sex *was* awesome.

"Holy shit," Tiara yelled, pointing to the ceiling as Queen began to sing *We Are The Champions*. "Unreal."

Tiara was correct. Floating down from the ceiling were two clouds of glittering magic. One hosted a beaming Mother Nature clad in a something she must have borrowed from Martha and Jane. Her exquisite loveliness was breathtaking, but the outfit was gag inducing. The yellow and orange sequined boob tube clashed horribly with her red hair and the bright green assless chaps hurt my brain. It was a total train wreck. However, my eyes were drawn to the performer on the other cloud.

His eyes bored into mine and his grin was positively feral. My hand went to my mouth and it was all I could do not to fly up to that cloud and attack him—in a very inappropriate way.

"*Dang*, he's hot and I don't even go for that," Tiara muttered as Claudia elbowed her with a giggle.

She was correct. Gareth was hotter than Hades on the summer solstice. Wearing only loose fitting pants and a grin that melted my panties, he was every kind of sex on a stick I could have dreamed up. His skin glistened and his gorgeous muscles were defined to perfection.

"I greased him up," Martha announced proudly, joining our group with Jane in tow. "Fucker didn't want me to, but I got him."

"Bastard's fast," Jane agreed with a grunt. "Had to chase him down for an hour to get the baby oil even."

"I'm sorry, what?" I stammered trying to picture the reality of what they'd just shared.

"Yep," Jane confirmed. "And if I were you guys, I'd stay out of the training facility until someone can mop that shit up. It's like a goddamned slip and slide in there. Dang near lost my undead life trying to get out of that mess."

"You greased Gareth?" Astrid asked, shocked. "And you're still alive?"

"Looks that way to me, Knockers McChesticle," Martha shouted over the music that was increasing in volume.

"We also dressed Mother Nature. That gal is a fucking hoot," Jane added.

Everything about this moment was so wrong and at the same time so right. I was with the people I loved and I had a beautiful future in front of me.

Not to mention I was about to see my man pole dance with Mother Nature. Unfreakinbelievable.

And then the show no one thought would ever happen started.

Hot didn't begin to cover watching my man work the pole like a Chippendale's sex god. Mother Nature only fell off her pole three times—this was good for her—normally she hit the floor at least six times. Gareth, ever the gentleman, helped her back on every time she took a spill. He was earning very big points from the mother of God and Satan. I had a sneaking suspicion he'd use his newfound popularity with the insanely delightful nut job to avoid having to pay up on the favors owed to Satan.

My man was all kinds of smart and all kinds of sexy.

And he was mine. Forever and ever.

And I was happy. My new nickname, bestowed upon me by the love of my undead life fit like a glove. I was Happiness. I would always be Happiness with Gareth at my side.

***

Once upon a time there was a girl and a boy.

He had loved her always and she had loved the boy as well even though she didn't know it was him until almost too late.

It took them many long years to get it right, but when they finally did...it was magic.

Happiness was theirs. They deserved it and they were humbled by it.

It was also very very hot.

Even though they still disagreed on a daily basis, they didn't mind because make up sex rocked.

And as in most wonderful Fairy tales—or Vampyre tales to be more accurate—they lived happily ever after and after and after and after.

--- The End... for now ---

Note From the Author

If you enjoyed this book, please consider leaving a positive review or rating on the site where you purchased it. Reader reviews help my books continue to be valued by resellers and help new readers make decisions about reading them.

You are the reason I write these stories and I sincerely appreciate each of you!

Many thanks for your support,
~ Robyn Peterman

Excerpt:
A TALE OF TWO WITCHES

Chapter 1

"My Virginia has a heart beat," I whispered, keeping my stance very wide. "I think I made a huge mistake."

Standing in the bright airy kitchen of my BFF's house, I decided to come clean. Zelda was a healer witch and I was definitely in the market for some magical restoration.

"I'm going to ask a question I *really* don't want the answer to," Zelda said, pulling on her wild curly red hair and staring at me like I'd grown two heads.

I got that look a lot—from everyone. Whatever. I was fairly certain I was clear. I wasn't sure how much clearer I could get than telling her my girly parts had a pulse.

"Go ahead," I told her, holding my position. It was the only one that was working at the moment.

"Why does your nether region have a heartbeat?"

"If you're going to speak French, I'm going to zap a massive hairy wart onto your chin. I'm having a crisis here," I squeaked. "I'm talking about my va-jay-jay, not the weather season, for the love of the Goddess."

"I said… never mind," Zelda grumbled.

I was pretty sure she was trying not to laugh. This was not a laughing matter. At all.

"I went to the Hooch sisters," I confessed, going ghostly pale at the recent memory.

"You did not," Zelda groaned with a wince.

"I did," I admitted, hanging my head in mortification.

It was not my best move, but I did it and I had to own it. My weather seasons were not going to let me forget it anytime soon.

"What were you *thinking*?" Zelda gasped and grabbed the table so her knees didn't give out.

"I don't know," I said, beginning to pace and then thought better of it. Movement was not my friend in this predicament. "I thought it would be sexy—that Jeeves would think it was hot. Goddess, I don't know what I was thinking. I guess I wasn't thinking at all."

"Well there's something new," Zelda mumbled.

"I suppose I wanted to surprise Jeeves. He's a total lights on kind of kangaroo. I thought an unvarnished Virginia would be a turn on."

"Did you just say unvarnished?"

"I did."

"Okay, never ever put the visual of you and Jeeves in any kind of compromising position in my head again. Furthermore, never refer to your bits being unvarnished in my presence in this lifetime. If you do, I'll turn your blonde hair green. You're a witch. Why would you go to the Hooch sisters when you could have done a little voodoo on your hoohoo and gotten the same result without having to walk like you've been riding a horse for a month straight."

Dang, she had me there.

"Well, I heard Wanda and DeeDee talking about it and I just…" I trailed off.

I had done a tremendous about of stupid things in my twenty-nine and three quarters years on the earth, but this may have taken the cake. Ever since spending nine months in the pokey for misuse of magic—or rather a penchant for blowing up buildings and stealing other witches boyfriends, I'd gotten a little bored and craved excitement. However, getting a Brazilian from the masochistic Hooch sisters was too much excitement even for me.

"Let me get this straight," Zelda said, taking a seat at the table and staring up at the ceiling. "You got your lady bits waxed and now said bits have a heartbeat?"

"Yessss. And it hurt like a mother humper. Those sisters are violent. They threw me all over the table and then they…"

"Stop," Zelda shouted, slapping her hands over her ears. "I do *not* want to have to go back to therapy because your Virginia got a hair cut. Trust me, I can imagine—no need to narrate."

"Virginia's bald."

"Right," Zelda replied letting her head fall to her hands. "And you're telling me this because you hate me?"

"No, I love you. You're my best friend. I'm telling you this because I need to be healed."

Zelda's head snapped up and she pinned me with a stare that made me think this was my second bad idea of the morning.

"You do realize that whatever body part I heal, I take on that pain," she said with her brows raised almost to her hairline.

"Really?" I asked, shocked. "That sucks."

"For you," she shot back. "I'm not taking on a throbbing Virginia because you're an idiot."

"I see where you're going with this," I told her. "Do you have any frozen peas?"

"Are you serious?"

"Yes. Very. If you're not going to heal me, the least you can do is let me ice my Virginia with your vegetables," I said, thinking it was a reasonable request. "I mean, I can barely walk. It was hell flying over here on my broom."

"Dude, why in the Goddess's name are you riding a broom if your Virginia is on fire? We don't even need brooms to fly, dorko."

Without waiting for an answer, Zelda stomped over to the freezer and ransacked it. Muttering something rude about fire crotches, she tossed me a bag of frozen mixed veggies. Easing myself to the floor while keeping my legs as far apart as humanly possible, I gratefully put the bag on my weather seasons. I was going to learn French soon. Zelda spoke it entirely too much for me to not at least try to learn a few words.

"I'll return this when I'm done," I promised.

"Umm, no. You can keep them."

"Great. Thanks. Listen, do not ever go to those women. Ever," I told her. "They're heinous. I'm pretty sure I created an entire new dictionary of swear words during my session."

"Sassy, I have no intention of going to the Hooch sisters. They're buzzard shifters and they have beady eyes, but thanks for the heads up," Zelda said biting back her laughter.

"That's what best friends are for," I told her, giggling. "We have to look out for each others Virginias."

"Can't say I've heard those requirements for a BFF, but you're my first best friend," Zelda said with a huge grin as she plopped down on the floor next to me. "You really are an idiot."

"Tell me something I don't know," I shot back with an eye roll and a laugh.

"I do have something to tell you that you don't know," she said, looking serious. "But I think it can wait until you only have one heartbeat."

"Will it be painful?"

"Define painful."

"Shit. Even I know that's not a good response," I mumbled. At least the peas and carrots were tamping down the inferno in my pants. Did I want to add more yuck to my plate this morning?

No. No I didn't. Avoiding the truth had worked out just fine for most of my life. I was finally happy. I had friends and a kangaroo shifter who adored me. Never in my witchy life did I think I would have a place to call home with people who truly cared. Crappy news could wait.

As soon as my crotch was mobile, I wanted to go home.

"Let's hold off," I said. "Are the babies awake?"

"Nope, the gorgeous little turds have their days and nights mixed up. Mac and I were up all night with them," she said in a dreamy happy voice.

Audrey and Henry were one month old twins and the cutest wolf shifter-witch babies in the world. Actually they were the only wolf shifter-witch babies in the world, but they were darn cute. It made me want some kangaroo shifter-witch babies, but Jeeves and I weren't mated yet.

And we had adopted four full-grown chipmunk shifters—Chip, Chad, Chunk and Chutney. My boys were as dumb as a box of hair, but I loved them and they loved me back.

"You're so lucky, Zelda," I whispered as she nodded off on the floor next to me.

I laid my head on her stomach and got comfortable. She smelled great and she loved me—well she liked me a lot. She liked me more when I didn't borrow her stuff. I was trying to give up my sticky fingered ways, but she had really good stuff.

"We're both lucky," she said groggily right before she conked out.

She was right. We'd been cellmates in a horrible prison for wayward witches and now we were BFF's with bright futures ahead of us in the beautifully run down Assjacket, West Virginia. I was never going to take my new luck for granted. Ever.

As soon as my Virginia stopped vibrating, or when Zelda woke up, I was going to get my magical hinny back to my little family and continue my new happy life.

No more life threatening or va-jay-jay ripping excitement for me.

I was a witch reformed—for the most part.

Visit **www.robynpeterman.com** for more info.

Excerpt:
MATCMAKER ABDUCTION

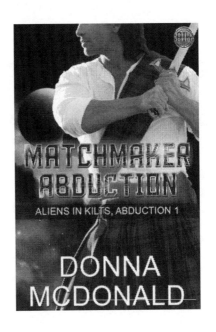

Note From Robyn...

Sci-fi romance wasn't my thing until I read this...

I literally spit my soda out of my mouth while reading the hilarious, sexy, silly spoof that knocks Sci-fi romance on its ass!!!

I'd love to crawl into Donna McDonald's brain for a day. It would be a wild ride! Check out Matchmaker Abduction.

You'll be so happy you did!

xoxo Robyn

Book Description

True love is said to defy time, but can it survive space, aliens, and being abducted? Angus MacNamara and Erin O'Shea are about to find out.

The big blue planet that most call Earth desperately needs matchmakers. There is only one small—okay, BIG—problem. No one wants the alien dating service job. No one. The original matchmakers are dead, and much worse, their DNA is no longer viable for cloning.

Solution? Go back in time to some of Earth's other—thankfully slower spinning—versions, and retrieve the alternates of the one couple in any universe who seems able to do the job.

Far easier said than done though, especially when the alternates are anything but a loving couple, and both are none too pleased to be thrown into the future.

Chapter 1

Universe 6, May 15,1958, on a hill outside Lisdoonvarna, Ireland...

Angus MacNamara pulled the pistol from the holster on his kilt belt. He checked the chamber, made sure his shot was loaded, then looked down at the grave and glared. Love and hate had always been intertwined in his life. The harpy he had married over forty years ago had been his greatest pleasure and his darkest curse.

Love weakened a man's resolve. There was no doubting that for him.

"Alright, woman. It's been nine fecking years, but I finally kept my entire promise to yer dying soul. Yer children are married well, even the stubborn ones. Ya have two grandchildren remembering yer name already, five still on the tit, and a few more on the fecking way because our sons and daughter are as lusty as we were in creating them."

Angus huffed. "What's that ya say? I hear ya fussing, even from six feet under. *Why did it take so long, Angus? What have ya been doing all this time?* This isn't the 1800s, you crazed old crone. I couldn't make them hardheads you bore do what they didn't want to. In fact, I had to fecking bribe most of their intendeds to take them on. Without yer guidance, the last four never got their edges rounded off as well as the first three."

Angus stomped his polished black brogue on the ground. The tassels of his father's clan flapped from the top of his pristine white stockings. His kilt lifted, bringing a welcome breeze under it. Wool in the early summer was never a good idea for a man his size. But he'd wanted to look good today. Being as much Scottish as Irish, he'd wanted closure to come in style, which meant while he was wearing his plaid.

"Pay attention to me, woman. Stop rolling over down there and laughing at my misery. Do ya think it's been easy for me all these years without ya? Well, it wasn't, ya cruel creature. I told ya not to die, but no… ya never did listen to me."

"I knew ya lost yer flipping mind years ago," a voice called. "Did ya call me out here to watch ya lose the rest of yer shit, Angus? I'd just as soon not be a part of yer descent into madness if I get a say in things. Plus, I have to tell ya true… the woman yar talking to will come back and haunt ya good if ya keep stomping on her grave like that."

Angus jumped back from the grave and raised the pistol from his side to point it at the mounded dirt on the ground. Most of him was sure it wasn't his Mary speaking to him from beyond the veil. He wasn't that many sheets in the wind… or at least he hoped he wasn't.

Suddenly a green-eyed glaring angel with shiny, golden brown hair and enormous breasts appeared. Instead of a robe of white, she was wearing some unfortunate man's stolen pants as she stepped up to face him down. Had he shot himself already and forgotten about it in his dying state? That would just be his fecking luck.

The angel glared at him over Mary's grave, but held up her hands at the pistol he finally raised and pointed at her. She wisely backed up a few steps which clued him in about what he was doing. One set of the angel's fingers gripped a note which she shook at him furiously. If it was a page from the great Book Of Life about him, his angel was sure fecking mad about what was written on it.

Lowering the pistol, Angus wavered on unsteady legs, wishing now he hadn't downed so many pints of Guinness. He'd thought it'd be easier to shoot himself if he was drunk. It never occurred to him that both heaven and hell would gang up against him and send a foul-mouthed angel his way as a final torment. He'd honestly thought ya got to settle yer accounts with St. Peter after ya passed on, but not *before* ya ended things.

He looked down at the grave again. "Ya could have fecking warned me about the avenging angel coming for me, Mary. What good is it being dead if ya can't help those ya left behind? She looks mad as the devil ever could look, and now I have to deal with her all by my fecking self. I'll not be forgetting this betrayal, ya laughing harpy."

Erin swore under her breath at the way Angus was dressed. Though a tall woman who dwarfed most men in height, she'd always felt dwarfed herself by the nearly two meters tall Angus MacNamara. That was especially true when he was looking every bit of his Scots-Irish self dressed in his best Prince Charlie outfit. It was criminal the way the man's long, sculpted legs were just meant for his stupid, fecking kilt.

Erin muttered a prayer for patience as she rubbed her forehead. Angus was a known horse's arse when he was drinking, but he usually had the sense not to pack a fecking gun around while in such a condition. What a day this was turning out to be. She didn't know whether to be worried for Angus's sanity or to be in mortal fear for her own life.

"Did ya call me out here to kill me, Angus? Is that what this shit is about? I always knew ya were a competitive sort, but ya could at least try to force me to move first. Yer meddling has nearly ruined my business reputation in this town anyway. Fact is... I've been thinking about leaving Lisdoonvarna anyway. No one believes me when I say ya have been buying off the suitors when I know fecking well, it's the only way ya could ever make a real match."

"*Erin? Erin O'Shea?* Feck ya for not saying hello. I thought ya were an avenging angel come to torment me."

Angus stumbled and had to plant his feet firmly to stay standing. He put a hand on his head, but it just wouldn't stop spinning. Worse, Erin's complaining always got through even the finest of liquors.

"Och... are ya daft, woman? Our relationship isn't that twisted. I would never call ya out to Mary's grave... not for any reason."

Erin O'Shea reached out her hand and shook the paper in it. "Yar a drunken liar, Angus MacNamara. This is yer handwriting asking me to meet ya here or I'm as dead in the head as yer Mary down there."

"*Liar? I'm no fecking liar,*" Angus barked. He shoved the loaded gun back in its holster, fuming because a man couldn't even kill himself in peace in this town.

Stepping across Mary's grave to get to the woman who'd both aided and hindered him in his matchmaking efforts, Angus yanked the paper from her steady fingers. Seeing them tremble a bit had him remembering that one night his weakness had decided to get the better of him. It had been so long since he'd had a woman, and the ale had gone to his head then too, and... feck it all. A living man had needs, didn't he? It had only been the one time, but Erin O'Shea made it seem like he'd ruined her forever.

He looked at his writing on the note, bemused and befuddled by the realness of it. Even as tipsy as he was, he had to admit it was a damn fine replication. "I can see why ya thought this was mine, but I swear on Mary's grave, I didn't write this. Tell me truthfully, Erin... ya had this faked to torment me, didn't ya?"

Erin fisted hands on her hips. "Why in the Goddess's name would I bother faking a note from ya that had me traipsing out here to watch ya talk nonsense to a bag of bones in the ground? No one's down there, Angus. Mary's spirit left this world at her death. I've tried to tell ya that for years."

Angus swung the letter around and shook it at her. "How should I know why ya would do something like this to torment me? Yar a woman, aren't ya? That makes ya do things no man could ever understand."

"Listen here, you drunken arse..." Erin began.

A throat clearing nearby interrupted her scolding and earned the interrupter a glare she usually reserved for her primary age students at the school where she taught. The throat clearer was just one of a group of five strange men staring hard at her and Angus. They were strangely dressed too. All looked like they were heading for a fancy French funeral.

The man who had interrupted them hid a smile as he coughed into his hand, but nodded at them both when he saw he'd finally gotten their complete attention.

"I'm Agent Black from Universe 1. And you are Angus MacNamara and Erin O'Shea from Universe 6. You're very recognizable and it's a pleasure to see you both in person."

Angus pulled his pistol. He held it at the ready at his side and didn't point it directly, but he wanted them to know he could... and would... use it if necessary.

"Who are ya and what do ya want?" Angus demanded. He watched the one who'd done all the talking so far turn to the nearest one behind him. Maybe it was the drink affecting his eyes, or the overcast day making everything dreary, but the men all looked nearly the same to him. He could scarcely tell them apart with their blackened glasses and blacker suits.

"Are we prepared to insert the U10 version?" Agent Black asked the one behind him.

"Yes, sir," his near twin replied.

Angus cocked his weapon and lifted it. "I don't think so, boy-o. None of ya will be doing any inserting on me or my lady friend here."

Erin put her hand on Angus's arm. "Stop. They outnumber ya. And ya don't even know what they're meaning. Lower yer pistol before ya do something ya might regret."

"Get behind me, woman. I'll take a few of them out before I go. Maybe they'll change their mind about what they intend to do to ya."

Erin snorted and hung on, tugging his arm harder. "If this is another of yer practical jokes to get me behind ya just so ya can fart in my general direction, I'll not be falling for it this time. Now I insist ya pull yerself out of yer Guinness haze. Lower yer fecking gun before the fecking thing goes off."

"It's alright, ma'am. I appreciate you trying to keep everyone safe, but it's not necessary. The single bullet he loaded earlier has already been removed from Mr. MacNamara's gun. He won't be able to harm anyone even if he tries to shoot," Agent Black said quietly.

Erin turned as Angus pointed the gun to the sky and shot. The trigger clicked, but nothing happened. He jerked from her grasp to examine his pistol.

"What the feck is going on here? It can't be empty. I just chambered that round," Angus declared.

Erin watched in stunned fascination as the one calling himself Agent Black calmly shrugged.

"Yes, sir. You did chamber a round. In the time space just after you performed that action and just before Ms. O'Shea arrived here, one of my men briefly inserted himself in a time stop and emptied the chamber while you were distracted with your speech. You were so determined to end your life that we thought it best to intervene a bit earlier than planned."

Erin turned to glare at the man beside her. "*Angus Ian MacNamara*," she said in shock. "Ya were going to end yer own life? Why?"

"My thoughts are my own fecking business... and none of yers... *or theirs*," Angus said tersely, his head tilting to the men dressed all in black.

Her single glance back to Agent Black caught the pitying look on his face. Fecking Angus. He was always landing them both in a giant pile of shit.

"I'm sorry to traumatize you, Ms. O'Shea, but your presence is now needed as well. That's why we sent you the note from Mr. MacNamara. Two matchmakers are required. It's been decided to take the pair of you while it's still possible."

Erin gasped at the admission and shook the note at all the men dressed in black. "I can't believe ya would be so conniving. May Brighid split ya from gut to gullet on my behalf."

"Yes, ma'am," Agent Black said cheerfully. "I am fully versed in ancient Celtic legends from your universe's timeline. Brighid was the goddess of the hearth and forge, but also the defender of women."

"I'll show ya a defender of women," Angus said, starting toward the man intending to beat the crap out of at least one of them so they'd know he wasn't fooling around.

"Wait... did ya just say that ya *fecking stopped time*?" Erin yelled the crazy query in disbelief. Then she started walking toward the man she was trying to save. "Angus, stop... I'm telling ya no good will come from yer impulsive actions." She picked up her pace, reached out, but Angus speeded up too. "Will ya at least try to control yer drunken self? They're obviously mad as diseased hens. Get your big arse back here."

"Shut up, woman," Angus yelled. "Can't ya see I'm trying to protect us?"

Erin shook her head fiercely. "No. All I see is an eegit walking half-cocked into a fight with a group of men half his age. Sure now, they're a skinny lot compared to ya, but I think it will only take a couple to bring ya down. Lay off the lads, you old fool. How much did ya drink today?"

"Actually, it will only take one of us to stop him," Agent Black said calmly. He motioned with his hand and another of the men pointed a device at a still advancing Angus. A few seconds later, Angus dropped face first to the ground, landing like a large stone.

Calling out in alarm, Erin ran forward and stooped down to check him. "Angus, talk to me," she demanded, but there was no answer. She looked up and glared at Agent Black. "Bastard. Ya didn't have to kill him."

Agent Black smiled. "Rest assured, Ms. O'Shea. I didn't take his life. I merely subdued Mr. MacNamara while we insert his alternate version from Universe 10 who died just this morning of natural causes. They don't bury their dead there, so we gathered the body up for our use before they could incinerate it. Mr. MacNamara's U10 self will show all the signs of having had a heart attack which will allow Mr. MacNamara's U6 self to travel back with us unmissed. His children will find the U10 alternate and bury him beside his wife. That's what would have happened anyway if he'd shot himself... probably. Whatever the case, that's the plan we're going with today."

Erin's mouth dropped open for the second time. Her brain was spinning, but she figured it best to go along with the crazies. "What do ya plan to do with the still live

Angus now? I didn't quite catch what ya said about the matter."

"You and he will accompany us back to Universe 1 where you'll serve New Earth and all its remaining people in a unique capacity using the acquired learning of your Universe 6 matchmaking professions."

"*Me?* Goddess… yar taking me with ya too?"

"Yes, ma'am. I'm really sorry to deliver this news so abruptly. Your Universe 1 self is also dead, as is the first Erin alternate we jumped there. In Universe 6, you'll unfortunately become one more missing person who vanished without a trace. That sort of incident happens naturally in all universes, so it's not like the scenario isn't feasible in Universe 6 space time. Those who miss you will assume you left because the love of your life died so suddenly and tragically of heart failure."

"Why would anyone believe such a thing? I've never had a husband. I have no love," Erin declared.

Agent Black smiled. "With all due respect, ma'am, I was speaking of Mr. MacNamara."

Erin was so shocked that she was speechless for a moment. She looked down at Angus still on the ground. Her inner harpy rose to the surface like it always did when someone pointed out her weakness for the most contrary man she'd ever had the misfortune to lust after.

"Yar speaking of Angus MacNamara? Ya think *he's* the love of my life? Now I know yar mad for sure."

Agent Black rubbed his chin and looked at the other men. They looked at each other and shrugged. Erin heard yet another one speak up, but his comment made little sense.

"In most multi-verses, Ms. O'Shea is with Mr. MacNamara at some point. This is one of the few where it might never have happened… without some intervention,

I mean. The risks are marginal and our options for Ms. O'Shea alternates are fewer."

Agent Black turned back around to face her as he spoke. "Then I remain committed to my plan to take you both, Ms. O'Shea. Hopefully you'll be a calming influence on Mr. MacNamara."

"And what happens to me if I don't fecking want to go with ya?" Erin asked.

Agent Black—the scoundrel—had the nerve to chuckle at her dare instead of answering her. The last thing she saw was him waving a hand to the man behind him without looking away from her. The dastardly device came up again and suddenly she was falling face first across Angus's plaid kilted ass.

Visit www.donnamcdonaldauthor.com for more info.

Book Lists
(in correct reading order)

HOT DAMNED SERIES

Fashionably Dead
Fashionably Dead Down Under
Hell on Heels
Fashionably Dead in Diapers
A Fashionably Dead Christmas
Fashionably Hotter Than Hell
Fashionably Dead and Wed
Fashionably Fanged

SHIFT HAPPENS SERIES

Ready to Were
Some Were in Time
No Were To Run
Were Me Out

MAGIC AND MAYHEM SERIES

Switching Hour
Witch Glitch
A Witch in Time
Magically Delicious

HANDCUFFS AND HAPPILY EVER AFTERS SERIES

How Hard Can it Be?
Size Matters
Cop a Feel

If after reading all the above you are still wanting more adventure and zany fun, read *Pirate Dave and His Randy Adventures*, the romance novel budding novelist Rena was helping wicked Evangeline write in *How Hard Can It Be?*

Warning: Pirate Dave Contains Romance Satire, Spoofing, and Pirates with Two Pork Swords.

About Robyn Peterman

Robyn Peterman writes because the people inside her head won't leave her alone until she gives them life on paper.

Her addictions include laughing really hard with friends, shoes (the expensive kind), Target, Coke Zero Cherry with extra ice in a Styrofoam cup, bejeweled reading glasses, her kids, her super-hot hubby and collecting stray animals.

A former professional actress with Broadway, film and T.V. credits, she now lives in the South with her family and too many animals to count.

Writing gives her peace and makes her whole, plus having a job where you can work in your underpants works really well for her. You can leave Robyn a message via the Contact Page and she'll get back to you as soon as her bizarre life permits! She loves to hear from her fans!

Visit **www.robynpeterman.com** for more information.